Merry Christmas, Mr. Lawrence

Merry Christmas, Mr. Lawrence

Laurens van der Post

QUILL • NEW YORK • 1983

The book as a whole to my wife Ingaret
Giffard for editing this Christmas trilogy
with such concern for its meaning; *A Bar of
Shadow*, as it was when first published, to
William Plomer

"Et venio in campos et lata praetoria memoriae."

St. Augustine

"And came upon him in the fields and palaces of my memory."

Contents

Christmas Eve

A Bar of Shadow

As we walked across the fields we hardly spoke. I, myself, no longer had the heart to try and make conversation. I had looked forward so eagerly to this Christmas visit of John Lawrence and yet now that he was here, we seemed incapable of talking to each other in a real way. I had not seen him for five years; not since we said good-bye at our prison gates on release at the end of the war, I to return to my civilian life, he to go straight back to the Army on active service. Until then for years he and I had walked as it were hand in hand with the danger of war and endured the same bitter things at the hands of the Japanese in prison. Indeed, when our release came we found that our experience, shared in the embattled world about us, fitted like a measured garment to the great and instinctive coincidence of affection we felt for each other. That moment of rounded nearness had stayed with me. There was no separation in it for me, no distance of purple leagues between him and me. I knew only too well the cruel and unnecessary alliance (unnecessary because either one of them is powerful enough) that time and distance contract for waging their war against our brief and brittle human nearnesses. But if I had managed to stay close, why should he have been set so far apart? For that is precisely what I felt. Although he was so near to me that I had but to half stretch out a hand to take his arm, never in five years of separation had he seemed so far away as now.

I stole a quick glimpse of him. The suit of pre-war tweeds which still fitted him perfectly, sat on his tall broad frame more like service uniform than becoming country garments and he was walking like a somnambulist at my side, with an odd unconscious deliberation and purposefulness, a strange, tranced expression on his face. His large grey eyes, set well apart under that fine and wide brow in a noble head, were blue with the distance between us. Even the light of that contracting December afternoon, receding from the day like the grey tide of a stilled sea from a forgotten and forlorn foreshore fuming silently in the gathering mists of time, glowed in his eyes not like a light from without so much as the fading tones of a frozen wintry moment far back in some calendar of his own within. Their focus clearly was not of that moment and that place and the irony of it was almost more than I could bear without protest.

I don't know what I would have done if something unknown within me, infinitely wiser and more knowledgeable than my conscious self marching at his side in bitter judgement over this resumption that was not a resumption of our relationship, had not suddenly swept into command and ordered me to ask: "You have not by any chance run into 'Rottang' Hara again?"

The question was out before I even knew I was going to ask it and instantly I felt a fool at having put it, so irrelevant and remote from that moment did it seem. But to my amazement, he stopped short in his tracks, turned to me and, like someone released from an emotion too tight for him, said with obvious relief:

"It is curious you asking me that! For I was thinking of him just then." He paused slightly and then added with an apologetic laugh, as if he feared being misunderstood: "I have been thinking of him all day. I can't get him out of my mind."

My relief matched his, for instantly I recognized a contact that could bridge his isolation. Here was a pre-occupation I could understand and follow a long way even if I could not share it to the end. Just the thought of Hara and the mention of his name was enough to bring the living image of the man as clearly to my senses as if I had only just left him and as if at any moment now behind me that strange, strangled, nerve-taut, solar-plexus voice of his which exploded in him when he was enraged, would shriek *"Kura!"* —the rudest of the many rude ways in Japanese of saying: "Come here, you!"

At the thought the hair on the back of my neck suddenly became sensitive to the cold air and involuntarily I looked over my shoulder as if I really expected to see him standing at the gate by the Long Barn beckoning us with an imperious arm stretched out straight in front of him, and one impatient hand beating the air like the wings of a large yellow butterfly in its last desperate flutter before metamorphosis into a creeping and crawling thing on earth. But the field behind us, of course, was empty, and the great, grey piece of winter, the tranquil and tranced benediction of a rest well earned by eager earth long wooed and well-beloved by man, lay over the tired and sleeping land. The scene indeed in that gently shrinking moment of daylight stood over itself as if it were an inner dream in the inmost sleep of itself, as if circumstances had contrived to make it conform absolutely to that vision which had made England a blessed thought of heaven on earth to us when we were in prison under Hara, and a rush of bitterness, rudely brushing aside the relief I had felt, went straight to my heart that Hara's twisted, contorted shape should still be able to walk this intimate and healing scene with us.

I said "in prison under Hara" for though he was not the Commandant he was by far the greatest of the powers that ruled our prison world. He himself was only a third-class sergeant in His Imperial Japanese Majesty's forces and nominally we had a young subaltern in charge, but that slight young man more resembled an elegant character out of the novels of the great Murasaki or the pillow book of her hated rival than a twentieth-century Samurai. We seldom saw him and his interest in us seemed focused only on the extent to which we could add in variety and number to his collection of wrist-watches. John Lawrence, who had once been assistant military attaché in Tokyo, said he was certain our commandant was not born in the great hereditary military classes of Japan but was probably a second-class Customs official from Kobe or Yokohama who could therefore not be dishonoured as a real soldier would have been by an ignominious appointment to command a camp of despised prisoners of war. But Hara, he said, was the real thing, not of the officer class, but the authentic feudal follower, unhesitatingly accompanying his master and overlords into battle. He had served his masters long and well, had fought in Korea, Manchuria, China, and this unexacting job now, presumably, was his reward.

I don't know how right Lawrence was, but one thing stood out: Hara had no inferiority complex about his officer. One had only to see them together to realize which was authentic, predestined military material and which merely deriving colour and benefit from war. Scrupulously correct as Hara was in his outward behaviour to his officer, we had no doubt that inwardly he felt superior. He never hesitated to take command of a situation when he thought it necessary. I have seen him on inspections walk rudely in between the Commandant and our ranks, haul out someone who had unwittingly transgressed his mysterious code of what was

due on these occasions, and in a kind of semiconscious epi-
lepsy of fury, beat the poor fellow nearly to death with
anything that came to hand, while his disconcerted officer
took himself and his refined-Custom-house senses off to a
more tranquil part of the parade-ground. No! Not he but
Hara ruled us with a cold, predetermined, carefully con-
ditioned and archaic will of steel as tough as the metal in
the large, two-handed sword of his ancestors dangling
on his incongruous pre-historic hip.

It was he, Hara, who decided how much or rather how
little we had to eat. He ordained when we were driven to
bed, when we got up, where and how we paraded, what
we read. It was he who ordered that every book among
the few we possessed wherein the word "kiss" or mention of
"kissing" appeared, should be censored by having the
offending pages torn out and publicly burned as an offence
against "Japanese morality." It was he who tried to "purify"
our thinking by making us in our desperately under-
nourished condition go without food for two days at a time,
confined in cramped and over-crowded cells, forbidden
even to talk so that we could contemplate all the better
our perverse and impure European navels. It was he who
beat me because a row of beans that he had made my men
plant had not come up and he put the failure down to my
"wrong thinking." It was he who when drunk would babble
to me endlessly about Greta Garbo and Marlene Dietrich
whose faces haunted him. He who questioned me for hours
about Knights of the Round Table, "606," Salvarsan and the
latest drugs for curing syphilis. He mounted and controlled
our brutal Korean guards, gave them their orders and made
them fanatical converts, more zealous than their only
prophet, to his outlook and mood. He made our laws, judged
us for offences against them, punished us and even killed
some of us for breaking them.

He was indeed a terrible little man, not only in the way that the great Tartar Ivan was terrible but also in a peculiarly racial and demonic way. He possessed the sort of terribleness that thousands of years of littleness might seek to inflict on life as both a revenge and a compensation for having been so little for so long. He had an envy of tallness and stature which had turned to an implacable hatred of both, and when his demon—an ancient, insatiable and irresistibly *compelled* aspect of himself that lived somewhere far down within him with a great yellow autonomy and will of its own—stirred in him I have seen him beat up the tallest among us for no other reason save that they were so much taller than he. Even his physical appearance was both a rejection and a form of vengeance on normality, a vaudeville magnification and a caricature of the Japanese male figure.

He was so short that he just missed being a dwarf, so broad that he was almost square. He hardly had any neck and his head, which had no back to it, sat almost straight on his broad shoulders. The hair on his head was thick and of a midnight-blue. It was extremely coarse and harsh in texture and, cut short, stood stark and stiff like the bristles on a boar's back straight up in the air. His arms were exceptionally long and seemed to hang to his knees but his legs by contrast were short, extremely thick and so bowed that the sailors with us called him "Old Cutlass-legs." His mouth was filled with big faded yellow teeth, elaborately framed in gold, while his face tended to be square and his forehead rather low and simian. Yet he possessed a pair of extraordinarily fine eyes that seemed to have nothing to do with the rest of his features and appearance. They were exceptionally wide and large for a Japanese and with the light and polish and warm, living, luminous quality of the finest Chinese jade in them. It was extraordinary how far they went to redeem this terrible little man from caricature. One looked into his eyes and all desire to mock vanished, for then one realized that this twisted being was, in some manner beyond European comprehension, a dedicated and utterly selfless person.

It was John Lawrence, who suffered more at Hara's hands than any of us except those whom he killed, who first drew our attention to his eyes. I remember so clearly his words one day after a terrible beating in prison.

"The thing you mustn't forget about Hara," he had said, "is that he is not an individual or for that matter even really a man." He had gone on to say that Hara was the living myth, the expression in human form, the personification of the intense, inner vision which, far down in their unconscious, keeps the Japanese people together and shapes and compels their thinking and behaviour. We should not forget two thousand and seven hundred full cycles of his sun-goddess's rule burnt in him. He was sure no one could be more faithful and responsive to all the imperceptible murmurings of Japan's archaic and submerged racial soul than he. Hara was humble enough to accept implicitly the promptings of his national spirit. He was a simple, uneducated country lad with a primitive integrity unassailed by higher education, and really believed all the myths and legends of the past so deeply that he did not hesitate to kill for them. Only the day before he had told Lawrence how in Manchuria the sun-goddess had once lifted a train full of soldiers over an undetected Chinese mine laid for them on the track and put them all down again safely on the other side.

"But just look in his eyes," Lawrence had said: "there is nothing ignoble or insincere there: only an ancient light, refuelled, quickened and brightly burning. There is something about the fellow I rather like and respect."

This last sentence was such heresy among us at the time

that I protested at once. Nothing Lawrence could say or explain could wash our *bête noir blanc* or even *jaune* for that matter, and I would have none of it.

"The troops do not call him 'Rottang' for nothing," I had reminded him severely. "Rottang" is the Malay for the kind of cane Hara was seldom without. The troops christened him that because he would at times, seemingly without cause, beat them over the head and face with it.

"He can't help himself," John Lawrence had said. "It is not he but an act of Japanese gods in him, don't you see? You remember what the moon does to him!"

And indeed I remembered. The attraction, both the keen conscious and the deep, submerged attraction that all the Japanese feel for the moon seemed to come to a point in Hara. If ever there was a moon-swung, moon-haunted, moon-drawn soul it was he. As the moon waxed—and how it waxed in the soft, velvet sky of Insulinda, how it grew and seemed to swell to double its normal gold and mystically burning proportions in that soft, elastic air; how it swung calmly over the great volcanic valleys like a sacred lamp, while the ground mist, mingling with the smell of cloves, cinnamon and all the fragrant spices of Insulinda drifted among the soaring tree trunks like incense round the lacquered columns of a sequined temple—Yes! as this unbelievable moon expanded and spread its gold among the blacknesses of our jungle night, we saw it draw a far tide of mythological frenzy to the full in Hara's blood. Seven days, three days before and three days after and on the day of the full moon itself, were always our days of greatest danger with Hara. Most of his worst beatings and all his killings took place then. But once the beating was over and the moon waning, he would be, for him, extraordinarily generous to us. It was as if the beating and killing had purged him of impurities of spirit, of madness and evil in some strange way and made him grateful to them. In fact, the morning after he had cut off the head of one of us, I remembered seeing him talking to Lawrence and being struck by the fact that he had an expression of purified, of youthful and almost springlike innocence on his face, as if the sacrifice of the life of an innocent British aircraftman the night before, had redeemed him from all original as well as private and personal sin, and appeased for the time the hungry bat-like gods of his race.

All this passed through my mind like a dream with the speed and colour of a dream and it was almost like a man half asleep that I heard Lawrence continue: "Yes. It is curious that you too should think of him just then; for I have an anniversary of Hara in me today, that I am not allowed to forget, try as I may. Have I ever told you?"

He had not and eager to consolidate any contact between us, even this grim, precarious bridge, I said quickly: "No! Please tell me."

Well, it was exactly seven years ago, he said, seven years within an hour or so, allowing for differences of Insulinda and Greenwich mean time. He was lying in a dream beyond the deep, raw, physical pain in his bruised and outraged body, when far away, like a bird perched on the daylight rim of a deep well into which he might have been thrown, he heard the first chee-chak call. Yes, that was it: a chee-chak, one of those agile, translucent little lizards that lived in every hut, house and even deepest dungeons in Insulinda. There were two of them in his cell and he loved them dearly. They had shared his solitary confinement from the beginning and in his affection for them he fancied he could tell them apart, the male from the female, just by the sound of their voices. They were the only living things not Japanese or Korean, not an active, aggressive enemy that he had seen for many weeks. So real had they become to him that he christened them Patrick and Patricia. He knew instantly when he heard the sound, that the sound came from Patricia, and at once he was out of the dream that had consoled and drugged his pain, and back on the damp stone floor with his bruised, stiff, aching and tired body, so tired that it could hardly take note even of the dismay which clutched at his heart the moment Patricia called. For she called like that only when it was well and truly dark, only when the jungle outside had closed its ranks and fallen back on its own black shadows between the purple volcanoes, the better to withstand that sheer, utter obliteration of outline and shape brought about by the overwhelming invasion of the moonless tropical night in the valley outside. It was as if then Patricia herself was afraid and wanted Patrick quickly to rejoin and reassure her that this great black nothingness abolished only the vision of the nearness of her mate and not the nearness itself. There! Patrick had answered her, and Lawrence knew his fear was justified. For this was the hour at which the Japanese usually came for him; this was the time of night when they usually did their torturing. Yes, the details of it were not important, he said, but for weeks they had been torturing him, and the interesting thing was they did it always at night.

I might smile and think him fanciful as I did about his belief that Hara was an embodiment of a myth more than a conscious individual being, even though I had seen for myself how moon-swung Hara and his countrymen were. But that was by no means all there was to it. That was only the elementary beginning of it all. The more complete truth was: they were all still deeply submerged like animals, insects and plants in the succession of the hours, the movement of day into night and of the days into their lunar months and the months into their seasons. They were subject to cosmic rhythm and movement and ruled by cosmic forces beyond their control to an extent undreamt of in the European mind and philosophy. He would have more to say of that presently, but all he had to stress at the moment was this: it was only at night that people so submerged in the raw elements of nature could discover sufficiently the night within themselves—could go down far enough with sun and sunlight into that deep, deep pit of blackness in time and themselves to the bottom of their own unlit natures, where torture was not only natural but inevitable, like the tides of the sea. I may not recognize it, he said, but Patricia and Patrick knew in the nerves and very swish of their tidal tails that a moment of great and ancient dread in the movement of the spheres had come. And hardly had they called, when he heard the jack-booted steps, untidy and slurred as if the boots were mounted on an orang-utan, and not a man, coming down the corridor towards his cell.

"Our Father which art in heaven," his lips moved instinctively. "Once more please be thou my shepherd."

As he said this prayer for the third time to himself, the door was unlocked and a Korean guard called out, in a mixture of the crudest Japanese and Malay and in the most arrogant and insolent tone: "*Kura!* You there, come here! *Lakas!* Quick!"

He got up slowly. He could not in his condition do otherwise, but it was too slow for the guard who jumped into the cell, pulled Lawrence angrily to his feet and pushed him out into the corridor, prodding him with the butt of his rifle and saying again and again: "*Lakas! Lakas!*" and "Quick! Quick!" as well as making other strange irritated abdominal noises at him. In a few minutes he was marched into the Commandant's office and there sitting at the Commandant's desk was not that girlish young subaltern, but Hara himself with a section of the guard, hat in hand and rifles at the side standing respectfully behind him. Lawrence, his eyes hurting as if stung by bees in that fierce electric light, looked round the room for the rest of the inquisition as he called them, that expert band from the Kempitai, the headquarters of the secret-police, who did the real torturing, but there was not a sign of any of them.

For the first time a feeling of hope so keen and unnerving that his conscious mind would not allow it, assailed him fiercely. True, Hara was one of the band but not the worst. He joined in too but only when that deep sense of an almost mystical necessity to participate in all that a group or herd of his countrymen did, forced him to identify himself with what was going on. It was as if they all were incapable of experiencing anything individually; as if a thought or deed in one was instantly contagion to the rest and the fated plague of cruel-doing like a black or yellow death killed their individual resistances in an instant. Hara, after all, was the Japanese of the Japanese among them and he too would have to join in the torturing. But he never started it and Lawrence knew somehow that he would have preferred killing outright to protracted torture. With all this in his mind he looked at Hara more closely and noticed that his eyes were unusually bright and his cheeks flushed.

"He has been drinking," he thought, for there was no mistaking in Hara's cheeks the tell-tale pink that drink brings so easily to the Japanese face. "And that accounts for the glitter in his eye. I had better watch out."

He was right about the flush in Hara's cheeks but wrong about the light in his eye, for suddenly Hara said, with a curl of the lip that might have been a smile strangled at birth: "Rorensu-san: do you know Fazeru Kurīsumasu?"

The unexpected use of the polite "san" to his name so nearly unnerved Lawrence that he could hardly concentrate on the mysterious "Fazeru Kurīsumasu" in Hara's question, until he saw the clouds of incomprehension at his slowness, which usually preluded frenzy, gathering over Hara's impatient brow. Then, he got it.

"Yes, Hara-san," he said slowly. "I know of Father Christmas."

"Heh-to!" Hara exclaimed, hissing with polite gratification between his teeth, a gleam of gold sparkling for a moment between his long lips. Then sitting far back in his chair, he announced: "Tonight I am Fazeru Kurīsumasu!" Three or four times he made this astonishing statement, roaring with laughter.

Lawrence joined in politely without any idea what it really meant. He had been lying there in his cell alone, under sentence of death, for so long that he hardly knew the hour of the night beyond the fact that it was normal torture hour, and he had no idea of the date or month; he certainly had no idea that it was Christmas.

Hara enjoyed his announcement and Lawrence's obvious perplexity so much that he would have gone on prolonging his moment of privileged and one-sided merriment, had not a guard presented himself at that moment in the doorway and ushered in a tall, bearded Englishman, in the faded uniform of a Group-Captain in the R.A.F.

Hara stopped laughing instantly and an expression of reserve, almost of hostility came over his features at the sight of Hicksley-Ellis's elongated frame in the doorway.

I could see Hara clearly, as Lawrence spoke; could see him stiffen at the R.A.F. officer's entrance, for of all of us he hated the tall, lisping Hicksley-Ellis, I think, by far the most.

"This Air-Force Colonel," he told Lawrence in Japanese, waving his hand disdainfully at the Group-Captain, "is Commander of the prisoners in my camp; you can go with him now."

Lawrence hesitated, not believing his ears, and Hara, confirmed in his own sense of the magnanimity of his gesture by the unwilled expression of disbelief on Lawrence's face, sat back and laughed all the more. Seeing him laugh like that again, Lawrence at last believed him and walked over to join the Group-Captain. Together, without a word, they started to go but as they got to the door, Hara in his fiercest parade voice called: "Rorensu!"

Lawrence turned round with a resigned despair. He might have known it, known that this transition was too sudden, too good to be true; this was but part of the torture; some psychologist among the secret police must have put the simple Hara up to it. But one look at Hara's face reassured him. He was still beaming benevolently, a strange twisted smile, between a quick, curling lip and yellow teeth framed in gold on his twilight face. With an immense, hissing effort, as he caught Lawrence's eye, he called out, "Rorensu: Merry Kurīsumasu!"

"Merry" and "Fazeru Kurīsumasu" were the only English words Lawrence ever heard him use and he believed Hara knew no others. Hara went pinker still with the effort of getting them out, before he relaxed, purring almost like a cat, in the Commandant's chair.

"But he knew something about Christmas, all the same," I interrupted Lawrence. "It was most extraordinary, you know. When the Padre, Hicksley-Ellis and I, thought of organizing some celebration of our first Christmas in gaol, we never thought for a moment a thug like Hara would allow it. But the curious thing was when we asked him, he exclaimed at once, so our interpreter said: 'The feast of Fazeru Kurīsumasu!' When the interpreter answered 'Yes,' Hara agreed at once. No argument or special plea was needed. He said 'Yes' firmly, and his orders went out accordingly. In fact, he was himself so taken by the idea that he went to the other camps that were also in his Officers command, camps with non-Christian Chinese, animistic Menadonese and Moslem

Javanese in them and forced them all to celebrate Christmas whether they liked it or not. The interpreter told us, in fact, that Hara even beat up the Chinese commandant. When Hara asked him who Fazeru Kurīsumasu was, the unsuspecting man quite truthfully said he had no idea. Whereupon Hara called him a liar, a crime in his code equal to 'wrong thinking' and 'wilfulness,' said all the world knew who 'Fazeru Kurīsumasu' was, and at once flew into one of his frenzies. It was odd, very odd, the value he attached to Christmas; we never found out where he got it from. Did you?"

"I am afraid not," Lawrence answered, "but odder still it saved my life."

"You never told us!" I exclaimed, amazed.

"No, I did not, for I didn't know it myself at the time, though I expected it of course from my own sentence. But I saw my papers after the war and they were actually going to kill me on December 27. But your putting the idea of Christmas into Hara's head saved me. He substituted a Chinaman for me and let me out as a gesture to 'Fazeru Kurīsumasu.' But to continue . . ."

He had followed Hicksley-Ellis out of Hara's office and joined up with me again in the common prison. Suddenly he smiled at me, a gentle, reminiscent and tenderly grateful smile as the relief of his release came back to him. Did I remember the moment? He could not but be amused in his recollection, for although we were all incarcerated in a Dutch colonial gaol for murderers and desperate criminals, so relative had our concept of freedom become, that we rushed up to him and congratulated him on his liberation without a trace on our part, or a suspicion on his, of the irony implicit in it.

Then not long afterwards Hara suddenly left us. He was put in charge of a draft of R.A.F. officers and men under

Hicksley-Ellis, and sent to build aerodromes in the outer islands. We did not see him again until near the end, when he returned with only one-fifth of the original draft left alive. Our men looked like ghosts or drought-stricken cattle when they arrived back. We could see their shoulder-blades and ribs through their thread-bare tunics. They were so weak that we had to carry most of them in stretchers from the cattle-trucks wherein they had travelled, trucks which stank of urine and diseased excretions. For not only were they so starved that just a faint pulse of life fluttering with a rapidly regressive spirit was left in them, but also they all had either dysentery, malignant malaria or both. One-fifth was all that remained; the rest were dead and Hicksley-Ellis had terrible things to tell of their treatment by the Japanese officers and N.C.O.s and their Korean underlings, and above all about Hara. Again, Hara was at the centre, the primordial Japanese core of this weird inspiration of distorted circumstances. It was he who was again *de facto* if not *de jure* ruler of their world; he who beat dying men saying there was nothing wrong with them except their "spirit," their "evil thinking," their "wayward wilfulness of heart" which made them deliberately ill in order to retard the Japanese war effort. It was he, Hara, who cut off the heads of three Aircraftmen because they had crept through a fence at night to buy food in a village, and after each head rolled on the ground brought his sword to his lips thanking it for having done its work so cleanly. It was he who day after day in the tropical sun drove a horde of men ailing and only half alive to scrape an aerodrome out of coral rock with inadequate tools until they were dying and being thrown to the sharks in the sea at the rate of twenty or thirty a day. But Hara himself appeared untouched by his experience, as if he had foreseen and presuffered it all in his mother's womb, as if life could neither add to nor diminish the stark wine in his legendary cup. He came back to us burnt black by the sun; that was all. For the rest he naturally took up the steely thread of command where he left it as if he had never been away, and drove us again with the same iron hand.

Even at the end when the prison was full of rumours and the treacherous, unstable Korean guards, scenting a change in the wind of time, were beginning to fawn and make up to our men for past misdeeds, were even whining to them about their own suppression under the Japanese, when the ground under the feet of Hara's war lords was cracking and reverberating from the shock of the explosions at Hiroshima and Nagasaki and when the legendary twilight of the submerged racial soul of Japan must have been dark and sagging under the weight of the wings of dragons coming home to roost, Hara never trembled nor wavered once. He must have known as well as anybody what was going on, but in that tide of rumour and wild emotion running free before the wind of change, he stood like a rock.

Only three days before the end there was a terrible scene with Lawrence. Lawrence had found a Korean sentry, one of the worst, prodding a dying man with his bayonet, trying to make the Aircraftman stand up to salute him. Lawrence had seized the sentry's rifle with both hands, pushed the bayonet aside and forced himself between the sentry and the sick man. He was immediately marched off to the guardroom, arriving there just as Hara returned from a tour of inspection. The sentry told Hara what had happened and Hara, much as he liked Lawrence, would not overlook this insult to the arms of his country. He beat up Lawrence with his cane over the face and head so thoroughly that I hardly recognized him when he joined us again.

Three days later the end came and we all went our inevitable ways. Lawrence did not see Hara again for nearly two years. When he saw Hara then it was in dock at his trial. Yes! Hadn't I heard? Hara was sought out and brought to trial before one of our War Crimes Tribunals. It was largely Hicksley-Ellis's doing of course. I could have no idea how bitter that mild, lisping, sensitive fellow had become. It was understandable, of course, after what he had suffered, that he should be truly, implacably and irretrievably bitter and vengeful, and he gave his evidence at the trial with such a malign relish and fury that Hara never had a hope of a mitigated sentence, let alone acquittal. But what was not so understandable was the bitterness of the official prosecution, for bitter as Hicksley-Ellis was, his temper was more than matched by that of the war-crimes sleuths.

"And that," Lawrence exclaimed, incomprehension on his broad brow: "was very odd to me. After all, none of them had suffered under the Japanese. As far as I know, not one of the particular bunch on Hara's trial had even been on active service but they were nonetheless a bloodthirsty lot. They were more vengeful on behalf of our injuries than I myself could ever be."

He said all this in such a way that I gathered he had tried to plead for Hara and had failed. It certainly seemed highly significant to me that when Lawrence held his hand out after the trial to say good-bye, Hicksley-Ellis had refused to take it and silently turned a neat, tense Air-Force back on him. I could not resist asking therefore:

"Did you tell the Court that Hara saved your life?"

"Indeed I did," he replied, surprised that I should have found the question necessary. "I did that and the judge-advocate looked me up and down over a pair of the most unmilitary glasses and said in a slow, precise voice, each syllable as distinct and pointed as a letter pen-pricked on a blank sheet of paper, a trace of ponderous irony, for which I can't blame him, in his voice: 'That, of course, Colonel

Lawrence, is a valuable consideration—most valuable, indeed hardly less valuable to this court than it must be to you; but it must not be overlooked that there are many others for whom life would have been no less valuable who are not here today as a direct result of the accused's actions.' "

No, there was obviously nothing to be done. Hara was inevitably condemned to be hanged.

"How did he take it?" I asked with the memory of the way others had marched to the fall of Hara's keen two-headed sword on the backs of their necks as fresh in my mind as if it were a picture painted that morning.

"Without a tremor or change of expression, as you would have expected," Lawrence said. "After all, he had pleaded guilty from the start. He had said, as that hopelessly inadequate interpreter told the Court: 'I am wrong for my people and ready to die!' He made no effort to defend himself except to say that he tried never to do more nor less than his duty. He called no witnesses, asked no questions even of me, and just went on standing silently and rigidly to attention in the box right to the end. Besides, all that too had been foreseen."

"Foreseen?" I asked, surprised.

Yes! He explained Hara had never expected anything except death of some kind in the war. In fact, in an unconscious way, perhaps he had even longed for death. I must please not be too sceptical but try and follow what he was trying to say with intuition rather than with conscious understanding. This was the other half of what he'd been trying to say in the beginning. It was most important, most relevant and the one foundation whereon his understanding either stood erect or fell. . . . He had always felt even when he was in Japan that the Japanese were a people in a profound, inverse, reverse, or if I preferred it, even perverse sense, more in love with death than living. As a nation they romanticized death and self-destruction as no other people. The romantic fulfilment of the national ideal, of the heroic thug of tradition, was often a noble and stylized self-destruction in a selfless cause. It was as if the individual at the start, at birth even, rejected the claims of his own individuality. Henceforth he was inspired not by individual human precept and example so much as by his inborn sense of the behaviour of the corpuscles in his own blood dying every split second in millions in defence of the corporate whole. As a result they were socially not unlike a more complex extension of the great insect societies in life. In fact in the days when he lived in Japan, much as he liked the people and country, his mind always returned involuntarily to this basic comparison: the just parallel was not an animal one, was not even the most tight and fanatical horde, but an insect one: collectively they were a sort of super-society of bees with the Emperor as a male queen-bee at the centre. He did not want to exaggerate these things but he knew of no other way of making me realize how strangely, almost cosmically, propelled like an eccentric and dying comet on an archaic, anti-clockwise and foredoomed course, Hara's people had been. They were so committed, blindly and mindlessly entangled in their real and imagined past that their view of life was not synchronized to our urgent time. Above all they could not respond to the desperate twentieth-century call for greater and more precise individual differentiation. Their view of life refused to be individual and to rise above their own volcanic and quaking earth, as if there was always a dark glass or the shadow of the great dragon's wings of their submerged selves between them and the light of individual mind, a long blackness of their own spinning globe between them and the sun, darkening the moon for which they yearned so eagerly, and some of the finest stars.

He was sorry if it sounded fantastic but he could put it no other way. Unless . . .

He paused and looked at the simple spire of the village church just appearing in a dip in the fold of the fields in front of us, as if its precise and purposeful shape presiding so confidently over the trusting and sleeping land, rebuked the shapeless, unformed and dim-lit region wherein his imagination moved so like a lone sleep-walker at midnight. Thereupon, he broke off the apparent continuity of his thought at once and asked me if I knew how the Japanese calculated the age of an individual? I said "No" and he explained that at birth they added nine months to a person's life, counted in all the days between his conception and emergence from the womb. Didn't I see the significance of that? Didn't I realize that such a system of reckoning life was not just an artless and naïve accident of minds more primitive than ours? If I paused to reflect how biology clearly establishes that we recapture and relive in the womb the whole evolution of life from amoeba to pithecanthropus erectus, surely I too would recognize implicit in this system of reckoning a clear instinctive acknowledgement of the importance of the dim past to the Japanese character. He certainly looked at it that way and until now he had been forced to think of them as a people whose spiritual and mental umbilical cord with the past was uncut; as a people still tied by the navel to the mythical mother and begetter of their race, the great sun-goddess Ama-terasu. Even in that they were characteristically perverse, reverse and inside out, for to most races in the past the sun was a bright and shining masculine deity, but to them only a great, darkly glittering mother. While the moon, so beloved and eternally feminine to the rest of mankind, was male and masculine to them. Perhaps it was that inside-out, upside-down subjection to the past which gave them their love of death.

If I had ever attended a feast of the dead in Japan as he had often done I would not be surprised at his use of so strange a word as love to illustrate his meaning. That feast was the gayest and most cheerful of all Japanese celebrations. Their dead were happy, cheerful, contented and benevolent spirits. Why? Because the living, one felt, really preferred dying to living as they had to live; not only preferred it but also thought it nobler to die than to live for their country. Not life but death was romantic to them and Hara was no exception. He had all this and more, deeply ingrained in him, underneath and beyond conscious thinking; he had more because above all he was a humble, simple and believing country fellow as well.

"I shall never forget one night in prison," Lawrence continued, picking up yet another thread of our prison yesterdays, and weaving it as if it were something new and freshly made into this pattern of Hara in his mind until my heart was heavy that so much should remain for him apparently immune to time. "Hara sent for me. He had been drinking and greeted me uproariously but I knew his merriment was faked. He always behaved like that when his heart and mind were threatening to join in revolt against his long years of exile from Japan. I could see that the drink had failed to blur the keen edge of nostalgia that was like a knife-stab in the pit of his stomach. He wanted someone to talk to about his country and for some hours I walked Japan from end to end with him through all four of its unique and dramatic seasons. The mask of cheerfulness got more and more threadbare as the evening wore on and at last Hara tore it from his face.

" 'Why, Rorensu,' he exclaimed fiercely at last. 'Why are you alive? I would like you better if you were dead. How could an officer of your rank ever have allowed himself to fall alive in our hands? How can you bear the disgrace? Why don't you kill yourself?' "

"Yes. He asked me that too once," I interrupted, more with the object of letting Lawrence know how closely I was following him than of telling him something he didn't know. "In fact he taunted us all so much with it that in time the Koreans picked up the habit, too, but what did you say in reply?"

"I admitted the disgrace, if he wished to call it that," Lawrence replied. "But said that in our view disgrace, like danger, was something which also had to be bravely borne and lived through, and not run away from by a cowardly taking of one's own life. This was so novel and unexpected a point of view to him that he was tempted to dismiss it as false and made himself say: 'No! no! no! it is fear of dying that stops you all.' He spat disdainfully on the floor and then tapping on his chest with great emphasis added: 'I am already dead. I, Hara, died many years ago.'

"And then it came out, of course. The night before he left home to join the army at the age of seventeen, that is after nine months in the womb and sixteen years and three months on earth, he had gone to a little shrine in the hills nearby to say good-bye to life, to tell the spirits of his ancestors that he was dying that day in his heart and spirit for his country so that when death came to claim him in battle it would be a mere technicality, so that far from being surprised he would greet it either like a bosom friend, long expected and overdue, or merely accept it as formal confirmation of a state which had long existed. To hear him one would have thought that this bow-legged boy, with his blue-shaven head, yellow face and shuffling walk, had gone to report to his ancestors his decision to enter one of the grimmer monastic orders like the Grande Chartreuse, rather than to announce his banal intention of joining a regiment of infantry. But you see what I mean, when I say the end too had been foreseen?"

I nodded silently, too interested to want to speak, and Lawrence went steadily on. Even that evening in prison Lawrence was conscious of a content, a sort of extraterritorial meaning to the moment that did not properly belong to it. It was as if Hara's end was drinking his wine with him, as if far down at some inexpressible depth in their minds the ultimate sentence was already pronounced. Looking back now, he found it most significant, that towards the end of the evening, Hara began to try his hand at composing verses in that tight, brief and extremely formal convention in which the popular hero of the past in Japan inevitably said farewell to the world before taking his own life. He remembered Hara's final effort well: roughly translated it ran:

"When I was seventeen looking over the pines at Kurashi-yama, I saw on the full yellow moon, the shadow of wild-geese flying South. There is no shadow of wild-geese returning on the moon rising over Kurashiyama tonight."

"Poor devil: as I watched and listened to him trying to break into verse, suddenly I saw our roles reversed. I saw as if by a flash of lightning in the darkness of my own mind that I was really the free man and Hara, my gaoler, the prisoner. I had once in my youth in those ample, unexacting days before the war when the coining of an epigram had looked so convincingly like a discovery of wisdom, defined individual freedom to myself as freedom to choose one's own cage in life. Hara had never known even that limited freedom. He was born in a cage, a prisoner in an oubliette of mythology, chained to bars welded by a great blacksmith of the ancient gods themselves. And I felt an immense pity for him. And now four years later, Hara was our kind of prisoner as well and in the dock for the last time, with sentence of death irrevocably pronounced."

So unsurprised, so unperturbed was Hara, Lawrence said, that as his escort snapped the handcuffs on him and ordered him to step down to his cell below, he stopped on the edge of the concealed stair, turned round with the utmost self-composure, sought out Lawrence and Hicksley-Ellis who were sitting side by side next to the prosecuting officer. When his eyes met theirs, he raised his manacled hands above his head, clasped them together like those of a boxer who had just won the world championship and waved gaily to the two of them, grinning a golden smile from ear to ear as he did so.

How clearly I saw him do it: that gesture was all of a piece with the character also as I knew it, for whatever it was that held Hara together, I too knew that he could never fail it. Suddenly I was glad, almost grateful to him that he had taken it like that, gone from our view with a gay, triumphant gesture of farewell, for somehow, I imagined, that would make it easier for us now to have done with his memory.

"So that was how he went," I remarked, not without a certain unwilled relief, "that then was Hara's that."

"No, not at all," Lawrence said quickly, a strange new ring in his voice, a passionate and surprisingly emotional undertone for so calm and contemplative a person. "That by no means was his 'that.' As far as I am concerned 'that' was only the end of the beginning of the 'that' . . ."

It came out then that the night before he was hanged, Hara got a message through, begging Lawrence to come and see him. Hara had made the request—his last—many days before but it was not surprising to anyone who knew the "usual official channels" as well as we did that the request did not reach Lawrence until ten o'clock on the night before the morning set for the execution. Lawrence got his car out as fast as he could; his chivalrous nature outraged by the thought that the condemned man would now most certainly have given up all hope of seeing him, and be preparing to die with the bitter conviction that even his last slight request had been too much. Hara's prison was on the far side of the island and he could not, with the best of luck, get there before midnight.

The evening was very still and quiet, rather as if it had caught its own breath at the beauty and brilliance of the night that was marching down on it out of the East like a goddess with jewels of fire. An immense full moon had swung itself clear over the dark fringe of the jungle bound, like a ceremonial fringe of ostrich plumes designed for an ancient barbaric ritual, to the dark brow of the land ahead. In that responsive and plastic tropical air the moon seemed magnified to twice its normal size and to be quick-silver wet and dripping with its own light. To the north of the jungle and all along its heavy feathered fringes the sea rolled and unrolled its silver and gold cloak on to the white and sparkling sand, as lightly and deftly as a fine old far-eastern merchant unrolling bales of his choicest silk. The ancient, patient swish of it all was constantly in Lawrence's ears. But far out on the horizon, the sea too went dark, seemed shrunk into a close defensive ring, in face of the thunder and lightning hurled against it by curled, curved and jagged peaks of cloud which stood revealed on the uttermost edge by the intermittent electric glow imperative in purple and sullen in gold. It was the sort of night and the kind of setting in a half-way moment between the end of one day and the beginning of the other, in which Lawrence's articulate knowledge seemed to hold the same urgent, spasmodic, and intermittent quality as the electricity and lightning quivering along the horizon; yet his inarticulate, inexpressible awareness of the abiding meaning, beauty and richness of life was as great as the vast, eager-footed and passionate night striding overhead like a queen to a meeting with a royal lover. All that we had been through, the war, the torture, the long hunger, all the grim and tranced years in our sordid prison, he found light and insignificant weighed in the golden scales of that moment. The thought that yet another life should be sacrificed to our discredited and insufficient past, seemed particularly pointless and repugnant and filled him with a sense of angry rebellion. In this mood and manner he arrived at the prison just before midnight. He found he was expected and was taken at once to Hara's cell.

Like all condemned persons Hara was alone in the cell. When the door opened to let Lawrence in, although there was a chair at hand Hara was standing by the window, his face close to the bars, looking at the moonlight, so vivid and intense by contrast to the darkness inside that it was like a sheet of silver silk nailed to the square window. He had obviously given up all idea of visitors and was expecting, at most, only a routine call from one of his gaolers. He made no effort to turn round or speak. But as the guard switched on the light he turned to make a gesture of protest and saw Lawrence. He stiffened as if hit by a heavy blow in the back, came to attention and bowed silently and deeply to his visitor in a manner which told Lawrence that he was moved beyond words. As he bowed Lawrence saw that his head had been freshly shaven and that the new scraped skin shone like satin in the electric light. Lawrence ordered the sentry to leave them for a while, and as the door once more closed he said to Hara who was coming out of his low bow:

"I'm very sorry I am so late. But I only got your message at nine o'clock. I expect you gave me up as a bad job long ago and thought I'd refused to come."

"No, Rorensu-san," Hara answered. "No, not that. I never thought you would refuse to come, but I was afraid my message, for many reasons, might not be delivered to you. I am very grateful to you for coming and I apologize for troubling you. I would not have done so if it hadn't been so important. Forgive me please, but there is something wrong in my thinking and I knew you would understand how hard it would be for me to die with wrong thoughts in my head."

Hara spoke slowly and deliberately in a polite, even voice, but Lawrence could tell from its very evenness that his thought was flowing in a deep fast stream out to sea, flowing in a deeper chasm of himself than it had ever flowed before.

"Poor, poor devil, bloody poor devil," he thought, "even now the problem is 'thinking,' always his own or other people's 'thinking' at fault."

"There is nothing to forgive, Hara-san," he said aloud. "I came at once when I got your message and I came gladly. Please tell me what it is and I'll try and help you."

From the way Hara's dark, slanted, child-of-a-sun-goddess's eyes lit up at the use of the polite "san" to his name, Lawrence knew that Hara had not been spoken to in that manner for many months.

"Rorensu-san," he answered eagerly, pleading more like a boy with his teacher than a war-scarred sergeant-major with an enemy and an officer, "it is only this: you have always, I felt, always understood us Japanese. Even when I have had to punish you, I felt you understood it was not I, Hara, who wanted it, but that it had to be, and you never hated me for it. Please tell me now: you English I have always been told are fair and just people: whatever other faults we all think you have; we have always looked upon you as a just people. You know I am not afraid to die. You know that after what has happened to my country I shall be glad to die tomorrow. Look, I have shaved the hair off my head, I have taken a bath of purification, rinsed my mouth and throat, washed my hands and drunk the last cupful of water for the long journey. I have emptied the world from my head, washed it off my body, and I am ready for my body to die, as I have died in my mind long since. Truly you must know, I do not mind dying, only, only, only, why must I die for the reason you give? I don't know what I have done wrong that other soldiers who are not to die have not done. We have all killed one another and I know it is not good, but it is war. I have punished you and killed your people, but I punished you no more and killed no more than I would have done if you were Japanese in my charge who had behaved in the same way. I was kinder to you, in fact, than I would have been to my own people, kinder to you all than many others. I was more lenient, believe it or not, than army rules and rulers demanded. If I had not been so severe and strict you would all have collapsed in your spirit and died because your way of thinking was so wrong and your disgrace so great. If it were not for me, Hicksley-Ellis and all his men would have died on the island out of despair. It was not my fault that the ships with food and medicine did not come. I could only beat my prisoners alive and save those that had it in them to live by beating them to greater effort. And now I am being killed for it. I do not understand where I went wrong, except in the general wrong of us all. If I did another wrong please tell me how and why and I shall die happy."

"I didn't know what to say." Lawrence turned to me with a gesture of despair. "He was only asking me what I had asked myself ever since these damned war-trials began. I honestly did not understand myself. I never saw the good of them. It seemed to me just as wrong for us now to condemn Hara under a law which had never been his, of which he had never even heard, as he and his masters had been to punish and kill us for transgressions of the code of

Japan that was not ours. It was not as if he had sinned against his own lights: if ever a person had been true to himself and the twilight glimmer in him, it was this terrible little man. He may have done wrong for the right reasons but how could it be squared by us now doing right in the wrong way. No punishment I could think of could restore the past, could be more futile and more calculated even to give the discredited past a new lease of life in the present than this sort of uncomprehending and uncomprehended vengeance! I didn't know what the hell to say!"

The distress over his predicament became so poignant in this recollection that he broke off with a wave of his hand at the darkening sky.

"But you did say something surely," I said. "You could not leave it at that."

"Oh yes, I said something," he said sadly, "but it was most inadequate. All I could tell him was that I did not understand myself and that if it lay with me I would gladly let him out and send him straight back to his family."

"And did that satisfy him?" I asked.

Lawrence shook his head. He didn't think so, for after bowing deeply again and thanking Lawrence, he looked up and asked: "So what am I to do?"

Lawrence could only say: "You can try to think only with all your heart, Hara-san, that unfair and unjust as this thing which my people are doing seems to you, that it is done only to try and stop the kind of things that happened between us in the war from ever happening again. You can say to yourself as I used to say to my despairing men in prison under you: 'There is a way of winning by losing, a way of victory in defeat which we are going to discover.' Perhaps that too must be your way to understanding and victory now."

"That, Rorensu-san," he said, with the quick intake of

breath of a Japanese when truly moved, "is a very Japanese thought!"

They stood in silence for a long while looking each other straight in the eyes, the English officer and the Japanese N.C.O. The moonlight outside was tense, its silver strands trembling faintly with the reverberation of inaudible and far-off thunder and the crackle of the electricity of lightning along the invisible horizon.

Hara was the first to speak. In that unpredictable way of his, he suddenly smiled and said irrelevantly: "I gave you a good Kurīsumasu once, didn't I?"

"Indeed you did," Lawrence answered unhappily, adding instinctively, "You gave me a very, very good Christmas. Please take that thought with you tonight!"

"Can I take it with me all the way?" Hara asked, still smiling but with something almost gaily provocative in his voice. "Is it good enough to go even where I am going?"

"Yes: much as circumstances seem to belie it," Lawrence answered, "it is good enough to take all the way and beyond . . ."

At that moment the guard announced himself and told Lawrence he had already overstayed his time.

"Sayonara Hara-san!" Lawrence said, bowing deeply, using that ancient farewell of the Japanese "If-so-it-must-be" which is so filled with the sense of their incalculable and inexorable fate. "Sayonara and God go with you."

"If so it must be!" Hara said calmly, bowing as deeply. "If so it must be, and thank you for your great kindness and your good coming, and above all your honourable words."

Lawrence stood up quickly not trusting his self-control enough to look at Hara again, and started to go, but as he came to the doorway, Hara called out: "Rorensu!" just as he had once called it in the Commandant's office after Lawrence's weeks of torture. Lawrence turned and there was

Hara grinning widely, faded yellow teeth and gold rims plainly showing as if he had never enjoyed himself more. As Lawrence's eyes met his, he called out gaily: "Merry Kurīsumasu, Rorensu-san."

But the eyes, Lawrence said, were not laughing. There was a light in them of a moment which transcends lesser moments wherein all earthly and spiritual conflicts tend to be resolved and unimportant, all partiality and incompletion gone, and only a deep sombre between-night-and-morning glow left. It transformed Hara's strange, distorted features. The rather anthropoidal, prehistoric face of Hara's looked more beautiful than any Lawrence had ever seen. He was so moved by it and by the expression in those archaic eyes that he wanted to turn back into the cell. Indeed he tried to go back but something would not let him. Half of himself, a deep, instinctive, natural, impulsive half, wanted to go back, clasp Hara in his arms, kiss him good-bye on the forehead and say: "We may not be able to stop and undo the hard old wrongs of the great world outside, but through you and me no evil shall come either in the unknown where you are going, or in this imperfect and haunted dimension of awareness through which I move. Thus between us, we shall cancel out all private and personal evil, thus arrest private and personal consequences to blind action and reaction, thus prevent specifically the general incomprehension and misunderstanding, hatred and revenge of our time from spreading further." But the words would not be uttered and half of him, the conscious half of the officer at the door with a critical, alert sentry at his side held him powerless on the threshold. So for the last time the door shut on Hara and his golden grin.

But all the way back to town that last expression on Hara's face travelled at Lawrence's side. He was filled with great regret that he had not gone back. What was this ignoble half that had stopped him? If only he had gone back he felt now he might have changed the whole course of history. For was not that how great things began in the tiny seed of the small change in the troubled individual heart? One single, lonely, inexperienced heart had to change first and all the rest would follow? One true change in one humble, obedient and contrite individual heart humble enough to accept without intellectual question the first faint stirring of the natural spirit seeking flesh and blood to express it, humble enough to live the new meaning before thinking it, and all the rest would have followed as day the night, and one more archaic cycle of hurt, hurt avenged and vengeance revenged would have been cut for ever. He felt he had failed the future and his heart went so dim and black on him that abruptly he pulled up the car by a palm-grove on the edge of the sea.

Sadly he listened to the ancient sound of the water lapping at the sands, and the rustle of the wind of morning in the palms overhead travelling the spring world and night sky like the endless questing spirit of God tracking its brief and imperfect container in man. He saw some junks go out to sea and the full moon come sinking down, fulfilled and weary, on to their black corrugated sails. The moon was now even larger than when he had first seen it. Yes. Now Hara's last moon was not only full but also overflowing with a yellow, valedictory light. And as he was thinking, from a Malay village hidden in the jungle behind there suddenly rang out the crow of a cock, sounding the alarm of day. The sound was more than he could bear. It sounded like notice of the first betrayal joined to depravity of the latest and became a parody of Hara's call of "Merry Christmas." And although it was not Christmas and the land behind was not a Christian land, he felt that he had betrayed the sum of all the Christmases.

Quickly he turned the car round. He would get back to the gaol, see Hara and atone for his hesitation. He drove recklessly fast and reached the gates as the dawn, in a great uprush of passionate flaming red light, hurled itself at the prison towers above him.

"But of course I was too late," Lawrence told me, terribly distressed. "Hara was already hanged."

I took his arm and turned with him for home. I could not speak and when he went on to ask, more of himself than of me or the darkening sky, "Must we always be too late?" he asked the question, without knowing it, also for me. It hung like the shadow of a bar of a new prison between us and the emerging stars and my heart filled with tears.

Christmas Morning

1. The Morning After

The Christmas morning after John Lawrence told me about Hara, I woke very early to find my mind not on the day but obsessed with the memory of Jacques Celliers. I rose quietly before it was light, before even our two children were awake, and went downstairs to my study. I unlocked the one compartment in my desk where I keep the things that mean most to me and took out seven cardboard folders. I opened the top one quickly to make certain the contents were intact and was instantly reassured to see Celliers' tense thrusting hand on the coarse yellow sheets of toilet paper which was the only paper the Japanese would allow us in our prison. Although the edges of the frail paper were frayed and partially rotted from damp under the stone floor of the prison cell wherein they had lain wrapped in a remnant of an army groundsheet, the hand was remarkably fresh and clear, as if it had only just penned the description of events instead of some eight years before. Just for a moment as I held this slim parcel of writing between my hands my fingers tingled as if with shock at the miracle which had enabled it to survive not only the heavy damp of the dark Javanese earth but also the fanatical search by our captors. Finally, years after the end of the war, the Javanese civilian mason who had found it had even been moved with enough wonder to take it to an official. And the official happened to have known me. When this man saw my name and address in England written on the outside and read the entreaty that it should be delivered to me he ignored the normal formalities, not without some risk to himself, and posted it off to me at once.

I sat there for a while, thinking deeply again as I had done so often since I received it, how strange it was that Celliers should have chosen me as his recipient. There must have been many people in his own country who had known him far better. Indeed for some months I wondered why he had not sent it to the brother who figures so disturbingly in his narrative. But when I myself went to his old home I discovered how little that would have helped, though it deepened the strangeness of his action by an implication of a clear foreknowledge of events still to come. But perhaps strangest of all to me, sitting there in the silence of the still Christmas dawn, was the fact that it should be there safe in my hands to show to John Lawrence. What he had told me about himself and Hara the evening before made me feel that Celliers might have written the document not for himself, not for me, not even for his brother, but specifically for Lawrence. I could hardly wait for full morning to come, to break away from the excited children, get out of church and, immediately after breakfast, to draw Lawrence to one side and ask:

"D'you remember Jacques Celliers?"

As he looked puzzled I hastened to add: "Surely you must! That tall good-looking South African officer who was with me on my first raids behind the lines in North Africa and afterwards with the 51st Commando in the Western Desert? He used to dine with me in our mess from time to time."

"Good heavens!" Lawrence exclaimed, his grey eyes quickening with interest: "Of course I remember him. He was a remarkable soldier. And apart from that he was almost the only man I've ever met whom one could call beautiful. I can see him now . . . walking about . . . almost like an animal, always on his toes and loose in the ankles. Had the guts of a lion too, and the endurance of a camel! That's the man you mean, isn't it? And didn't he have some nickname . . . ?"

I nodded. "That's Celliers all right: 'Straffer Jack' the troops called him." I gave Celliers the name he was popularly known by all along the precarious Libyan front in 1941.

"D'you know," Lawrence went on: "I've thought of him a great deal lately. Only yesterday I found myself wondering what had become of him. I always had a feeling he'd never come through alive. I never knew him as you did, of course, and as you know he never said much, at least to me. Indeed for a person who could talk so well when he wanted to I remember him as an oddly silent man . . ." He paused. "But he seemed to me to behave sometimes as if he wanted to get himself killed."

"Perhaps you're not far wrong," I said quietly.

"Did he get himself killed then? What happened to him? Why d'you ask me now if I remember him?" Lawrence questioned quickly, his imagination plainly roused.

"Look!" I said. "I'd rather you first read this document that he wrote before I answer your questions. What we talked about last night made me feel that you, rather than I, should be its keeper. Read it. It won't take long. And then we can talk."

I left him alone sitting with his fine head and responsive face on which time had written its own meaning with such intimacy, bowed over the yellow paper. Behind him the soft, grey Christmas Day was lifting over the accepting fields which, in prison, had haunted my memory like a vision of heaven on earth. This, then, is what Lawrence read.

2. A Brother

I had a brother once and I betrayed him. The betrayal in itself was so slight that most people would find "betrayal" too exaggerated a word, and think me morbidly sensitive for so naming it. Yet as one recognizes the nature of the seed from the tree, the tree by its fruit, and the fruit from the taste on the tongue, so I know the betrayal from its consequences and the tyrannical flavour it left behind it in my emotions. That is one of the fundamental things about betrayal, and which perhaps is better set down here, beyond doubt, right at the beginning. Though I say it without pride or humility but merely as a fact of my life, I speak now as an expert in this matter. And as such I can assure you that one of the most significant characteristics of betrayal is that it is neither spectacular nor presumptuous in origin. Indeed those treacheries destined to reach furthest in their consequences prefer not to be obvious or dramatic in their beginnings but rather to wait, humbly and unostentatiously, until they are ready to bear their bitter fruit in maturity. They seem to favour presenting themselves to the unguarded heart selected to become their own private seed-bed as trivialities in the daily routine of life, as insignificant occurrences so self-evident that no question of a choice and so no chance of rejection arises out of their appearance on the familiar scene of everyday events. In fact betrayal behaves as if it were worth no more than the miserable thirty pieces of silver that were paid for the greatest and most meaningful betrayal of all time. That I suggest is not only a fundamental but also one of the most frightening aspects of it. Contrast betrayal, for instance, with something else which also grows great out of very little, namely faith. No matter how far awareness pursues faith, even if it is to the outermost ends of being, faith still stands positively on the threshold of the world. There faith still will move mountains provided it has some substance in the heart. But betrayal has no need of anything particular in order to exist. It can begin most effectively as a mere refusal to be, a casual negation, as the insubstantial pollen of the deadly nightshade of nothingness. Like the geometric point in the intuitive heart of Euclid betrayal needs neither magnitude nor size for its existence but only position. Here then is the moment, the place and the circumstances; here the position in my own life of the betrayal of which I wish to speak.

There were four of us children in my family. I was the first, then came two girls and lastly my brother. But both my sisters died in one of those typhoid epidemics which were inflicted upon our remote African world, like one of the plagues of Egypt, before each of our fanatical droughts. So my brother and I were left, as my mother one day put it under an emotion that I was too young to share, not only to be brothers but also sisters to each other. I mention this here not out of a belated recognition of what she must have felt but because I had reason to remember the remark many years later. Between my brother and myself there was a difference of seven years and these seven years now had a difference of their own because of the tender flesh and blood so brutally extracted from them. They moved lean and hungry in my memory with the slow, mediumistic pace of the famished out of the river-bed of time, like the gaunt herd in Pharaoh's dream which warned Joseph of the great hunger and thirst to come. This, then, added a particular nuance to this separation in age between my brother and myself, making it a difference not only of life but of death as well. However, this was only one of the many differences between us all of which I have to mention because they contribute to my story.

To begin with I was born fair with dark blue eyes. I was well-made, and I grew up tall and strong without hurt or impediment to assail the physical confidence implicit in my step and carriage. My body was at home in the wide physical world about us, and my person at ease with the people in it. I seemed to move as appropriately to my environment as does a gilt-edged fish with its silky swish in an amber sea. From an early age I played, rode, shot and worked with the best of my childhood peers. In my response to the challenge with which the disdainfully cunning and infinitely experienced old earth of Africa teased and provoked the life it contained, I'm told that I was tireless and fearless. I was also well-spoken and good-looking. In fact this last sentence is so much of an understatement of something which had an important effect on my character that I ought really to enlarge on it.

The truth is that from an early age most people found my looks disturbing and many of them were strongly attracted to me on account of my appearance. This again is one of those things I say without pride or humility, without vanity or self-satisfaction. I have long since come to the diamond point of the tumult within myself where facts alone, and nothing but the facts, accurately observed and truly interpreted, can move me. I know that only fact can save me and I long passionately to be able, from the facts of my being, to forge a weapon strong enough to enable me to fight back against the power and pomp of unreality which is marching so boastfully against both me and the spirit of my time. But over this matter of my appearance, if I do recognize any other emotion in myself it is one of subtle and pervasive distaste. Perhaps this sounds ungrateful to life which has conferred such favours on me? Yet the truth remains. Part of me strongly resented my looks and blamed them too for what became of me. We had a neighbour who was born a dwarf and, as a child, whenever I saw him I used to pity him and feel grateful that I had not been given his shape. Yet today I am not sure that I should not have envied him. I simply do not know which constitutes the greatest danger to the integrity of being: to attract or to repel; to incur the dislikes or likes of one's fellow men. The dwarf, after all, had only pity to fear and, men being what they are, that is never excessive. But I had their instant, magnetic liking for my enemy and before I knew where, or even who I was, I had become a prisoner of the effect I had on them. The dwarf was firmly shackled to his deformity. But I was shackled not so much to my good looks as to what people, after seeing me, first imagined and then through their imaginations compelled me to be. I know now that from my earliest age the effect that I had on those about me enticed me away from myself, drew me out of my own inner focus of being, and left me irrevocably committed to the role that my admirers and the obscure laws of their magnetic attraction automatically demanded of me. To this day I shiver at the recollection of the cold impersonal power and efficiency of the mechanism of this compulsion, both in me and others, which forced me to lend my little measure of irreplaceable flesh and blood to the shadowy desires, phantom wishes and unlived selves of those around me. Slowly but surely I grew into a bitter estrangement from myself: a prodigal son in a far country of famished being, without any inkling of the dream that could have worked on my errant raw material. I suffered, as it were, from the curse of

Helen whose face launched a thousand ships and burnt the topless towers of Ilium, that Helen whose image still haunts the eyes of men wherein she was held prisoner for so long.

Yet I was not Narcissus-bound to any lilied reflection of my physical body. I never saw myself as good-looking. I have stared often enough in mirrors and shop windows but not with pride, only furtively, as if afraid of seeing also in the reflection what I felt myself to be. For, despite the plausible objective evidence to the contrary, I have known always that I was also an ugly person. I knew that what others found so attractive was only an outer aspect of something greater to which both it and this other ugliness were equally and irrevocably joined. In some mysterious way I was conscious that there was never one but always a pair of us, always a set of Siamese twins sitting down nightly to sup at the round-table of myself, a pair of brothers designed to nourish and sustain, yet also inexplicably estranged and constantly denying each other.

Yes, despite all provocations, I could never see myself as others saw me. The reflection that has become my master-reflection is not silver-quick in the crystal light of a modern mirror but is somewhat withheld, like the slow gleam behind the glassy surface of a particular pool which used to lie in our black bush-veld wood like a wedding ring in the palm of a Negro's hand. Oh, how clearly I remember that pool and that far distant dawn when I first dismounted from my horse to quench our thirsts at its golden water. I was kneeling down, my right hand held out to scoop up the burning water and my left holding the reins of the steam-silver horse beside me as, before drinking, it carefully blew the dawn-illumined pollen of spring in a rainbow smoke across the flaming surface. And suddenly, there, beyond the rose-red bars of the rhythmical vibration set up by my horse's fastidious lips, I saw my own reflection coming up out of the purple depths of the pool to meet me. I could not see clearly. The reflection remained shadowy, very different from my bright morning figure bent low over it. It stayed there, a dark dishonoured presence straining in vain for freedom of articulation against that trembling, dawn-incarnadined water as if the corrugations on the surface were not the bars of a natural vibration but rather those of a cage contrived to hold it forever prisoner. At the time it made me sad. It would have been better, perhaps, if it had made me angry. Who knows? Certainly not I.

But to return to the differences between my brother and myself. In appearance he was not at all like me. He was very dark in accordance with an unpredictable law which seems to dominate reproduction in both my father's and mother's families. His hair was as thick and dark as mine was fair and fine. His skin was a Mediterranean olive and his eyes, which were his best feature, were wide and of an intense radiant blackness. I could never look in them without feeling curiously disturbed and uncomfortable. I wish I could say why, but the discomforts of the spirit are beyond reason. Suffering is only a stroke of Time's implacable Excalibur dividing meaning from meaninglessness. I am forced, nonetheless, to attempt an explanation. There were moments when those deep eyes of his seemed to me to be unbearably defenceless. They seemed too trusting, too innocent of the calculation and suspicion of our civilized day. And because of this they seemed (though I am never sure regarding the personal emotions or intentions of my brother) to hold a kind of reproach against me and the world wherein I was so conspicuously at my ease.

I wish I could deal more firmly with this subtle discomfort but I cannot. I only know it was there from the beginning and as far back as I can remember it expressed itself from time to time in an involuntary feeling of irritation which, no matter how unreasonable and unfair, no matter what precautions I took to the contrary, would break out impatiently from me. What made it worse was that my brother never seemed to mind. He would take it all quite naturally, almost as part of his own dark, impervious birthright. When I begged his pardon awkwardly, as I invariably did, he would look at me warmly and say quickly, "But it was nothing, Ouboet, nothing at all. Don't worry so." In fact he would behave as if I had just rendered him some great service, as if my very impatience and irritation had given us both an opportunity which otherwise might never have existed. It was all very mysterious and I have had to make my peace with it by accepting it as something inevitable. But the flaw (if it is a flaw) inflicted by life on me is also, I suspect, incorporated in the master-seed of the being and greater becoming of us all, just as is the infinitesimal flaw that first gave birth to a pearl in the shell. One has said that there is "no greater love than that a man should lay down his life for his friends." Yet is it not, perhaps, as great a love that a man should live his life for his enemies, feeding their enmity of him without ever himself becoming an enemy until at last enmity has had surfeit and his enemies are free to discover the real meaning of their terrible hunger—just as my brother provoked and endured my strange hostility without ever becoming hostile to me? However, I am expert not in love but in betrayal and as little entitled to make points on the specialist's behalf as he would on mine, so I shall not press the issue unduly. Yet, for the sake of the proportions of my narrative, I must add that I was not alone in my reaction to my brother. He had much the same effect on most people with whom he came in regular contact.

I grew up, as I indicated, tall and gracefully made. He from the beginning was a square, short, awkwardly shaped person, immensely strong but ponderous and inclined to

be clumsy in his movements. He was not, I fear, prepossess-
ing to look at. What magic he had was in his eyes and they,
unfortunately, made one uncomfortable. His head was too
big even for his broad shoulders, yet his face after such
roughness of stature was disconcertingly tender, while his
brow, with a double crown of hair at the centre, was from
birth deeply furrowed. The effect was of a face profoundly
still though darkly withheld. Yet it could become startlingly
light, even beautiful, when he laughed and showed his even,
white teeth. But unfortunately, in public he rarely laughed.
Laughter appeared to be something he kept for the two of
us when the tension between us lessened. So, as a rule, his
face seemed folded, brooding over his nature rather like one
of our black African hens over her nest, head cocked slightly
towards the earth, senses deaf to the music of the sun
stroking the great harp of light in one of our feverish summer days, listening only to the electric expectancy of life
within her.

At school I was good in most things, games as well as
studies. My brother had great difficulty in scraping through
his examinations and could take no interest and acquire no
skill in sport. I was fast and a first-rate sprinter; he was slow
and an indefatigably plodding walker. I loved animals, the
flame-flickering game and sun-fire birds of Africa. He took
no great interest in them but from childhood was absorbed
in all that grew in the earth. I had no patience for planting
and sowing: he loved to plough and to sow. It was remarkable too, how successful his clumsy fingers were: whatever
he put in the earth seemed to grow and blossom. He used
to walk behind his favourite span of roan-purple oxen from
dawn to sunset, his deep single-furrow plough turning over
waves of Africa's scarlet earth like the prow of a Homeric
blackship the swell of a wine-red morning sea. He would
come home in the twilight after a day's ploughing deep in

content. Often I've found him resting, silent on the handlebars of his plough. "A penny for your thoughts, Boetie," I would greet him.

He would never answer at once. Then he'd say slowly, "Just smelling the earth. You know, there's not a flower in the world that smells so good to me as freshly turned-over earth!"

Then I would notice it too, that smell of Titanic perspiration in the glandular earth of the ancient land charging the fiery air all around us like the black quintessential of a magician's spell. Finally, when the rough old greatcoat of the earth was turned inside out and its antique lining lying velvet in the sun, he would stride across the naked land sowing his first corn like someone in an illustrated New Testament parable. I would watch him bestride the passionate soil, noticing his awkward, lumbering gait as if his being always had presupposed this heaving earth beneath his feet even as a sailor's feet always presupposes the swinging sea. His intuition in regard to the land too was uncannily accurate. As a child I have watched him standing absorbed over a patch of earth for so long that in the end I have exclaimed impatiently: "Are you going to stand there all day dreaming? Wake up, for God's sake!"

"Sorry, Ouboet," he would say equably, "I was wondering what we should suggest planting here. It might grow something pretty good. But what?"

"Well, we'll have to try before we can know," I would reply unmollified.

"All the same, looking does help, Ouboet," he would answer mildly, or words to that effect, and despite my sniff of unbelief I had an uncomfortable suspicion that perhaps he was right. In a way that I could not understand he and the earth had their own magnetic exchange of each other's meanings. When we got home he would suggest a crop to our father and that crop, as often as not, is growing there fruitfully to this day in the course of its lawful rotation.

Besides all this he possessed a remarkable gift of water-divining. I remember so well the day when we first discovered that he possessed this power. I was already almost a man but he was still a boy. Our father, anxious to add to our existing supplies already weakened by a succession of droughts, was looking for new water. Accordingly he had called in the help of one of those water-diviners who were always drifting through our land in the service of their strange intuition like Old Testament prophets.

We watched the gaunt old man arrive with a donkey led by a tiny black boy, watched him cut a forked stick from the nearest wild olive tree and strip down the stick from its precise classical leaf. Then he strode down to the selected site like Moses to the rock in the vermilion desert at Horeb. Once there, he gripped the fork, a prong placed tightly in the palm of each hand, but the stick itself pointed up at the blue sky like the hands of a pilgrim joined in prayer. Then, with a slow ritualistic step, he walked across the scene from east to west, the fitful whirlpool eddies of the hot afternoon air irreverently clicking his long beard out of the focus of his trance-like movement. When the critical moment came, the knuckles of his hands went white from the effort he was making to prevent the prongs of the fork turning in his grasp. But slowly the point of the stick began to vibrate and waver until suddenly, despite all his exertions to prevent it, the point plunged straight down quivering like an arrow in a drawn bow over the earth at his feet. As it happened an involuntary murmur went up from the white people present and a marvellous "Ye-bo!" came from our uninhibited black servants followed by a laugh which was not only a laugh but also a release of tension as if the charge which had mounted so mysteriously in the blood of the old man had welled up unbearably in them, too.

Unperturbed by the reaction of the onlookers, the old man stopped instantly at that point, drew a long line with his finger east and west in the earth, retreated thirty paces to the south and repeated his tense, hypnotic walk to the north. His gift did not fail him. The stick plunged a second time, and there again he drew another line south and north in the earth. Where the two lines crossed, he dug his heel into the ground and said to our father: "There is good water here. Two strong arteries meeting about a hundred feet down."

I had just completed my first year of Law at the University and my newly awakened reason was irritated by the old man's air of simple assurance. I thought at once that he was just putting on an act to disguise a guess that could be no better than our own. I whispered so to my brother but he, without emotion, quietly disagreed, "You're wrong, Ouboet."

"Don't be so silly, how could anyone know?" I replied irritated.

"But I know," he answered mildly. Then seeing the irritation mounting in me he added quickly with an odd note of surprise as if the explanation were news to him, too: "I know because—because I believe it would work with me, too."

"What?" I looked down at him but there was no mistaking that he was in deadly earnest. "Let's prove it then," I said quickly thinking it would do him no harm to make a fool of himself.

Instantly he went up to the diviner without a trace of embarrassment. "Oom," he said, "would you mind if I tried it, too?"

The old man looked at him with quick surprise. Then he

gave me a glance which somehow disturbed me before turning back to my brother. "Certainly," he answered. "Here's the stick. Be careful to hold it like this." He put the prongs of the stick in my brother's hand. "Grip it tight; keep your eyes on the point and walk steadily. A step with each breath and you will not fail to confound the unbelievers in our midst."

Then we all turned to watch the awkward, lumbering figure of my brother imitate the diviner's performance.

Intangible as these things are, there was no doubt that my own disapproval was beginning to communicate itself to the others and there was an increasing feeling that the boy was being allowed to presume too much. However, my brother seemed unaware of this mood in the watchers. Young as he was I could not help remarking the odd authority in his bearing. In fact he repeated the diviner's performance faultlessly and at the end of it all the fork twisted earthwards and where the old man had bent to make his cross, he too drew another like it in the earth with his forefinger. Then he stood up to look at us, no doubt expecting some acknowledgement for what he had done. But, as if in mutual agreement that to give him too much credit for what had happened might add to his boyish presumption, after a few words we passed immediately into a busy discussion of the arrangements necessary for boring on the chosen spot.

I do not know what my brother felt but the scene has stayed with me, and often in a guilt-quick memory I have remembered him stooping awkwardly and with his clumsy finger making again his first sign of the cross in the thirsty sand. Oh! the mysterious inevitability of those crosses in our blood! This deep game of noughts and crosses played unremittingly, night and day, from one dimension of being to another of becoming. First the flaming sword of an archangel making a cross over the gate to the forbidden garden of our lost selves. Again a cross over the doorway of the first ghetto to keep away the angel of death on the night of terror before exodus from nothingness in the bondage of Egypt's plenty to another country of strange, unlikely promise across the desert. Then another Cross where darkness gathers steeply over the very promise itself. Always, the significance of a long journey from bondage to a country not yet known: the negation which can only become positive when a cross has been nailed against it. Always, it seems, in the blank space at the end of the inadequate letter lies a large cross for a kiss from that terrible lover, life, who will never take "No" for an answer. So here, too, at the beginning of the boy about to become man was a cross made to mark the possibility of water in problematical sand.

Yet if on that day automatically we tried to make nothing of my brother's gift, he was unaffected by this.

He came up to me and said: "Look, Ouboet. It was much stronger than me!"

I looked unwillingly and saw that the bark had been stripped off the olive as it twisted and turned in his fist and there, in the broad palm turned upwards before my sceptical eyes, was stigmata of the deed, the skin torn and the flesh red and watery from its struggle with the fierce earthbound wood.

"Looks as if you'd scratched yourself," I said coolly.

Yet that night as we lay in the shared bed on the wide open *stoep,* looking up at a clear sky with the stars crackling and the Milky Way coming down like a river in flood, I begged his pardon. I admitted grudgingly that he may have been right—though it couldn't signify what he and the diviner thought it did.

He replied, "Oh, that was nothing," and turning on his side he fell instantly asleep, leaving me wakeful and dissatisfied.

For there are degrees in nothingness. Nothingness has its own backward inevitability of erosion. On this occasion there was something specific for which I could beg his pardon. But the master-nothing to which all these apprentice occasions are bound is so insubstantial that no question or thought of pardon arises.

There remain still two essential differences between my brother and myself to enumerate but before I do so I must add that when my brother became a man his gift for water-divining was much in demand in our remote world. He put it at the service of whoever needed it. But he would never accept any reward. Uncomfortable as it made many rich people to be under an obligation to him, he would never charge, saying always: "I can't take payment for it. The gift isn't mine. If I took money for it, I know it would leave me."

I have mentioned already that physically I was well-made and my brother not so favoured. Now I have to confess that he had a slight deformity. It was not in the least obvious, and my mother was able to conceal it almost entirely by arranging that his clothes were always slightly padded along the shoulders. It was not discernible as a specific deformity and yet in some way it formed a sure centre round which not only all that was odd in his appearance but also all that in his nature was at variance with the world seemed to meet. It was amazing how, whether other people knew of its existence or not, sooner or later their eyes were compelled by the laws of my brother's own being to fasten on this spot between his shoulders. I don't know who was the more sensitive about it: he or I. All I do know is that between us we never referred to it by name. We always designated it by an atmospheric blank in our sentences. For instance, I would say, "But if you do go swimming there wouldn't they see . . . blank." Or he to me: "D'you think if I wore that linen jacket it would . . . blank . . . you know?"

Instantly we would both know that we were referring to the razor-edged hump between his shoulders. Self-contained as he was in his spirit, yet this deformity was a breach in my brother's sufficiency which he could never man, and any enemy from without who discovered it could walk through the breach at will.

I have said we were both extremely sensitive about it but perhaps it would be more accurate to say he was afraid because of it, irrationally afraid of what the world might think, feel and be provoked to do on account of it. My own sensitiveness, on the other hand, although I passed it off to myself as a form of "minding for him," was of a different order. This, after all, was a problem in a dimension which was peculiarly my own. I could not readily endure the thought of people setting eyes on this razor-edged hump behind my brother's broad shoulders because I must have feared that it would reflect on me. I could not bear that anything related to me was not of the best. I had not learned to fear my lack of physical blemish as my brother did his deformity. And the scales, in this matter of our appearance, seemed so unfairly loaded against him. We could never appear together without people being reminded of it. Though it was an inequality which was not of my making and the blame (if such a word can be used for so impersonal a process) lay with life, yet the fact remained that I was, no matter how unwillingly, the main instrument whereby this manifest inequality was kept alive. I think again of the Man from Palestine when He said, "It may be that offence has to come in life but woe to him by whom it comes." He might have spoken the words for me. My discomfort over my brother's deformity had yet another powerful stimulus. I must have known instinctively that however much people sympathized with my brother on a perfunctory level, underneath, in the more spontaneous world of their emotions, they often felt embarrassed and even threatened by his departure from the norm. They could even secretly resent it and wish him out of the way. I say this confidently because I have found since both in myself and others that the greater the need for individual differentiation from a stagnant normality, the more we struggle and resent those who represent this difference. I have even noticed the same tendency in the behaviour of animals, and I think now of one animal in particular who played a brief, mysterious role in my story. But all I submit here is that, in those far-off days, I and those around me in our behaviour to my brother confirmed this paradoxical law without ever knowing what we did. I grew up showing an excessive solicitude on behalf of my brother's deformity, firmly believing it was his feelings that I wanted to protect. Yet without realizing it I was obliquely asserting values and defending feelings which belonged to me and my own world. In doing so I was extremely popular with my fellow men. My brother at best was tolerated. It was most noticeable that the moment he entered a room wherein I had company restraint came in with him like winter's fog. I immediately began to defend and explain him without appearing to do so, and found myself acting out an elaborate apologia on his behalf. My friends then began to feel that they had a duty to deny the effect caused by his odd appearance and soon the conversation became too artificial and self-conscious to be enjoyed. My brother grew up apparently a lonely, friendless person. Yet it sometimes seemed that I had more interests and friends than my life could contain.

And now I come to the final difference between us. I was tone-deaf. I could not sing in tune. It may sound a slight matter scarcely worthwhile mentioning. But for me it was an odd and difficult handicap. Secretly the fact that whenever I tried to join in any singing I spoilt it, made me surprisingly unhappy. If I persisted, as I often did when I was younger, I merely provoked a titter which forced me quickly to desist. It was an added irony too, that I, who was so well adapted to my world, was utterly at odds with it in my singing whereas my brother, whose nature always stood at such an acute angle, through his singing became completely at one. Even as a child he had a clear, unhesitating soprano which developed as he grew older into a manly and pleasantly rounded tenor.

I remember going to look for him once in our garden on my first day home from school on the long summer vacation. The garden was immense and I thought I would have difficulty in finding him. But I had just come to the edge of the orchard with its great yellow apricots, ruby peaches, purple plums and figs, pears, scarlet and pink cherries and pomegranates all shining like Persian jewellery in the morning sun, when I heard his voice, lovely as I had never heard it before, soaring up from the centre of the garden. He was singing something I didn't recognize which had that curiously simple yet urgent up-down rhythm of the African idiom. To me it sounded like primitive music before the mind and worldly experience had worked upon it.

I stood there listening to him singing, feeling more and more shut out from I knew not what—but something that I recognized to be urgent and vital. In the end I was overcome not by a nostalgia for the past (that is simple and well within the capacity of our awareness) but by a devouring homesickness for the future which is precipitated in our hearts through a sense of what we have left uncompleted behind us. The little song became for me, to borrow a platitude of the present day, a signature tune reminding me always of my brother as well as my own unrealized longings.

"Ry, ry deur die dag,
Ry, deur die maanlig;
Ry, ry deur die nag!
Want ver in die verte
Brand you vuurtjie.
Viriemand wat lang al wag."

The words, as you can see, even if you do not know our mother tongue, are simple enough. I can translate them freely in prose: "Ride, ride through the day, ride through the moonlight, ride, ride through the night. For far in the distance burns your fire for someone who has waited long."

"Where on earth did you learn that tune and who wrote the words?" I asked as I came on him watering seedbeds beside a tree sullen with the weight of its yellow fruit.

"Ag, Ouboet!" he answered, smiling in welcome, putting down his watering can and stretching his absurd frame: "It's just something that came bursting into my head one day while you were away."

As he spoke he had the same look on his face as when he made his cross beside the diviner's in the sand. But if he was waiting for some sort of acknowledgement from me he was again to be disappointed.

"It's not bad," I replied.

"Glad you think so," he answered. But he looked intently at me for a moment before he resumed his watering.

I suppose, therefore, it was no accident that my brother's first serious brush with the world of his boyhood was caused by his sense of the musical fitness of things.

In church the family who occupied the pew behind us had remarkably loud voices but no sense for tune. They all sang hymns loudly, usually slightly behind the rest of the congregation and almost two tones out of true, or so my brother said. One Sunday morning they were singing with such magnificent unawareness of their crime against the laws of harmony that my brother was first silenced, then set sniggering and soon we were both shaking with that convulsive merriment which sometimes assails one in places where it is strictly forbidden to laugh. The whole of the offending family gave us a very hard disapproving look after church but I thought no more of it. Yet from that Monday onwards I had an uneasy feeling of something amiss in our village life which I discounted as fantasy whenever it thrust itself upon my attentions and certainly did not connect with the episode of our merriment in church. Yet despite my determination not to recognize it, this feeling steadily grew. Unfortunately I did not know then, as I do now, how surely and wordlessly a change in the popular mood can communicate itself to those with whom the change is most concerned. During our school vacation neither my brother nor I had great occasion to go out into the streets, but whenever I did so I came back with a sense of uneasiness. It was as if some hostile force were secretly mobilizing against us. On occasions I would find myself in the main street at the sunniest hour of the day looking over my shoulder because of a sudden suspicion that I was being followed. Instantly I would laugh at myself for being so jumpy since invariably all I saw were the familiar figures of some of the village lads dodging artfully behind the glistening pepper-trees or swiftly round the corner of a wall which stood out like a rock in the sea of summer heat. "Obviously playing hide and seek," I told myself. And so ridiculous did any other interpretation seem that I mentioned my apprehensions to no one. Nor did I connect them with an added reserve in my brother's withdrawals.

Then one Wednesday morning from the moment I stepped into the street to carry out some errands for the house, I found this feeling of uneasiness subtly augmented. The manner in which I was greeted by the village, the looks I received, the words spoken, seemed to carry some new content of climax whose existence I could no longer deny. In the afternoon I was sent with my brother to take some horses to the blacksmith who lived a little distance outside the village. The village itself was very silent, half-asleep in the summer heat. The streets were empty and our horses' hooves echoed loudly from the walls of the white-faced houses. In the main grocer's window between the drawn blind and the panes, a large orange tabby cat lay fast asleep in the sun. As we passed, the edge of the blind was suddenly drawn back and the red head of the grocer's boy appeared, no doubt curious to see who rode out so loudly at so somnolent an hour of the day. He recognized us, and at once vanished so quickly that the blind whipping back into position flicked the sleeping cat smartly on the flank and sent it vanishing in a prodigious leap from the window shelf. Soon the hatless red-head emerged from the shop door, jumped the steps and came running after us.

"Hey!" he called out, and then when he caught up with us: "Off to the farm already?" he asked breathlessly.

Everybody asked everybody their business in our world and the question appeared to me no more than routine curiosity.

"Only taking the horses over to the blacksmith," I replied.

He stood there for a moment, repeating the words over and over to himself. Then he gave my brother a sly glance, broke off hurriedly, "Well, I must be off—Totsiens," * and disappeared in a golden blur of dust down the street.

Again I felt uneasy but merely shrugged my shoulders. What did it all mean?

I had been told to leave the horses at the blacksmith's and at once return home with my brother because some

* *Totsiens:* Au revoir.

cousins were coming that afternoon to call on us. But when the moment came I felt myself oddly reluctant to return. The smithy stood on the main cross-road at the edge of the bush-veld about a mile from the village. Leaning, hesitant, in the open gateway outside the smithy I saw that the country between us and the village was empty of people. Only a donkey and a cow with its calf were moving slowly about in a dream of after-dinner sleep, while an unfed grey falcon, suspended in a trance of blinding blue, trembled over their heads. It was all so silent and still that I stood on to let the familiar scene repulse my strange uneasiness. Then, distinctly, through the vibrations of light a cock crowed on the marches of our village. It has never been my favourite sound. In the indeterminate dawn hour between sleeping and waking it is bad enough. But breaking out suddenly as this crowing did, reminding me that yet another uncomprehended afternoon was about to plunge steeply into fathomless night, I found it almost more than I could endure. The crucified sound coming straight out of the heart of unrealized animal-being seemed appropriately a prelude to some inevitability of suffering. I looked up to the top of the spire of our village church which flaunted a cock rampant with a comb of stainless steel on its head, and for some reason I felt myself both reproached and warned by the sight.

I stirred. I couldn't go on standing there all day, but I turned to give a last glance at the smithy behind me. The smith was drawing a shoe, made magic in fire, from the forge. Placing its eager gold on to the black anvil he began expertly to batter it into shape for a horse stamping in the shade outside. Leaning on the bar of the bellows, a black apprentice flashed a smile at me. My brother, too, was watching and had the excitement of the fire glowing in his eyes.

I beckoned to him and, turning, we took the road to the village. Just before you enter our village the road dips steeply to disappear in a dry river bed emerging a hundred yards or so further on almost at the beginning of the main street. As we were walking I noticed in the distance dark figures hurriedly coming out of the village in clusters of three or four and taking the road down into the river bed. I thought nothing of it until I realized that none of the figures emerged on our side of the river bed.

I stopped short in my tracks and turned to my brother. Looking down, I saw that his face had gone suddenly white under its olive shadow. His eyes were wide open and the anguish of an unknown fear walked naked in them.

"Have you seen what I've seen?" I asked, my lips oddly dry.

He nodded.

"Any idea what it means?" I asked curtly.

"Yes, Ouboet. They're after me." His voice was still with certainty as water is still with depth.

"What?" I exclaimed, feeling my own uneasiness of the past few days rush in fast to confirm his reply.

Then in the same breath I asked, "But why?"

"Because of Sunday," he answered slowly. "I laughed at them in church on Sunday. They say I've insulted them and they must teach me a lesson."

"Nonsense," I protested. "What about me? I sniggered too."

"It's me they're after, not you," he said darkly. "They like you, but they don't like me. Two of the sons stopped me in the village on Monday and asked me what the great joke on Sunday had been about. When I told them they got so angry."

"You told them?" I exclaimed, hardly believing my own ears.

He seemed genuinely surprised at the hardening tone of my voice. "I just told them what had happened," he explained. "And that I couldn't help laughing. Of course I said I was sorry if—if I hurt them—but it—it had sounded so funny——"

He broke off, but despairing of his want of tact I prodded him: "What did they say to that?"

"They said so much and so fast I can hardly remember, Ouboet," he answered miserably. "They said I was a liar and dared me to repeat what I'd said. They asked if I thought I knew more about singing than their parents did . . . and when I said that honestly they'd all been——"

"I see," I interrupted. There was no need to know more. "And now they're all waiting down there in the river bed to teach you, or both of us, a lesson, eh?"

He nodded his head sombrely. Then added, "Not both of us, Ouboet, only me. They like you, I tell you, but they don't like me. The singing is just an excuse really——" He faltered. "They don't even want to beat me—they want to . . ." His voice dropped to a whisper. "To pull the clothes off my back and make fun of . . . you know."

"No! No!" I protested appalled, for after all the same ghost had burrowed for so long in the foundations of both our minds. For a moment I thought of retreating on the smithy, waiting for our horses and then riding back fast through the crowd of young lads that had collected for the sort of brawl that was one of their favourite sports. I thought also of taking some roundabout path and thereby avoiding the dry river crossing between us and our home. But just at that very instant, as if Fate had commanded it, one of the older boys came out of the river bed, climbed on to a boulder sparkling like a fabulous garnet in the sun, saw us, put his hands to his mouth and called out loudly and provocatively in unmistakable challenge.

I have been over this phase of the incident many times in my mind. I know that the sensible thing to do would still have been to avoid the crowd of boys, or even to wait for the storm to blow over as these village upsets sometimes did. Yet once that boy had seen me and knew that I had seen him, I was no longer a free agent but a prisoner of the situation. It was impossible for me to do anything else but go on, because every one expected that and nothing else of me. Whatever price the drama was going to exact from us all it was pre-supposed that I would play my part exactly as I did. The ancient pattern conditioning the minds of the youth of our village from that fateful Sunday onwards was such that they were instinctively, without any special word of command or active leadership, committed to a conspiracy wherein they would all serve a moment when my brother and I could be confronted together, and alone, without any chance of interference from our elders. But I knew none of this at that time. I knew only that under that empty and unseeing blue sky from which even the witness of the hungry falcon had been withdrawn, I had to go on and get over that crossing with my awkward brother as best I could.

Feeling sick in the stomach I moved forward. My brother however still blanched at the prospect. Putting his broad ploughman's hand on my arm to restrain me, he said in an incredulous voice: "But, Ouboet, if you go on they'll tear the clothes off my back and mock me for——"

I pushed his hand roughly away and said with bitter resignation: "It's too late now for anything else. But I'll not let them touch you if I can help it. Look! When we get to the river bed I want you to go straight on. I want you to promise me to walk straight on home . . . and not look back whatever happens. If you're right and they've nothing against me then you've no need to worry."

He opened his mouth to protest but I shook him roughly

and said, "For Christ's sake, do what you're told! You've already caused trouble enough."

It was the oath that did it. That form of swearing is absolutely forbidden among decent people in my country. I don't think I had ever tried it before. To this day I find it strange that I should have used it then and that, hearing it, my brother should have come forward without demur to walk like a shadow at my side.

Some minutes before we came to the dip in the road we could hear the quick buzz which comes from an excited crowd. The sound rose high into the bright air around us and harmonized uncannily with the feverish tempo of the light and constant murmur of heat which always trembles in our bush-veld afternoon silences. But as we came nearer the buzz quickly detached itself from the general rhythm of the day and hit us like the noise of a crowd at some public demonstration. Nevertheless, directly my brother and I came out on the river bank someone called out joyfully: "Look: Oubtjies,* they're here!"

Instantly the crowd went as silent as a tomb. I had not much eye for detail at that moment nor indeed for anything save the sullen shade and earthquake rumble of the dark necessity which drew my brother and myself. Yet as I took in the general outline of that mass of oddly expectant faces arranged in a half-moon on the level surface of the river bed I saw that not a boy under sixteen from our village was absent and that some pimply over-seventeens had been thrown in for the generous measure that fate reserves for these occasions. I remember also that the glare in those eyes focused on me and my brother seemed fired with a blazing cannibal hunger which I had never seen before on human faces—though today I know it only too well. Then quickly I marked down two figures standing apart from the rest

* Little old ones: Afrikaans term of endearment among boys.

and facing us. Bitterly I recognized the principals in the
scene, the two toughest of the occupants of the pew behind
ours. As my eyes met theirs one shifted his hobbledehoy
weight uneasily on to another foot, and the other licked
his lips with apparent nervousness.

"Remember," I whispered to my brother: "Not a word
to anyone. Walk past them and straight home. I'll do all the
talking that's necessary."

He made no reply. Silently we approached. Though we
had known those present all our young lives no one called
out a greeting: they just sat or lolled against the river banks
staring at us with that strange hunger in their eyes. My
brother, devastated by the brilliance of that massed impersonal stare, tried desperately to look for comfort in some
eye not hostile to him. But those faces were not glaring so
much at us but at the event that they longed to bring about
through us. At last we came close to the two standing apart
waiting in the middle of the river bed. I could hear their
hard breathing. My brother and I stepped to the side in
order to pass them. At that a hiss of imperative meaning
escaped from the crowd like steam from a high-pressure
boiler. Automatically the bigger of the two grasped my
brother by the arm and said: "Not so fast—you misshapened
bastard!"

As if long rehearsed for the part I moved in between
them, pushed him aside and said quietly to my brother:
"Remember. Your promise." In the same breath I turned to
face his opponent.

The crowd sighed with relief. Tongues licked expectant
lips as quickly as those of our lizards when they deftly flick
some ripe insect-sparkle from the air into their saffron
mouths. The occasion was developing according to their
satisfaction.

"Get out of my way, Cousin," the youth growled at me.

"Our quarrel isn't with you but with that abortion of a brother of yours."

"I shan't get out of your way," I told him, my heart beating wildly. "You're not going to touch my brother. He's much younger and smaller than you."

I forbore to add that my opponent was also a good deal bigger than I.

For a moment he stood there undecided, looking first at me and then at my brother who was walking fast up to the far bank and towards the village with an apparent willingness so different in spirit from the reluctant promise which I had extracted from him that even I was surprised and perhaps somewhat shocked. Then my enemy looked back from my brother to the one-eyed crowd and in its glance read his instructions. I had just time to see my brother scramble up the far bank and break into a run, when he exploded in hoarse, militant sarcasm: "Well, you've asked for it!" and came for me hitting out fast with both hands.

Excitement heaved the crowd to its feet and sent it rushing to form an eager ring around us. He was, as I said, bigger than I and I never had much hope of beating him, quite apart from the fact that while we fought his brother danced around exhorting him to finish me and threatening to join in if the other failed. I don't know how long we fought. I am told that after the first few minutes I was clearly the loser, but I was unaware of the fact. In me some stranger had taken over. He did the thinking and the hitting for me and robbed me of all feeling. Yes, someone of infinite experience became master of my situation. Then suddenly on the far perimeter of the storm of my senses came a new sound.

Someone was bellowing like a bull at the crowd of boys and hitting out at them. Simultaneously we stopped fighting, and looking round in amazement we saw the crowd scattering fast and the big figure of the village lay-preacher lashing out right and left with his horsewhip as he came towards us, my brother following close behind him.

"Are you all right, Ouboet?" my brother implored even before he reached me.

I don't know why but at his words rage boiled over like water in a kettle inside me.

"You'd no business," I told him panting furiously, "to fetch him here!" The village moralist was still pursuing the fleeing multitude with his whip. "Why didn't you go home as I told you?"

A few of the boys who had not yet fled apparently heard my words for on the way home whenever we passed groups of excited boys in the street obviously discussing the fight and the respective merits of the two performances, they gave me a look of approval. But for my brother there was only a scornful glance. He did not protest but walked silently beside me like a condemned person. Occasionally I could feel him trying to get me to look at him. However, I kept my outraged eyes firmly on the street watching our shadows thrown up by the fast-westering sun behind us growing longer and longer, darkening the scarlet dust of Africa and taking the colour out of the pink, red and white berries of the heavily scented pepper-trees which lay like the beads of a broken necklace around our feet. To this day I have only to smell the whiff of green peppers in the air to see our shadows, side by side, staining the hungry dust, and to feel again the retarded horror of the inflexible condemnation in my heart.

When we did get home my brother rushed straight to our father with an account of what had happened. He made me out to have been a kind of David who had faced a village Goliath. Before he had finished, the whole family had come in to listen, absorbed, to his tale. As I went to bathe my bruised face in the bathroom I heard the murmur of their spontaneous approval. The tone of their words warmed me through like wine. Even so I noticed that no one expressed approval of my brother for his deed of rescue in my need.

That night, as we lay in our bed on the *stoep* listening to the jackals barking with frantic mournfulness on the margin of our little village so deeply marooned in the black bush-veld sea, I heard a sob break from my brother.

"What's the matter, ou klein Boetie?" * I asked, quickly turning over towards him.

The unexpected note of concern in my voice was too much for him. He began sobbing without effort at self-control, and then gasped out, "I don't want you to have to fight for me. . . . Please don't always fight for me. If you do you'll end up by hating me one day. And—and I don't want you to hate me too, Ouboet . . ."

I was a witness then of the starry prancing impis † of the night throwing down their assegais and watering the heroic heaven of Africa with their gentlest tears.

* Generally: Old little, little brother: term of great endearment.
† An Impi is a Zulu or Matabele regiment of war.

3. The Initiation

Halfway through my last year at school my family decided to send my brother to join me. He could have done with another six months or year at the village school because he was still backward in his studies, but my family thought it would be easier for him if he had me to introduce him to life in a great public institution and help guide his awkward paces. I was not consulted but merely told of the decision, because, I expect, my family took it for granted that I myself would like the idea. It was another instance of what everyone expected of me and I received the decision, as far as I am aware, with an ease which confirmed my place in the estimation of my elders and betters.

The year had gone well for me at school. I had never been more successful and popular both with boys and masters. I was in the first eleven, captained the first fifteen, won the Victor Lodorum medal at the annual inter-school athletics, and was first in my final form. I was head of the senior house and would have been head of the school, I think, if I had not been a year or two younger than most fellows in my form. Both masters and boys confidently predicted that at the close of the year I would be awarded the most coveted prize of the school, that for the best all-round man of the year. It was to this brilliant and crowded stage that I returned from vacation with my strange brother at my side.

We arrived the afternoon before the re-opening of the

school. I don't think I was over-sensitive as a child except, perhaps, to the reaction of people and the world to me. But as the school slowly became aware that the awkward, graceless shadow at my side was indeed my brother even I could not help feeling the surprise that merged into the ineffable condescension of public pity in the atmosphere around me. More subtly still, I got an inkling of the relief that can surge through the hearts of the many when they begin to suspect an infliction of fallible humanity on the lives of their popular idols. My contemporaries were surprised and for one brief moment I was able to see how ready are the mass instincts to seize an excuse for pulling down the very thing that they themselves have need of elevating. Perhaps I imagined myself to be beyond the reach of all these influences. But they had their effect on me. They could not, to put it at its lowest, make me love either myself or my brother more. I was young enough to hope that once he had gone through the various rites and the tough period of initiation which tradition prescribed for newcomers to the school, his oddness would be accepted as part of the daily scene, and that the qualities which endeared him to his family would have their chance to emerge. Yet, from the very first evening, the start was not encouraging. First impressions are important to the young and never more important then when there are initiation rites to perform.

After all, the purpose of initiation ceremonial is first, by a process of public humiliation, to make the victim aware of his inferiority and then to extract from him, through some painful form of ordeal, proof of the courage which alone can entitle him to redemption from his shameful singularity in membership of the privileged community. Moreover, I have noticed that among those to be initiated there is always one who seems to be pre-destined to bear an extra burden of ritual because he alone appears to personify most clearly the singularity that has to be humiliated and sacrificed. I use the word "appears" deliberately because in my school it was this appearance, this first impression, which decided the degree in initiation that the candidate was to be forced to endure. All crowds seem to possess an instinct for determining with diabolic accuracy the most suitable sacrifice among its prospective victims. My school was no exception. Even if I had not been apprehensive I could not have helped noticing how everyone who met my brother soon found their eyes drawn in puzzled focus to the spot where his padded coat concealed his deformity.

I watched one boy after another come up to him and fire the usual questions: name, age, address, form in school, games, favourite books, hobbies and so on. My brother answered them all in that artless manner of his without concealment. Yes, his name was the same as mine: he was indeed my brother. Was that so surprising? He was eleven, and in the first form. Yes, he probably should have been out of it long ago but he was no good at books. No, he didn't play any games either. He didn't like games much and never played them unless forced to. His hobbies were music and growing things, if you could call that a hobby!

This catalogue of unorthodox answers completed, his questioners hastened away to spread the news of how strange a fish had been thrown up on the school beach in the shape of the brother of the head of the senior house. Soon I was left without doubt that he would have to bear the main burden of initiation if the school were free to have its way. Only one thing stood between my brother and such an unenviable fate: the fact that he was my brother.

Now to be fair to myself I had discussed initiation many times with my brother. He knew all there was to know about it. He knew the details by heart and even remembered some that I had forgotten. He was as ready for it, intellectually, as any newcomer could be. Also, he had great physical strength and resistance to pain. Nothing I had told him about running the gauntlet in pyjamas with the school drawn up in two long rows and hitting out hard at the runners with wet towels plaited to a fine lash-like point; about waking up at night and finding some boys sitting with pillows on his head while others put a slipknot of a fishing line round his toes and pulled at them, one by one, until they bled in a perfect circle; nothing about being made to measure the distance from school to town with his toothbrush on his half-holidays, or having to wear boot-laces instead of a tie into town, or being forced to look straight into the sun without blinking for as long as some older boy commanded, or being trussed up and left on the frosty dormitory balcony all night, none of these things, I repeat, had unduly dismayed him. There was only one thing he truly feared: exposure and mockery.

When we were told he was accompanying me to school the first thing he asked was, "They won't make fun of . . . you know . . . will they?"

"Of course not," I'd replied vehemently. "You're going to a decent school, not a village kalwerhok." *

The relief in his eyes was so intense that I quickly looked away. Was there far back in the long tunnel in my mind a faint cackle of cock-crow? Was I really so certain? But I gave myself no chance to discover doubt and repeated firmly: "We're not at all that kind of school."

Later, on the day of our return to school, as our train came to a standstill at the platform and we got ready to leave our compartment, again his broad hand clutched my arm and he asked: "They won't—will they, Ouboet?"

* Kalwerhok: calfpen.

It was on that occasion, for the first time, that I pretended not to know what his question meant.

I exclaimed irritably: "Won't what?"

He was utterly taken aback. For a moment he stared speechless at me, then said in a frightened whisper: "Mock me because of—Oh God, you know what, Ouboet!"

"Oh, that!" I answered noticing how heavily he was taking it to heart and continuing as if it were all too trivial for words: "I've told you already, we're not that kind of school."

I think the question was again on his lips when I did my rounds of the dormitories last thing that night. But if it was he dared not ask it. He just looked at me with such eloquent apprehension that I turned away hastily and bade him a curt: "Good night."

My rounds done I went to join the heads of the other three houses in the study of the Captain of the school. I had done that walk between my house and the school many times, yet that night it felt to me as if I had never done it before. Every detail had taken to itself the mystery of all things. The moon was so bright that I could see the shadow of our greatest mountains at the end of the plain many miles away. The round white-washed stones beside the gravelled drive might have been skulls adorning the approach to a barbaric court. The cactus in the rock-garden raising its arms high to heaven was a Maya priest, knife in hand, sacrificing to the moon. The shadows of the trees were inky pools of tidal water lying forgotten among glistening rocks, and the whole night was hissing urgently as if the moonlight were the sea and the earth an outward-bound ship parting the surf at the bar of some harbour mouth. Between the school and distant town, night-plovers cried continuously, like gulls over the stormy Cape.

It all made such an overwhelming impression on me that I stood for a while in front of the Captain's door, wondering.

Even the stars moved as if they were sparking off messages in their own confidential code. Noticing it, I was sharply harried by the fancy, which came out at me like a watchdog in the dark, that perhaps they really did carry some special message for me? Impatiently I dismissed the notion as clearly absurd. I was there to discuss with the Captain of the school and others the ordinary business of the term. The five of us had met, thus, on the eve of each re-assembly for the past eighteen months. The idea that there would be any extra significance on this occasion even made me impatient with the splendour of the night.

I rapped on the door and went in to be warmly welcomed by the Captain and heads of the other three houses. After a cheerfully busy hour or two the Captain said: "This brings us now to the little matter of tomorrow's initiation. I take it you've all interviewed the newcomers in your houses. Have you any youngsters you think should be excused?"

Yes, said the man next to me, he had a boy with a weak heart who'd brought a doctor's certificate to that effect. The next, grumblingly, said he'd got a chap who was as blind as a bat, with lenses thick enough for a septuagenarian! He'd probably better be excused all the physical rites though there was no reason why he shouldn't be available for the rest of the fun. The third pleaded similarly for a boy still recovering from a long fever. Then came my turn. Firmly I said I had no one needing to be excused.

The Captain looked keenly at me. "No one?"

"No," I repeated carefully veiling the surprise I felt at his question and looking him steadily in the eye. But to my amazement he didn't leave it at that.

"You've got a young brother in your house, haven't you?" he asked.

"I have," I answered, my whole being springing to attention.

"What about him?" the Captain asked.

"Well, what about him?" I parried so sharply that the others laughed.

The Captain smiled. "I was merely wondering if he was all right——"

"Of course he's all right." My answer was quietly vehement yet the Captain persisted.

"Forgive me, old chap," he said, almost shyly. "I don't want to badger you. If you say he's all right we all accept it. But, knowing you, we realize the last thing you'd ask for would be special dispensation for a relation. So if you've any reason for wanting your brother excused tomorrow we'd none of us think of it as favouritism."

A spontaneous murmur of applause went round the table. I found myself blushing. "Awfully decent of you but there's no reason, honestly."

"Well, then, that's that," said the Captain, evidently well satisfied with the way the claims of business and decency had been met, and he bade us a hearty good night.

On the way back I found myself perturbed and not a little sad, and I was unable to explain it to myself. It is only now that I know that between my impatient rap on the Captain's door and the moment when it opened and shut behind me again as I stepped out into the unbelievable moonlight of that wheeling night, the master-nothing of which I have spoken previously had caught up with me and was moving fast into place.

A second example of this, if I may use so positive a phrase for so negative a phenomenon, arose next morning right at the beginning of school.

Prayers over, the Captain came up to me and said: "I've got to see the Head immediately after classes this afternoon. Would you keep an eye on things for me until I get back?"

He was referring of course to the "round-up" of newcomers which always took place on the opening day between the last class and the first prep.

"D'you mind if I don't?" I asked at once.

"Of course not." He paused. "I didn't really think you'd want to. But as you're head of the senior house I felt I had to ask you." He smiled and put a friendly hand on my shoulder before moving on.

I had a suspicion of his feeling but my intimates saw to it that I soon knew the full meaning of his words. Apparently after our conversation the Captain had told them all of my refusal to take charge of the school during the "round-up," and he had explained that he was certain it was done out of respect for the traditions of the school and in order to ensure that my popular presence in a position of authority should not influence the crowd to treat my brother differently from any other unprivileged newcomer. He had even added that it was exactly what he'd expected of one with such a scrupulous sense of fair play.

Slowly that first day at school passed its peak midday hour. I had not seen my brother at all since early morning when I stopped an over-spirited scrummage between some older boys outside his dormitory before breakfast, until a moment or two before the school dismissed at the end of the day. There were, of course, dozens of good reasons why the head of a large house has no time for personal affairs and private considerations on the opening day of school. If anyone had accused me then of trying to avoid my brother, I could have rebutted the charge without difficulty. Today I might accept the result of my actions as proof enough of my real intention no matter how hidden it may have been from me at the time. I have no idea what my brother felt during all that busy day because we have never discussed it. In a way I can imagine it from my own experience of my first day in the same school. After all I had

had to endure the start of school without a brother for comfort and a lot of good had come to me out of so elementary a test. Obviously there was a lot to be said for leaving my brother to fend for himself. True, he had his extra dimension of fear to make horror of his anxieties but, believe it or not, ever since that moment on the platform when I had refused to understand his meaning, this aspect of his problem had slipped from my memory, almost as if I had been secretly resolved not to remember it.

When finally I did see him that day, it was just after school had ended. He was standing against a pillar close to the door of the senior Science laboratory in which my form was doing practical chemistry. He was standing very still as always when possessed by only one thought. Occasionally his eyes left the door to try and peer through the windows of the laboratory but because the light flamed and flared in the cool mauve glass he could not see anything in the shadows behind it. Obviously he was waiting for the class to come out to seize a chance of speaking to me before the "round-up" which, judging by the noise coming from the quadrangle on the far side of the laboratory, was rapidly getting under way.

For a moment I felt a desperate pity. He looked so incongruous and helpless, his young arm clasped round the iron pillar for support. I knew, too, that he had no chance of seeing me. Some minutes before I had already gone to the science master and offered to stay behind after class and prepare the laboratory for the next morning's class. The idea had come to me quite suddenly. I could pass it off as pure impulse. Yet the result deprived me of my last chance of seeing my brother before the "round-up" and ensured that I was detained on duty elsewhere until it was all over.

As the laboratory door opened and the class hurried out my brother desperately searched among them to make quite certain he should not miss me from among those jostling figures. When the last one sped by him and I was not there the same look of utter finality came to his eyes as on that afternoon before crossing the dry river bed at home, when he had said tonelessly: "They're after me, Ouboet." He stood peering at the emptiness round him as if he couldn't believe his eyes. I doubt if he saw the science master come out and shut the laboratory door almost in his face. He just stood there looking irrevocably lost while I watched him, unseen, from within, wilfully denying the validity of his need of me or of my chance of helping him. Indeed, suddenly I found my spirit hardening against him. I wished he would go and get his trivial fate over as we had all had to do before him. . . .

Almost as I wished it, an exultant shout went up nearby. There was a rush and scurry of heavy school boots: heads and faces of a crowd of young lads appeared outside the window. Whooping, jeering, screaming, tearing, they pulled my brother towards them. He stumbled. As he went down his face was like that of someone who cannot swim being swept out to sea on an unsuspected current.

I turned my back on the window thinking: "Well, that's that. It'll soon be over now and he'll be better for the experience." I began to tidy up. But I didn't get far.

I found myself standing, a retort in hand, listening. The noise coming from the quadrangle which before had been like a great roar, now had a new subdued tone. Not that it was dying down. On the contrary it maintained itself in waves, at the same savage pitch. It was the sound of a people all of one mind—or rather of no mind at all. Yes, this united voice came before mind and its cry was filled with the strange cannibal hunger of those who have not yet lived themselves. It was the sound of diverse beings made one through the same appetite, and though it issued from young throats the sound itself was old and worn threadbare with time. It was even older, I felt, than the grey old mountain looking down on the school.

I had helped at these "round-ups" often enough. But this was the first time I had had to listen to it apart, and alone. It was the first time, too, that my own flesh and blood had fed its hunger. At the thought I nearly dropped the chemical retort in my hand. Swiftly I wondered what my brother could have wanted of me? What good could seeing me have done? Could my familiar, brotherly face in that sea of unknown ones have made him feel that he was not quite alone in his experience? Could my awareness of his own most secret fear have made him feel, in some measure, safe against the excesses of the mob? These seemed such fantastic lines of reasoning that I told myself impatiently: "A fat lot of good it is arguing. He's just got to go through with it. My being there might even have made it worse."

In this way I completed my betrayal. So confident was my negation that it did not even fear drawing attention to itself by argument. But as it settled down comfortably within me, a great silence suddenly fell over the school. I knew that silence well. The victim designate, the sacrifice supreme, the symbol round which the herd ritual turned, was about to be proclaimed. Despite all my resolutions to the contrary, I moved quickly to the one window which gave on the quadrangle. I looked out. My brother, hatless, dishevelled and whiter than I had ever seen him, was lifted shoulder-high by some of the bigger boys in the quadrangle. The moment the crowd saw him a fresh roar burst from it and everyone began mocking him according to their own particular gift until, in a flash, all the streams of insult and humiliation became one, and the whole school, as my brother was carried through the crowd, began chanting derisively:

> *"Why was he born so beautiful,*
> *Why was he born at all?"*

At the far end of the quadrangle were two long deep water-troughs, relics of the far pioneering days when bearded "boys" rode to their classes on horseback, guns slung across the shoulder. Between the two troughs were two sets of taps, side by side, in the wall. This, by tradition, was a favourite place for sport with newcomers to the school. The taps were convenient for display, and the troughs handy for ducking. My brother was soon forced to stand on the taps and roughly pushed up against the wall, facing the crowd.

I was too far away to see his expression. I know only that, from a distance, he looked like a caricature of a schoolboy. His dark face which had gone startlingly white was all the more so by contrast with his great head of thick black hair. His nose was invisible to me, but his mouth and large black eyes showed up like three blobs of darkness in the centre of his moon-white face. His head was tilted awkwardly on one side and he looked awfully like a clown. When he was firmly in position on the water-taps one of the bigger boys climbed on to a trough beside him, held up his hand for silence and said: "Chaps, this newcomer has got to do something for our entertainment. What shall it be?"

After a moment several voices cried out: "Let him sing. He says he likes singing. Let him sing!"

"Right!" The speaker turned at once to my brother as if expecting him to start singing straight away. My brother, I suspect, was swallowing hard with nervousness and far from ready to sing. The speaker at once punched him with a fist on the shoulder, shouting: "Come on, Greenie, you've had your orders. Sing, blast you, sing!"

Music as I have told you was peculiarly my brother's own idiom. With the prospect of singing, even in such circumstances, his courage appeared to come back. He obeyed at once and began to sing:

> *"Ride, ride through the day,*
> *Ride through the moonlight,*
> *Ride, ride through the night*
> *Far, far . . ."*

The opening notes were perhaps a trifle uncertain but before the end of the first line his gift for music confidently took over. By the second line his little tune sounded well and truly launched. But he didn't realize, poor devil, that the very faultlessness of his performance was the worst thing that could have happened. The essence of his role in the proceedings was that of scapegoat. He should not only look like one but also behave accordingly. Anything else destroyed his value as a symbol and deprived the crowd of any justification for its fun. The boys, quick to feel that the clear voice singing with such unusual authority was cheating the design of its ritual uttered an extraordinary howl of disapproval.

My brother faltered. Even at my distance from the scene dismay was plain in his attitude. He tried once again to sing but the din was too much for him. So he stopped altogether, his long arms dangling like sawdust limbs at his sides, and stared in bewilderment from one end of the quadrangle to the other, searching wildly, so a sudden sickness in my stomach told me, for my face. At that moment the crowd felt itself again to be in command.

The howl of disapproval became a roar of relieved delight and the school now began to press towards the troughs chanting joyfully:

> "Greenie's a liar and a cheat,
> He can't sing a note.
> Greenie's a fraud: drown him,
> Drown him in the moat!"

For a moment my brother's white face remained outlined against the afternoon fire flaming along the red-brick quadrangle wall, his eyes ceaselessly searching the screaming, whistling mob of schoolboys. Then he vanished like the last shred of sail of a doomed ship into a grasping sea. I don't know if you have ever listened to a crowd screaming when you've been alone and divorced from the emotion which motivates it? At any time it is a sobering experience. But when the scream is directed against your own flesh and blood—— At that moment my heart, my mind, my own little growth of time all seemed, suddenly, to wither.

I could not see what was happening. My experience told me that my brother was being ducked vigorously in the troughs as we had all been before him. I knew the "drown" in the chant really meant "duck." All the same I was extremely nervous. I watched the struggle and tumult of yelling heads and shoulders by the water-trough, wondering whether it would never end.

Then suddenly again the crowd went motionless and silent. Some of the broader shoulders by the trough heaved, an arm shot up holding aloft a damp coat and shirt, and behind it was slowly lifted my brother's gasping face and naked torso.

"Look chaps!" a voice near him rang out with a curious intonation. "Look! Greenie has a boggeltjie." *

For a second there was silence as the boys stared at my brother held dripping in their midst. Then, as if at a signal,

* Boggel: hunch; Tjie: diminutive.

they all began to laugh and shake and twist and turn with hysterical merriment.

I had never seen my school go to these lengths before. I stood at the window as if nailed to the floor while the merriment transformed itself into one of the favoured chants:

> *"Greenie has a boggeltjie,**
> *boggeltjie, boggeltjie,*
> *Greenie has a boggeltjie: one*
> *two and three and*
> *Greenie has——"*

Then it stopped. The noise fizzled out and the crowd in the quadrangle became uneasily still. A window on the second-floor of the main building had been thrown open. The head and shoulders of the English master were leaning far out of it.

"Who, might I ask," he demanded in a voice precise and icy with anger, "Who is in charge here this afternoon?"

"I am, sir," the head of a certain house answered contritely.

"Well, dismiss your rabble and report to me in my rooms at once," the master told him slamming down the window.

However, there was scarcely need to dismiss the school. It needed no telling that it had exceeded itself. It was dispersing of its own accord, taking my brother away with it.

I remained at the window for a while in a state of irresolute agitation. I wanted to rush out and do something to make good what had just happened. I was angry and humiliated and wanted to take it out of all and sundry in the school, not excluding my brother. I wanted also to rush out and comfort my brother. But it all came back to the fact

* The tjie of Boggel is pronounced like key.

that I still had a duty in the laboratory to perform. The fact of duty won. I tidied up the laboratory, set up the apparatus for the next morning's experiment and in the process came to the convenient conclusion that by far the best way of helping my brother would be to make light of his experience.

It was evening before I saw him again. He was coming out of the Matron's room carrying a complete change of clothing on his arm. The long corridor was lit only by the reflected flames of a cataclysmic sunset flickering in the tall windows over the main stairway at the far end of the landing. My brother, recognizing my steps, stood still in the open doorway. The light from the Matron's room fell sideways on his face and left the rest of him indistinct in the rising night-shadow. He stood so still that his face looked like an antique mask hanging on the door behind him. I expected him to greet me as he always did but on this occasion he just stood there, silent.

"Well," I said, assuming the gay nonchalance that I'd decided would be good for him. "How did you get on today?"

"Then you weren't there?" His question was flat.

"Not where?" I answered, seeking respite in evasion.

"At the round-up." He peered hard at me in the twilight.

"Oh, there!" I replied easily. "No, I was in the science lab most of the afternoon. Had a job for the Science master to do. In fact, I've only just finished."

I stopped. Something in his face, looking up at me out of a past and forgotten dimension of time, stopped me. We stared at each other in a silence so great that I could even hear the Matron's alarm clock ticking on her table inside the room.

"I see," he said at last with, for one so young, an odd note of finality in his voice. "Well, I must hurry or I'll be late for supper."

He walked straight past me and ran for the stairs. I was so taken by surprise that I never stopped him. I might even have followed him if the Matron, hearing my voice, hadn't asked me in to discuss some petty matter.

I saw him again late that night. He was in bed and either asleep or pretending to be. Twenty-four hours before I would without hesitation have called him by name, softly. Now, somehow, I had not the confidence to do so, and so my last natural opportunity for coming to terms with myself vanished.

The school, however, did not abandon the incident with ease. For a few days I was continually being stopped by fellows with sheepish faces all muttering some sort of an apology.

On the night after the round-up at the Monitors' meeting the Captain of the school addressed me amid a murmur of approval, saying: "I'm sure I needn't tell you, old man, what the school feels about this afternoon. We're horribly ashamed of letting you down, particularly seeing how you trusted us," and so on.

Yet no one begged my brother's pardon. I seemed to gain in popularity by the incident, but not so my brother. To him the school behaved as if it blamed him, and not itself, for the outrage, almost as if he had tricked them into doing something which otherwise they would never ever have dreamed of doing.

As for myself, that night, just as I was about to drop asleep comforted by the warmth of my reception at the Monitors' meeting and the Captain's concern for my feelings, I suddenly heard my young brother's voice saying again in a tone that I had never heard before: "I see."

Instantly I was wide-awake. That was a phrase he had

never used before. Always in the past, when anything went wrong between us he'd shrugged his shoulders and said, "It's nothing, Ouboet." But now a new realization followed me like a ghost across the flimsy threshold of my sleep. Dear God, had my truth always got to be my brother's untruth? My untruth his truth? Was something of this sort implicit in the nature of all betrayal?

I got my prize at the end of the year. My father and mother were there, beside the Governors of the school, to hear the headmaster make a pretty little speech before he announced that I had been chosen as the best all-round man of the year. Amid the shattering applause of masters and boys I climbed on to the school platform for the last time to receive the award. I felt drunk with satisfaction at my achievement, yet, as I turned to go back to my place in the hall, I was sobered instantly by the sight of two faces in the applauding crowd. One was my brother's. He was cheering as if the achievement were his own yet there was something in his eyes which made me uneasy. The other was that of the master who had thrown open a window and intervened on my brother's behalf on the day of the "round-up." Subsequently he had come to take a close interest in my brother and he was looking at me now with an enigmatic expression on his sensitive face while he politely clapped his hands. It came to me that he looked almost sorry for me.

That night, for the first time, I went with my closest "buddies" to a private bar at the principal hotel in town. There we pledged ourselves in strong drink to be forever one for all and all for one. In the morning, with strangely poignant feelings, many of us, and I was among them, left the school for good.

As I wished my intimates "good-bye" on the platform I felt a lump in my throat and noticed that even the eyes of the school Captain were unusually bright. Then my brother and I climbed, with our parents, into the train and for the last time we all journeyed home together. Yet, not even then in the intimacy of a family re-united did we ever discuss what had happened to my brother on his first day at school. Neither he nor I ever mentioned it to my parents nor in our talks with each other. We both behaved as if we had no other desire than to forget the incident as quickly as possible. But we reckoned without the incident itself.

That is another aspect of betrayal. It has a will of its own which feeds on the very will that seeks to deny it. I might have succeeded in forgetting the event if it had not so obstinately persisted in remembering me. As for my brother, I believe that his success was no greater than mine.

There was, for instance, the episode of "Stompie." *

On the broad acres of my father's high-veld estate we had immense herds of springbuck. Unlike many of our neighbours, my father and his grandfather before him had preserved the indigenous game on their land with the greatest care and affection. There was hardly a view from the high-raised *stoep* stretching all round our white house, which did not show a group of springbuck peacefully grazing in the safe distance. I was never tired of watching them. They were seldom still, yet never appeared restless, for their movements were consistently rhythmical. The patterns they made on the blue and gold veld possessed a curious heraldic quality and on some of our crystal days the herd, from a distance, would appear to open and shut like the flower of chivalry itself. In summer when the distances were set on fire by the sun, when grass, bushes and sequined savannahs were reflected in the quicksilver air in an endless succession of crackling coloured flames, the springbuck held their position in the centre of the tumult with pastel delicacy and pre-

* Stompie is the diminutive of stomp—stump, but it is also slang for the discarded fag-end of a cigar or cigarette and is used as both here.

cision. In winter, when the fires of summer were drawn and the fine dust of burnt-out ashes stood blue and high in the air, they would still be there maintaining a glow of living fire on the raked-out hearth of my native land.

In the spring the scene was made poignant with the keen thrust of new being in the flickering herds. First, the young bucks would emerge to challenge the old rams. They would bound out into the open from the herd like ballet dancers from the wings of time. Backs arched and a ruff of white, magnetic hair parted along their quivering spines to fall like snow upon their fiery flanks, they would dance their challenge in front of the established but ageing rams. The older ones would ignore them as long as possible, but finally the whiff of disdain emanating from the wide-eyed does waiting alertly for the outcome, would sting them into obeying the implacable choreography of spring in their blood. The battle that followed, then, was deadly. The horns of the two males would interlock with speed and clash as swords of heroes in some twilit Celtic scene. The herd, entranced, would follow closely in impassioned rushes, taking every advantage of ground which gave them a better view of the combat. I have often sat on my horse, watching, with the whole herd normally so fearful of man pressing tightly round me for a closer view of the fight, snorting, and sighing with excitement and suspense. The fight over, I have watched the young does, their hieroglyphic eyes under long lashes shining with the tension of spring without and fear of the uncompromising fires within, display their charms to the winner. Passing and re-passing repeatedly in front of him, tails tucked with becoming modesty under their buttocks, they would keep their glances fixed firmly on the ground.

But in the autumn the herds would contract, drawing young and old together in a circle the centre of which turned on their fear of death implicit in the coming winter. All differences among them vanished. Steadily they gave the homesteads an even wider berth, and became acutely wary of our movements as if they sensed that our season of killing, too, was about to begin.

But there was one odd phenomenon that I noticed had maintained itself for some years in the seasonal re-groupings of the herd. There was one buck who was never allowed to join the herd in any circumstances whatsoever. Whenever he came near the main herd the bucks, young and old, would combine to drive him away with a ferocity most unusual in so gentle and lovable a species. For a year or two he persisted, often trying several times during a day to rejoin the herd, but each time he was driven off with the same determined ferocity. In the end he gave up trying and was always to be seen following the main body of his fellows at a safe distance. At first I thought he must be some old ram who had incurred unusual hatred by maintaining a dominant position in the herd extending beyond the normal span. However I soon found out that I was wrong.

One day I was lying in ambush for a particularly cunning jackal who for long had been creating great havoc among both sheep and buck, when the main herd of buck came grazing so close by me that I could hear them cropping the grass with quick lips and a crunch of eager mouths. I know of no more attractive sound for it has always brought back to me a sense of being briefly restored to the abiding rhythm and trust of nature. As the sound receded, leaving me alone with only the faint sigh of afternoon air in the spark-ling broom-bushes wherein I lay, I felt strangely forsaken. I had decided to abandon my ambush when another faint crunching reached me. Coming towards me, closer even than the herd, was the lone buck. I was amazed to see, then, that he was not old at all. He was young with a lovely, shining coat and glistening black velvet muzzle. Whenever he stopped grazing delicately to sniff the air, he would first stare forlornly at the herd before searching the vast shimmering horizon trembling on the rim of high-veld like an expanding ripple in a pool of blue water. There was no doubt as to his nostalgia. He went on cropping the grass and only when he was immediately opposite me did he stop, lift his head and turn it in my direction. Instantly I knew the reason for his rejection by the herd. He was deformed. One horn lay crumpled behind a saffron ear; the other was stunted and stuck out crookedly in the air. As for his eyes—— On that day I was not ready to allow myself to know of what they reminded me.

My brother did not care much for animals, particularly game, but when I first told him all this, he was greatly interested. This buck henceforth found an assured place in his imagination. He began to keep a close and affectionate watch on it. It was he who first called the buck "Stompie." Soon he surprised me by telling me things about the buck which even I had not noticed. It was he, for instance, who one day observed that although the herd had rejected "Stompie" yet he was bound more closely to the herd by that rejection than any of the other animals. They all mated and fought and roamed away on long foraging parties with comparative freedom. But "Stompie" felt compelled to do only what the assembled herd did. When we rounded-up the main body of buck for shooting and drove them down towards the line of guns lying in wait for them, although we ignored Stompie and left him safely outside the ring of mounted drovers, nevertheless he would insist on taking the same fatal route that the herd had taken and, undeterred by the sound of firing ahead, he would come up from behind and with extraordinary and solitary courage run the gauntlet of deadly guns. He would have been shot many times over had we not all contracted for him the compassion which his own kind so conspicuously denied him. So he was spared to live a sort of moon existence, a fated satellite, condemned to circle forever the body which had expelled it. In this role he was not without great value to the herd. Exposed to the danger of man and beast, constantly alone, he developed a remarkable intelligence and heightened presentiment of danger. He was always the first to feel it and then to give the alarm by making a series of prodigious bounds into the air, his pastel coat, sea-foam belly and black-lacquered feet of Pan flashing in the sun. Often an exasperated gun would threaten to shoot him for spoiling our chances in this way, and sending us back to an empty pot. But a curious compassion for the deformed animal always restrained us.

Then came this vacation at the end of my school career. On the first morning I came out of the house at dawn to see the great herd mistily burning in the shadows of the veld. I took a deep breath. It was wonderful to see everything again as it had always been. At that very moment the first level ray of the sun picked out Stompie, standing like a statue on a pedestal of golden earth far to the left of the main herd. Immediately the feeling of contentment fell from me. I could not account for it. All I know is that at that moment I felt about Stompie something I had never felt before. Somehow he spoilt the view for me. In the past I had tended to feel reproach of the herd and even some slight gratitude to the lone buck for giving us the constantly recurring opportunity of displaying a certain magnanimity to life. Now the sight of him in the natural vista that I had loved so long disturbed me. I took it to be merely a temporary emotion but the reaction gained rather than diminished in vigour.

At the end of my vacation I went to continue my studies

at the University. For six months I never gave Stompie a thought. I came back on holiday again as ready to accept the familiar as ever before. It happened to be our first shooting season since I had left school. On the night of my arrival I was asked if my brother and I couldn't try next day to relieve the monotony of our winter diet with a taste of the venison we all loved. No sooner had we ridden out into the open than I saw the forlorn shape of Stompie standing to attention in the distance.

"He's seen us," I remarked to my brother with a trace of exasperation that drew a surprised glance from him. "He's getting more cunning each year. I bet you we're going to find it difficult to come up to the herd today."

I had hardly finished when Stompie suddenly left the earth, almost vanished for a second from our startled gaze, and then reappeared flashing high in the blue air. He must have turned round completely in the course of one of the greatest jumps of his life. Again and again he repeated this astonishing performance until the shimmer of fire on the coats of the herd was arrested and it steadied into a front of unwavering flame. For a moment it remained so, a thousand delicate heads moving backwards and forwards between us and that far empty flank where Stompie was dancing out his concern for the safety of the herd. Then the alarm beat too, in the hearts of the animals. Fear is the deepest of our vortexes and determines its own cataclysmic dance in the heart. I never cease to marvel at the immediacy with which terror turns the animal soul inwards upon an empty centre with whirlwind paces. But the speed with which the herd before us contracted even after a cycle of seasons free from fear, seemed to me unusually poignant. It spun across the sleep-indifferent veld like a cyclone of fire, turning and re-turning upon itself in an anti-clockwise direction as if it believed that there was magic strong enough

in devout movement against the sun to turn back time to
its Elysian source and leave behind the threatening present.

"Told you so," I remarked with gloomy satisfaction to my
brother riding silently at my side. "It's no good going on."
I paused. "Unless you go on alone and drive the herd to the
far side of the farm. Remember that ant-heap near the
boundary fence where we dug out the ant-bear last year?
I'll lie up there, and if you can send the herd streaking by
between the ant-heap and the fence, I'll do the rest."

I had no fear my brother would reject the suggestion
since he disliked shooting intensely. Now, to my amazement,
however, he seemed to hesitate.

I asked brusquely: "Well, what is it?"

"Sorry, Ouboet, I was just wondering——" He made no
effort to ride on.

"What?"

"I don't know——"

I asked deliberately, "Would you rather do the shooting and I'll round them up?"

A shiver of distaste went through him. "No, it's all right.
We'll do as you said first." He pulled his horse into a
gallop and rode off.

Watching him go I felt rather sorry for him. Poor devil,
he rode so badly! I could see daylight between his seat and
the saddle at every stride of the horse! Then I wheeled
about, put my horse into a brisk canter and rode for the hills.

The long line of hills ahead my brother and I called the
"dinosaur hills." We called them that because in the light
of Africa's Götterdämmerung sunsets they looked like the
vertebrae of some fabulous prehistoric fossil. I rode quickly
through them, the incense of wild-olive and black-leopard
ferns stinging in my nostrils and my horse's hooves sounding
almost blasphemous in the silence. I read an Arabic scribble
of wind in the grass's silken parchment as I emerged, alone,

on the great plain beyond. It was as if I had burst a time barrier and come out into a world that had existed before the Word and man's articulation of it. Far as the eye could see the plain was empty. Not even a lone wanderer's smoke hung over it. Above, the sky was filled to the brim with blue and only the morning air feebly complained in my ear for neglect of sound.

I rode steadily across the plain towards a tall clump of wild-raisin bushes near the ant-heap of which I had spoken. At the clump of bushes I dismounted, put my horse under cover and then walked to my pre-arranged position behind the ant-heap. I got there none too soon for as I unslung my rifle, carefully laid it down out of the sun's sparkle and stood up for a last look round, the head of the herd was just emerging from the dark eye of the pass in the hills. For a moment I stood immobile watching them. All our high-veld buck are from birth afflicted with claustrophobia. This fear was drawing them now strung out in a long line through the pass as fast as they could go. At that distance the hills were a smoky purple and the buck themselves a coral and white glitter, but so swiftly did they follow on one another's heels out into the glittering plain that they looked like a twist of silk threading some ancient needle. However, once clear of the pass they slowed down, stopped, re-formed their tight circle, and faced about.

They had barely done so when Stompie came bounding out into the open. Not far behind came my brother. The lone buck saw him first. Again and again he flashed his warning colours high in the air in a series of prodigious leaps. The herd, unsettled, needed no persuasion. Almost at once the buck were on the move again, not running full out but trotting with their easy, elegant, long-distance stride. Occasionally they would stop, look quickly over their shoulders as if to make certain that indeed a horse and a man with a gun were really on their spoor. Then the sight of my brother still darkening the blue of their day as he came doggedly onwards would huddle them together in panic, and they would mill about uncertainly, as if demanding of that empty sky and lonely plain what they had done to merit such a situation. But then, inevitably, some natural leader would emerge, and provoke the herd into following him, at the trot, deeper into the open veld and nearer to me.

This was for me, always, a most moving sight and full of real excitement. Until the very last moment I could never tell what the herd would do. Often when the buck were nearing reasonable rifle range they would suddenly change their instinctive plan, break away at right-angles from their line of advance, out-circle their drovers, and go back the way they had come. It needed only one mistake from my brother to bring this about. He had only to press them too hard, or appear too eager to turn them on one particular flank rather than another, to make them suspicious of his secret intent. Then in a flash they would wheel, break through that wide gap between him and me, and make for the familiar ground from which they had been driven. Considering how indifferent my brother was to sport of this kind the risk of this happening was never remote. Perhaps it was awareness of this that made me over-anxious and, as I watched their progress, tempted me into exposing myself once too often over the shoulder of the ant-heap. Suddenly Stompie began to run as never before, coming fast round on the far flank of the herd which was still trotting easily towards me. Soon he appeared at its head and with arched back and glistening coat did his warning dance in full view of the main body. The herd stopped in a ragged, irresolute line looking rapidly from Stompie to my brother and back. Again Stompie bounded. At that moment he was barely two hundred yards from me and as his finely moulded and superbly arched frame appeared high above the grass, the lace of the white ruff on his pastel coat flying wide open from the violence of his bound, I saw him cross and uncross his finely pointed feet twice in the air before he came down to earth again. It was a difficult and brave act, beautifully executed, and perhaps possible only to some lonely outcast denied other forms of expression in life. But, unhappily, on that day it only filled me with fury.

No sooner had he landed and bounded away again at an incredible angle to his descent, than the herd reacted. It wheeled right like a battalion of Royal Guards on parade and charged at incredible speed in the direction that Stompie was pointing, straight for the hills and the invisible plains of home. In fact, so rapidly did the herd change course and run that it got between my brother and Stompie, who in obedience to herd tabu had now stopped bounding and had dropped into a slow walk behind the herd whose hooves were still making the plain reverberate like a drum. Then, when he was once more rightly distanced from the fast receding herd, he did not follow them as he normally did, but turned and stopped so that he was standing sideways on to me. From this position he looked first at the pink and sea-foam surge of buck on the fringe of the blue hills, and then straight back at my ant-heap with, as I believed, a look of pure triumph. It was more than I could bear.

In my way I, we all, had been good to that buck. Yet, before I knew what I was doing, I had laid my sights on him thinking, "You've bloody well asked for this!" and pressed the trigger. I have always enjoyed the smack of the bullet as it hits the game I'm after, particularly game that has tested my patience and skill. On this occasion I liked it too, but only for as long as the sound lived in my ear. Stompie took the shock of the bullet without a bound or a stagger. For one second he remained in position looking at me without surprise as I stood up from behind my ant-heap. Then his fore-legs began to give way. He struggled to remain upright, gave one last, wild glance at the hills where the herd had fled, before he sank down on to his knees. Like a destroyer holed in the bows and sucked down into smooth waters so his body took a swift glide forward to sink steeply into the hissing grass and vanished from my sight.

Immediately I ran forward to put him out of unnecessary pain. However, he was dead when I reached him, lying on his side with large brown eyes wide open, filled with hurt and turning purple between the blue of the day without and fall of night within. I cut his throat quickly. I stood up to wipe my hands and knife. The last of the herd was vanishing down the pass. Behind me a horse snorted and jingled its bridle chain. I swung about. My brother was there sitting on his horse his face white as chalk, looking at Stompie.

"Well?" I asked, pretending to take it for granted that he was about to dismount to give me a hand cleaning the buck: "Not much of a bag for all that work, is it?"

He made no answer but went on staring past me at the stained earth.

That put me on the defensive. "What's biting you?" I said. "Aren't you going to help?"

He shook his heavy head and said with difficulty, his eyes bright with the unanswerable rhetoric of tears: "No, Ouboet. I'm not going to help." Then he burst out suddenly, "How could you? How could you do such a thing?"

"Don't be an ass," I answered, more perturbed than I cared to show. "Stompie asked for it. Besides I probably did him a kindness. He can't have enjoyed himself much. No one wanted him around."

It was then that my brother became more violent than I had ever seen him. "How d'you know?" he asked passionately. "Life must have wanted him or he would never have been born."

This time there was no holding his tears. I became so upset that I sent him off home on his own, thinking I could then clean and truss Stompie at peace. But all the time I was haunted by that look of living hurt still lingering in the dead buck's eyes. I seemed to have known that look all my life though never so poignantly or at such close quarters. For instance, had I not seen something of the sort a year before in my brother's eyes at school? The question of it gripped my mind like the first nip of winter frost in the shadows cast by a watery autumn sun. It made me shiver and I tried to dismiss the association as sheer fantasy. Yet from that time onwards, although I continued shooting for years, I never again enjoyed it as before. I shot purely out of habit. My liking for it ended that morning with Stompie on the wide plain on the far side of the prehistoric ridge at the back of the white walls of our home. And my liking for Stompie? How and when had that died? Was Stompie perhaps condemned on the afternoon when I abandoned my brother to the school's strange hunger? But I am better at questions than answers. All I know for certain is that it is on such dubious trifles as these that the "nothingness" of which I have spoken feeds and grows great.

4. The Growth of Nothing

My brother and I never spoke of Stompie again. The incident seemed to glide into place naturally beside the other unmentionable episode and to form a pair of creatures waiting in the shadow of my mind for their native night to fall. There were even long periods when I succeeded in forgetting them altogether. I was aided and abetted in this by the fact that life afflicts the young with appetites and longings so violent and vivid as to lend reality to the illusion that they are permanent and that their satisfaction is purpose enough. I had my university to get through, then my law studies to conclude and finally my own legal practice to set up. I did all this in a manner which satisfied the high expectations everyone had of me. True, towards the end of my law examinations I was conscious for the first time of a slightly sagging interest in the mechanics of learning. From time to time I wondered whether what I was doing was as important and urgent as it seemed to be. This may even have been noticeable in the results of my examinations. However, the change was so slight and there were so many valid excuses to be made for it since I had so many interests that it escaped both particular and general comment. Yet sometimes in the very midst of my activities and at all sorts of odd and unexpected moments, something would stir in the shadows: there was a movement of things long forgotten as if to remind me that they were still waiting for their own nightfall. This awareness always was accompanied by a feeling of indefinable dismay, a startling of my whole being. And I never got used to it. Perhaps because what we call "forgetfulness" and "neglect" are the favourite sustenances of a certain part of ourselves. Suddenly, in a street crowded with traffic, my step would falter because some leopard light on a white wall reminded me of that morning when my brother and I rode out of the white gates to shoot on the other side of the hills on the great plain. Sometimes at the climax of a complicated plea for the prosecution I would find myself stammering and forced to play for time by drinking a glass of water I did not need because the look in the black eyes of a handcuffed African prisoner waiting his turn in the dock had reminded me, poignantly, of my own past with my brother. I told myself that it was absurd, even unjust that such remote events should be allowed to keep such determined pace with my grown-up self. But none of these admirable and undoubtedly valid considerations influenced their behaviour or their effect on me. They lived on from year to year, thriving apart from the main stream of life within me, with a volition and dark reason all their own and in time their self-announcements seemed to gain in vigour. But even worse than their disconcerting reappearances in a recognizable dimension of my spirit was their invisible subversion.

As I grew older I became more and more afraid of being either alone or unoccupied. I found that my leisured moments were invaded by a strange uneasiness and bleakness. Particularly I could not bear to be alone during the hours of mid-afternoon, for this period seemed to acquire its own bleak, masterful intent which lived itself out quite apart from me. I could no longer hear the wind rising (a sound I had always loved) without feeling unbearably sad because now my spirit seemed to be incapable of response. And the sound of a cockcrow, even in bright daylight, always gave me the feeling that I was groping in a crepuscular sleep gripped by a horror for which there was never a name.

At the time, of course, I did not understand this sabotage in the invisible dimensions of my being. That came about only many years later. So I became a sufferer denied even the comfort of knowing the name of his disease; and that feeling of uncertainty promptly planted its own colony of uneasiness on the mainland of my spirit. I became, if you like, a haunted person. Yes, I know the meaning of ghosts. And we who discount them do so only because we look for them in the wrong dimension. We think of them as a return of the bodily dead from their graves. But these dead have no need to return to life for they are not the dead. As I see it what has once given life to the spirit can never again be dead in the dimension of the spirit. So we mistake the shadow for the substance; confuse the reflection and the reality. Ghosts do not follow physical death, but rather they precede life. The only death the spirit recognizes is the denial of birth to that which strives to be born: those realities in ourselves that we have not allowed to live. The real ghost is a strange, persistent beggar at a narrow door asking to be born; asking, again and again, for admission at the gateway of our lives. Such ghosts I had, and thus, beyond all reason, I continued to be haunted.

It made no difference that I worked hard, that I took good care never to be idle and seldom alone, that I did my duty conscientiously wherever I saw it clearly, that I earned the envy and esteem of my fellow-men in almost equal measure, that I took my vacations regularly in good company by the sea. . . . This subtle chill of "nothingness," of a cold, phantom presence silently trying and re-trying the handle of my door, turned the warmth of my ardent living tepid. Yet for many years I doubt if any of my contemporaries suspected that anything was wrong with me. Occasionally a woman would catch me out. In the midst of some cheerful gathering she would ask with curious urgency: "What's happened? You look as if something awful had happened?" I would laugh off the question, for how could I explain that I myself had no inkling of the truth and that in the past, when I had tried to track down the answer, it had led only to a jumble of unrelated visions.

It was only the forward thrust of youth in me and the support, visible and invisible, which the approval and expectation of our community gave me which enabled me to carry on, without wavering, until I was thirty-two. Then, for the first time, I was not merely saddened but frightened. The spirit of play declined in me. I began to be increasingly worried that what I had achieved was without meaning and my success merely an illusion. I would find myself waking up in the small hours of the morning not knowing where I was or who I was. I would appear in court or attend a public function with the feeling that I was not really there at all. I would look at the church clock and think: "But that's not my time at all; that's not the hour I keep." Or glance at the weathercock swinging complacently on its perilous perch and long to cry: "For God's sake teach your kind to be as silent as you are."

For the first time, too, the world around me began to indicate that it might have misgivings. One day an old acquaintance buttonholed me in the club to say with flattering solicitude: "You know, young fellow-me-lad, we all think you're overdoing things a bit. All work and no play makes Jack a dull boy! Why not come up north with me and put in a month's shooting on my ranch?"

I could only protest and decline with polite gratitude. Impossible to explain that for years now I had shot only from necessity, for, if there was one thing more than another which made my life seem like the endless repetition of a meaningless pattern, it was this automatic yearly recurrence of a long shooting excursion up north.

Later one or two elderly women, interested in my welfare, began to urge me to marry. "You're not looking after yourself properly. You need someone to take care of you." And then, with a touch of archness, "Don't leave it too long!" I forced a laugh at their concern and said that as soon as I met the right person I wouldn't hesitate. But on these occasions the question which always rose immediately to the surface of my mind was: "How take on somebody else when I can't even know myself?"

Yes, the paradox which more than any other disturbed my nights was just that: my familiar self was a stranger to me, and the more deeply I felt this the less inclined I was to visit my home. While my parents were still alive I went occasionally to visit them though always with reluctance. When they died I sold the home in the village where I was born and only once went to stay with my brother on the farm which he had inherited. Of that night I remember clearly only one incident. One evening, after a dinner party, I asked my brother to sing for us. Before he could reply a girl flashed me a surprised look and said: "But didn't you know, Cousin, he never sings any more." The answer went deep into me like a knife-stab in the dark.

I never visited him again after that although I was repeatedly pressed and as often promised to do so. I claimed pressure of work which, in the past, would have been a reasonable excuse. But at this period the bitter process of cancellation within me had reached such a point that there were times when I could barely summon up the energy to get up in the mornings or, once dressed, to get through the day. Often, the day over, I was unable to undress for bed. This distaste of life, joined to my fear of the distaste, lengthened in my heart like my own evening shadow cast behind me on a great, yellow plain of the high-veld. When at last one September our African spring came, it fell on my torn and tattered senses like the rap of a policeman at my own door with a warrant for my arrest. I was at my wits' end—and my wits, as my career showed, were not inconsiderable.

At that moment the War came.

War is animal, not vegetable or mineral. It should be proclaimed as such by the beast blowing his own apocalyptic trumpet and sending scarlet heralds on coal-black horses to spread the news from one land's end to the other so that all can recognize him for what he is.

It came to us, however, quite differently. We read the news on the club teleprinter whose main duty it was to keep us posted of the latest market prices, as we crowded round it that Sunday before lunch, glasses of wine in hand. I joined with the rest in the many expressions of horror that went up in the room. I, too, called it a crime against God and humanity. I warmly supported the oldest member when, tears streaming down his smooth pink cheeks, he called Heaven to witness that the war was not of our seeking and had been thrust on us despite the most honourable efforts to avoid it. But even as he spoke and I agreed, I was aware of a barely perceptible sense of relief, a feeling as if an obstruction which had been damming the waters of life and rendering them stagnant had now broken through and the stream was once more flowing fast towards the sea.

Not that I want to exaggerate. This is an issue of war and I want to be dead accurate. But it is not easy. In order to be so I have to deal in a currency which the civilized, Christian heart considers counterfeit; to pursue considerations to which no decent mind will wittingly own. Yet my impression that Sunday morning was that the company in the teleprinter room shared with me a lifting of tension. This, of course, had its legitimate aspect. For a long time the fear of war had been hanging over our heads: the removal of that uncertainty was accompanied by a certain relief. Yet, now that doubt was slain and the ancient theatre, closed for so long, was open once more and yet another great drama of life and death was about to be acted, it was noteworthy how the feeling of having a definite part to play in a world-première quickly invested the many persons in the room with a new sense of importance and an emotion of differences overcome. I saw two bitter enemies in the club who had not spoken to each other for years, simultaneously pledge themselves, with moist eyes, in an extra measure of wine. I myself felt the burden of meaninglessness which had been growing in me so alarmingly of late fall away and the savour returned to my tongue. I felt a new reinstatement of purpose in my life, and a promise of greater significance to come.

I stood at the window of the club. Alone for a moment, absorbed in my own thoughts, I listened to sirens and factory hooters breaking the Sunday calm to announce the news. Their tones of sinister hysteria affected the whole community. People walking in the street suddenly swung out into a stride, cars doubled their normal speed, all the leisurely, Sunday traffic began to hasten. I saw a policeman overlooking flagrant breaches of traffic regulations, and all sorts and conditions of men who had never before mixed together now gathered spontaneously on the street corners talking with extraordinary animation and gesticulating dramatically in a manner unknown in our community. Behind me, too, the club buzzed like a beehive. The sound reminded me of—of—— I could only think of the noise in the quadrangle at school the afternoon just before the "round-up." I felt my body stiffen as the finger of the implacable memory touched me. Then deliberately I forced myself to relax. The war—real fighting—I told myself savagely, would soon put an end to this shadow-boxing that I had endured for so many years. Yes, I even felt a kind of grim satisfaction at the thought.

I was just about to heed the voices of my friends calling me back to the bar when, among all those animated fast-moving and quickly changing figures without, my eye was caught and held by one inconspicuous scene. A woman and a child by her waiting no doubt for a man, were sitting apart from the crowd in the swirling streets on an iron bench under the Royal Palm in front of our imposing gates. The woman had her arm thrown out protectively round the child. Her shoulders were shaking. Clearly she was crying. When I turned away she was still crying. It was a scene I never forgot, and that went to join the other shadows in my mind, fighting for recognition.

All that Sunday my mind worked with a vigour and a precision I had not known for long. I did not worry at all about my own personal safety. I had an idea I would be all right in battle and good at killing. Ignorant of the origins of this terrible need of life for death in the living issue that was upon us, I dismissed them. All my instinct for action and my confidence seemed promptly to return to me. I left the club after a quick lunch, went to my chambers and wound up my affairs. I gave my clerks and juniors detailed instructions in writing as to how to carry on in my absence. It was nearly midnight when I finished, and yet for the first time in years I did not feel tired. I went home, still curiously exhilarated, woke up my housekeeper and repeated my performance there. I did not get to bed until four in the morning. Even so I was up by seven with a small suitcase packed with a few essentials. Soon after, still filled with this curious new eagerness, I presented myself at our military headquarters. I was nearly an hour too early and a sleepy sergeant, impatient for his relief, angrily told me so. However, I insisted, with such an assumption of authority, on seeing one of the duty officers that he had no option but to fetch him. As a result I was the first volunteer to be enrolled for the war in our city. In all this I behaved as if in accordance to a plan worked out years before for just such an emergency. I never thought about what to do next; each step presenting itself to me in an unhesitating sequence of an apparently predetermined logic, even down to this question of volunteering and entering the army through the ranks. I do not suppose that I really anticipated being left there long. Perhaps if I had I would have enlisted as an officer straight away, as it was easy to do in my country. Indeed, probably the more normal thing to do would have been quietly to apply for a commission and patiently wait my turn with the rest of my friends. But my instinct for the drama of the occasion, my yearning to keep close to this revived feeling of purpose, would have none of that. It exacted this precipitate gesture from me and persuaded me, at the same time, that this was the natural thing to do. The persuasion seemed more than justified when that evening, sitting in barracks in a brand-new uniform, I read in the evening newspapers: *City's youngest K.C. leads nation-wide rush to the colours: Famous barrister joins the ranks.*

I was sent for the next day. I could then have had a good administrative post for the duration in the Adjutant-General's department. They told me it was the branch of the service which could best use my experience and training. But resolutely I refused all such suggestions and insisted that I would remain in the ranks unless I could be commissioned in the infantry. Didn't they know, I asked with a grin, that it was killing, not clerking I was after? I had my way and within a few days was back in the club in officer's uniform, standing round after round of farewell drinks, hearing from everyone both appraisal and approval of my behaviour.

Even my brother, in one of his rare letters, had written on the day war was declared: "We've just heard the news and by the time this reaches you I expect you'll have joined up, so I want to hasten to wish you God speed. I can't, of course, go with you all. Someone has to stay behind and grow food, and I expect it's right that a bloke like me should be the 'someone.' I can only promise you that the thought of what thousands of gallant chaps like you will be doing for the stay-at-homes will make me work harder than ever. I have already thought of a way of bringing new land under the plough that will double, if not treble, our yield. I don't expect you'll have time to come all this way to visit us and I am sure it would be wrong for me to press you, but please remember, always, that you're constantly in our thoughts and prayers. Write when you've a moment and God bless you, Ouboet."

You see? In doing what I'd done I was fulfilling even my brother's expectations of me. No wonder that, for the moment, I was composed, even content. Yet I never answered the letter. I put if off from day to day and in the end merely sent him a telegram on the day I embarked.

I shall pass over the weeks of training that followed, the detail of embarkation with the first division of infantry and our voyage to the battlefields of North Africa. I do so not because that period is without interest but because it is irrelevant to my story. I am concerned only with betrayal, with the seed of negation within me, with a particular botany both of my own and of the human spirit, and in that connection I have nothing further to add until I come to my first taste of action. The action was not much of an affair except to me and my battalion. My role in it, moreover, was of my own choosing and execution. For days our Directors of Intelligence had been complaining about the dearth of prisoners to give them information. We were new in the field and took their urging more seriously than we might have done later on. My Colonel seemed profoundly bothered about the whole thing and so I volunteered one night to take out a special patrol and collect the bodies Intelligence wanted.

The offer was accepted gladly and again I was struck by how easily my mind planned and carried out the operation. It was as if I had done it all a thousand times before. That, coupled with my lifetime's experience in stalking the game of my native land made the task seem elementary and the success a certainty. After observing an advanced post of the enemy for some days, procuring a couple of aerial photographs of it, personally reconnoitring at night the ground between us and it, I crawled one moonless midnight out of our position with a section of seven hand-picked men behind me.

Within half-an-hour, still undetected, we were close to our target. The tide of a not unpalatable excitement ran high in my blood. I felt rejuvenated, my emotions as fresh and vivid as the day, nearly twenty years before, when I had stalked and killed my first Kudu bull. I halted my patrol and turned on my back to rest making sure we were all in full breath before going in to capture and kill the outpost whose low parapet was looming darkly before us like the outline of the backs of a bunch of ruminating kine. I remarked that the stars, too, were participating in the venture and trembling on the tips of their toes with excitement. In this strange northern sky they were mostly strangers to me and all appeared in the wrong places but, as if for encouragement, there was my favourite constellation, the great hunter Orion, gliding smoothly, with his Red Indian swing through the black wings on the edge of the Milky Way, unheeding of the clear song and bright twitter of lesser stars on the bright stage before him. I do not think I had ever known a purer or more complete moment than I did then. I mention it because I think now that it was all part of the greater plan to perfect and refine the irony of what had to follow.

All around us the desert, so appropriately a setting for battle in the bankrupt spirit of man, was oddly still. As I lay there the noise of an aeroplane coming fast towards us from behind the enemy lines broke in on the quietude.

"We'll go in the moment it's overhead," I whispered to my men. "It'll drown the sound of our movements. But get this clear. You three come first with your knives. You others follow, covering with your guns; no shooting if we can help it."

I turned over. Knife in my right hand, I rose softly into position like a runner braced for the starter's pistol on the edge of the track. Three dark shapes conformed beside me. The plane was flying low and fast towards us. Just before it was overhead I said "Now!" and leapt forward. The enemy position was only a shallow machine-gun pit scraped out of the hard desert rubble. My hand briefly on the parapet, I cleared it at the run and landed in the midst of a platoon of sleeping enemy soldiers. My feet barely touched bottom when the aeroplane dropped a landing flare almost immediately overhead. Instantly the shallow pit and its huddle of dusty little men and the desert far and wide around us were illuminated with a bright magnesium glare. The sentry leaning against the bank by the parapet was struggling out of a desperate sleep, terror on his face. In the strange phosphorescent light floating down from above us, I could see every line on his unshaven face. He was a small dark man, his face broad and his eyes wide open to the horror quaking within him. Something in me hardened instantly at the sight of him, as if he were not a reality of war without but a puppet in a shadow-show against the ecto-plasmic light of my own mind. He raised his rifle, perhaps to protect himself and he tried to call out, perhaps, that he was surrendering. The sound was strangled in his throat. I have always been exceptionally fast in my physical reaction to situations. Although this takes time in the telling, it all passed off in one continuous movement. I leapt at him and before he was clear of the bank, had ducked past his rifle, pinned him against the earth and driven my knife into him beneath his ribs with a swift upward thrust and all my weight and speed behind it. For one infinitesimal frag-ment of time a terrible stillness held between us the sort of stillness no doubt wherein God's monitors at their lis-tening post at the exit of the world could hear a sparrow fall or even the first faint footstep of evil setting out on its labyrinthine way. In the midst of that stillness I heard his skin squeak at the point of my knife and then snap like elastic. A look like the brush of a crow's wing passed over his face—and for a moment he reminded me of my own brother. Flashes of visions of my brother, Stompie, the woman crying under the Royal Palm came and went in my mind like children playing hide and seek in the twilight. They vanished just in time. My men were following my own ex-ample like automatons attacking with their knives the terri-fied men coming out of their sleep with upraised hands. I had to stop them at once. More I feared the fever of killing would upset the four covering us with their guns. Once they opened up there would be no survivors and our chances of getting back to our lines greatly diminished. As I ordered them to stop the landing flare went out and thank God a generous fall of blackness covered us all. We disarmed the seventeen enemy soldiers still alive. We made them take off their boots and marched them in their socks deftly back to our lines. My men went behind purring like kittens with their triumph. I went like someone profoundly preoccupied walking unaware with one foot on a pavement, the other in a gutter; one mind content with my men in that moment, another hopeless and strangely defeated in another epoch of time. In that time-gutter of my own, the prisoners in front of me seemed freer than I. I, a prisoner of myself and my own gaoler. Was this war waged in a cause of which I had had such ardent expectations, to show itself in my first encounter not to be the battlefield I sought? Would it not enable me to do the killing I needed? Was it about to cheat me merely into murdering enemy proxies of my own brother, and be but another turn of the same meaningless screw?

Back in our lines the Colonel came out to congratulate us on the success of the venture but for the first time I found praise hard to swallow. I was nearly rude to him. When my brother officers wanted to celebrate my first mention in despatches I could hardly force myself to drink with them.

And so it went on. I got better and better at killing. In particular I was so good at the kind of raid I have described that I was taken away from my battalion and set to plan and lead raids further and deeper behind the enemy lines. I came back each time impatient of offers of leave and rest, asking only to be kept active and employed. I volunteered for every difficult and hazardous operation. For more than a year I was continuously engaged either on operations against the enemy or busy preparing them. I gave myself no time for anything except war, hoping thereby to escape from my shadows, but they were too adroit for me. After waking, in the midst of battle, in the faces of men fixing their bayonets behind a sand dune, in the mindless sound of the cry as they charged, in the sight of the enemy caught in our concealed fire wheeling like springbuck, or at the sight of a peasant woman sitting with her child by the smouldering ruin of her home, right through the gateway of my deepest sleep and in the heart of my most tender dreams the shadows followed deftly swishing and fluttering their long skirts as they passed. I do not know where it would have ended if, despite all my resistances, I had not been suddenly ordered out of the desert and sent on a special mission to Palestine.

5. "The Day Far Spent"

I have often been overawed in the silences of a sleepless night by the thought of the precision with which chance and circumstance work in human lives. They will contrive, for instance, that a person such as a Maori I knew should be born on the other side of the world just in time to meet a German bullet in his forehead thirty years later in a Libyan desert, while I, who was leading him, was delivered with as nice a calculation. But of the many imposing expositions I have witnessed of the working of these precision instruments of life none struck me as so subtle as those which took me to Palestine. I went against my will and yet no assignment could have fitted more neatly into the jig-saw pattern of my desperation than this posting to Palestine. I found myself stationed at a monastery called Imwash. The monks had moved out only a few days before to their parent monastery a mile or so back at a place called Latrun. There was still a smell as of frankincense and myrrh from their centuries of occupation hanging about the cool corridors and the grey stone halls when I moved in with my band of cut-throats.

For some weeks I and other men younger than I but with even older faces, taught these desperate characters the kind of killing and clandestine warfare in which we had become specialists. They were a strange lot, all with their own idea and aptitude for killing. For instance the best shot among them was a boy with a squint and a contortionist's body who had had a Jewish father and an Arab mother and who aimed his gun with his right eye from his left shoulder. In him, as in them all, the normal proportions seemed inverted with a macabre logic to serve all the better their mission of death. In the mornings I marched them out and taught them how to handle explosives, lay booby traps, set time-fuses and delayed action bombs, together with unarmed combat and other tricks of silent killing. In the afternoons I lectured them out of my experience and tried to make their imaginations at home in the background against which they would have to do their work. At night I would take them out into the hills behind the monastery and play at stalking human game in the deep gullies, wadies, orchards of olives and fig trees on their terraced slopes. Usually between lectures and night manoeuvres I would march them out before sunset to watch the time-fuses and delayed charges, that we had set in the morning, explode. The dust of the explosions would hang golden between us and the sinking sun in the still air. I had always thought our African high-veld light was the purest in the world. I was wrong. There is nothing so lovely as the autumnal evening light in Palestine. I remember on the first evening standing there apart from my soldiers looking beyond the dust to the olive trees, figs, vineyards and slender cypresses, feeling the explosions still reeling in my senses, and thinking that this was a strange way to treat a holy land. Once the feeling was sharpened almost unendurably by the sight of a lone gazelle, one of the loveliest of the lean buck of the Palestinian hills, startled by the sounds and leaping high on a crest of purple hill, just as Stompie had once done in the great plain behind the prehistoric hills at home. Oh, it was ever-present, this prick of memory which had been tempered like a surgeon's needle in the general nightmare of betrayal in my being. I would be grateful, then, for the odd charge which had not exploded and the duty which compelled me to go and examine it, because, as Commanding Officer, it was I who had to execute this most dangerous of all tasks in our training mission.

One evening, so still and clear that the light standing brimful between the hills around us was like crystal water and the slight air of evening sent a faint but rhythmical tremble through it like the tail of a fish in a clear mountain pool, I was counting the explosions, thus, and felt almost relieved to find that one had failed. I was closing in on it fast when it went off and a rock the size of a rugger ball just missed my head. As the dust and shock cleared from my eyes I saw sitting on a boulder some two hundred yards away a civilian who had no business to be there at all. I went over to him quickly. He was a monk but despite his priest's clothes I spoke to him sternly, so relieved was I to find an outlet for the mixed emotions of shock and chagrin within me. He was a tall, middle-aged man with a slight stoop, yellow hair that fell to his shoulders and a pair of fine blue eyes in a wide forehead. He was heavily bearded as well and as a result the only light in his face came from his eyes and forehead.

He listened to me patiently and at the end said in English with a German accent: "I am sorry if I have done anything wrong, sir, and give you concern. But for many years now, long before our superiors in Jerusalem handed over our monastery to the military for thirty pieces of silver, I have come here every evening to look both at it and the view. You need not be afraid I'll do anything stupid. I know all about explosives. I too have been a service man once. But I'll not come here again if you forbid it."

With that he turned as if to go to where the greater monastery sat snugly a mile away below a hill securely tucked in behind screens of flickering cypress, glistening olive trees and wide autumnal vineyards of gold. However, his manner had made such an impression on me that I asked in a more conciliatory tone: "You say you have been a service man too? How, when and where?"

He turned round at once and said slowly: "I was a German submarine officer in the '14–'18 war."

"And in this?" I asked beginning again to feel aggressive.

But he was impervious to the change of tone and said, "I became a monk in 1919 and have been here in the 'Holy Land' ever since."

He paused and we stood there looking at each other.

He broke out of the silence first and asked: "Do you think you could possibly tell me how the war is going?"

I started, willingly enough, to give him the latest war news without realizing that I was on the wrong track.

He interrupted me again, saying: "I'm sorry, I didn't mean that war. I meant your war?"

"And your country's too," I answered sharply, thinking that, like many Germans, he was disclaiming responsibility for it.

"Forgive me," he answered quietly, "if I have presumed too much on a priest's privilege and intruded into your private affairs. But I thought I recognized a look on your face that I seemed to remember on my own in 1917 . . ." He paused. "It was then that I first realized that the war I was fighting was in me long before it was in the world without. I realized that I was fighting it in a secondary dimension at reality."

"Oh, that's all right," I said uncomfortably, not at all prepared to continue such a disturbing line of conversation with a stranger even though the stranger were a priest. So I went on instead to say: "Look, if you've been coming here every evening, don't let us break the habit. I can easily arrange for my men to practise these explosions at a safer distance."

At that a new expression came into his sombre eyes. He thanked me saying he would appreciate greatly such permission and begged me to allow him to explain why he so valued coming there in the evening. For twenty years, he told me, he had been coming here because this dip in the land where we practised our combats was, for him, the most hallowed ground in Palestine. It was there, he said, that Christ first revealed Himself to His disciples after the Resurrection. He waved his hands, now almost transparently white from the many years of concealment in his monk's sleeves, at the land below us. The sun was just going down and the shadows were already running deep like flowing water in the wadies. He said that there exactly where the monastery stood the disciples, some as stunned by their private hesitations and evasions during those critical hours between Christ's apprehension and His crucifixion as by the crucifixion itself, and all like sheep at nightfall in a world of wolves without a shepherd, were gathered fearfully together. Then suddenly He came out of a sunset sky and appeared before his anguished followers.

They did not recognize Him but out of their own deep hurt, and in their fear, welcoming any addition to their numbers, they made him welcome, saying, "Abide with us, for the day is far spent."

Here there was a pause and then my companion went on to say that as for himself, he came there every night to relive that hour. He came to remind himself of his own evasions and failure to recognize the Resurrected One during the day and to wait until he was ready to fall on his own knees for pardon of his daily acts of unbelief.

"But how do you know that this was the place?" I asked abruptly.

The great bell had suddenly begun tolling the dark hour in the monastery and I rather shot the question at him because I felt that the emotion roused in me by his tale and the manner of his telling it, would disturb me unless I clung to what were still to me the main facts of life.

"The first pilgrims discovered it and marked the place," he replied. "The crusaders followed to build this their first church and monastery on the designated spot, exactly where you now do your work."

His words again made me uncomfortable. His capacity for disconcerting me seemed unfailing yet I wanted him to say more. However, he excused himself gently, asking if I had not heard the bell? That was his call to duty as I had mine over there. He pointed to where my men huddled restless on the slope. If I liked, he concluded, we could meet again any evening I chose, in the same place, for now that I had been so good as to give him permission, he would keep up the habit. And with that he walked, still with a marked seaman's roll under his monk's dress, into the growing dark, the bell tolling all the time and shaking the brown air with wave upon wave of urgent sound.

But I did not see him again. I woke the next morning with one of my periodical recurrences of malaria, the worst I had experienced since I left the bush-veld. We had no doctor attached to my staff for we were only a small oddly select unit, an aristocracy, if you like, of killers, nor would I allow my adjutant to telephone to Jerusalem for one. I had had malaria so often in the past that I felt I knew better than any doctor what to do. I promptly dosed myself with quinine, got my batman to pile my bed high with rugs and greatcoats and settled down to wait confidently for my ague to stop and the sweat to burst out and break the fever. But as the day wore on it soon became evident that this was no ordinary attack. The ague got worse, my temperature rose and no sweat relieved the fever.

In the afternoon an age of ice seemed to have entered my blood and to be rattling my bones. When I am really ill, my instinct always is for life and not man to nurse me. When I come to die I hope it may be in the open, face to face with sky and stars and so I may be able to commit my spirit without reserve to its keeper, the wind.

So now with the help of my batman I struggled out into the open to lie under the sky facing the lee of the slope where the monk and I had met the evening before. There at last I felt my fever had room to spread its wings. For that is what fever needs. Fever is Time grown strange wings, the mind feathered to range great distances between an anguished brittle moment in the present and one's first drop into being. Hardly was I laid in the open than such consciousness as I had took flight. I forgot my aching and my shivering vanished and I just went with a single overwhelming thought swiftly backwards until I came to the moment where once a great darkness had gathered over the land on which I lay. I could feel the earth heave itself in agony beneath my ear, hear the temple rent with a lightning sound to be followed by a terrible silence wherein the only murmur was the blood hissing in my ear like an angry sea among the rocks. The silence became so frightening, so full of the nothingness of which I have spoken, that I could endure it no longer and flung myself up in my bed to look for something to fill it.

I saw the sun setting and realized my fever had brought me out at the moment where a little huddle of stricken followers were preparing for the night on the place where the monastery, my future workshop of war, was to be built. Then, in the focus of my fever, I saw first the huddle of men and then He Himself, coming down a footpath winding through figs and sparkling olives just as the monk had described it to me. The sunset was like a halo around His head. And yet now that He had come the occasion was so ordinary that I was not surprised that He was not recognized. How hard to learn that our own brief wonder is not worked in heaven but in the grains of sand at our feet; the miracle is not in the stars but in the fearful flesh and blood piled on the moon-bone beneath our own shrinking skin. The men huddled about Him now could not see the miracle for, in their fear, they were looking too far or too high.

Then I heard one of them, dark with bereavement like a crow at nightfall, say to Him: "Abide with us for the day is far spent."

But his tone implied no recognition.

As I watched it all, His presence crackling like a fire within my senses, I began to understand more fully their failure in recognition. He was the same: but He was translated. The perishable script of Himself was left in the archives somewhere around Gethsemane, and only the translation was now present. He had been rendered into a new idiom which could not yet be read and which it could need eons of both inner and outer Time to decode and absorb.

It was at this moment that He asked suddenly, "But why are you not all here?"

"Indeed, we are all here," one of them replied.

He shook His head decisively, answering, "Judas is not here."

The amazement on their faces was great partly, perhaps, because of the implication in tone that He wished Judas to be there, and also, perhaps, because He evidently did not seem to know of Judas's fate which was by now common knowledge throughout the land.

Then, in my fever, I saw one of them stand slowly to his

feet and answer, "But surely, Master, you know Judas is dead. He hanged himself."

Both by his action, words and tone I knew that at last revelation had come to that questioner.

At this the Resurrected One turned His back on the speaker and spoke out clearly yet with anguish. "This cannot be true! If I fail in this I fail in all else besides!" He looked up. "This life which You have set beyond men needs Judas just as it needs Me. His deed, too, is redeemed in the love which exacted it of him."

Saying this He half-turned again and I was able to see that His eyes were entirely without light.

While the others huddled together still dazed by revelation I got up unhesitatingly and, shivering, I went and knelt at His feet, saying, "There are many rumours in Jerusalem and Rome that are not true. See, I am Judas . . . I am alive and I am here."

As I spoke the light came back into His face and leaning forward He took both my hands in His and helped my fever-shaken body to its feet. Then, looking upwards, he exclaimed, "Thank you, Father. Now at last we can both be free."

"But I'm not free," I hastened to add. "I had a brother once and I betrayed him——"

"Go to your brother," He said at once, "and make your peace with him even as I have had to do with my need of you."

At that I felt the sweat break out on my skin and run down my body like tropical rain. I began slowly to grow warm again and I could hear the cool wind of an autumn nightfall stirring down the slope and through the leaves. For long I had feared the voice of the wind, but now I was grateful for the sound. It was almost dark and the stars were dropping their light like tears of compassion upon the night. Amazed,

I looked around me. There were no people to be seen. I was quite alone, yet for the first time in many years I did not feel lonely. I stretched back into my blankets and lay down watching the stars go down behind the hill between Imwash and Bethlehem. I don't think I slept at all and yet it was the shortest night I have ever known. The day came so swiftly that night could have been the mere shadow of a cloud passing across the sun. My own darkness had been overtaken at last.

When morning came I knew clearly what I was going to do. I felt like a ship long becalmed, reeling in the wind that had at last found its sails. I was going at once to my brother. War and the clash of the world's armies seemed insignificant in comparison with that slight deed. For the first time I feared lest I be killed before I could accomplish it. Death, I now understood, was a moment of supreme truth that one could only meet with equal truth. I prayed that I should not carry this secret, this lie of my betrayal with me into death.

My resourcefulness which I had thrown so wholeheartedly into destruction was now diverted towards quite another course of action. Before breakfast I had summoned a doctor from Jerusalem. That same day I had his order for a month's convalescent leave in my pocket. Though everyone declared it impossible, I managed to get from Palestine to Egypt and from Egypt, with the help of old friends in the South African Air Force, by stages to my home.

Barely a fortnight later I got out of a train one morning at the little railway siding near my brother's home. Everyone stared hard at my uniform which they found it as difficult to recognize as they did me. I managed to hire an old car for the day because that was all the time I could allow myself if I were to be back before my leave expired, and I drove to my brother's farm. During all this period I scarcely had eyes for the outside world at all but now even I could not help noticing how dry was the world. There was no grass left on the veld and the scrub was twisted and burnt black in the sun's fire; sheep and cattle were so thin that their ribs and bones seemed about to pierce their taut skins. Vultures, crows and buzzards circled the sky wherever some drought-stricken creature lay and wherever I got out of the car to open a gate the smell of death assailed my nose. Yet despite the tragedy of the thirsty land and the half-starved animals, as the morning wore on and I passed through great grey plains between shimmering blue hills and came nearer to my brother's home, a strange excitement began to rise in me. In the north-west, where our rains come from, I saw the snow peaks of a range of thunderclouds mounting in the sky but by the time I got to my brother's home they were turning black. Almost in their shadow I drove up an avenue of trembling poplars grown tall and broad since my last visit, drew up sharply before the wide *stoep*, jumped out and ran up the steps. Before I could knock, the front door opened and my brother's wife came out.

I had never known her well but I remarked what an austere spirit their joint struggle with the difficult earth had made of her. She recognized me immediately, yet in the very act of recognition her expression hardened in a way that was not promising. She did not even offer me her cheek to kiss but held out a cool hand and then managed to collect herself to explain: "This is a surprise. Come in and I'll go and call your brother. He'll be amazed to see you! Why didn't you send us word you were coming?"

"That's a long story," I said quickly, "and I can explain later. But where is he? I'll go and find him."

"Then I'll go on seeing to the dinner," she answered, not without relief. "He's in the garden at the back, leading the last of our water to the trees and vegetables. We've had a terrible time, as you've noticed I expect. No rain for a year. Sheep and cattle dying and all this lovely garden practically dead." She looked at me as if I'd been away enjoying myself somewhere instead of fighting a war.

"It must have been terrible," I agreed at once. "But it looks as if the rain is on its way at last."

"It has come up like this a dozen times recently only to be blown away by evening," she answered grimly.

I left her on that note and went to look for my brother. I found him in the centre of the garden leading a trickle of water with infinite patience and care from one parched, withering tree to the other. I saw him before he saw me. Of course he looked older, more bent, in fact almost twisted like one of the indigenous thorn-trees of our thirsty land. Indeed, he appeared to be so much a part of the earth that he might have grown out of it. I noticed the hump on his back was more pronounced than before but at that moment he heard me and turned round with the disconcerting adroitness so unexpected in one with so awkward a frame. He saw me and went still with shock. His dark eyes looked into my blue ones and I saw their light was still imprisoned in a moment far back in time. How well I knew it and how clearly I understood it now that I was free. Had I not learnt lately that death is not something that happens at the end of our life? It is imprisonment in one moment of time, confinement in one sharp uncompromising deed or aspect of ourselves. Death is exclusion from renewal of our present-day selves. Neither heaven nor hell are hereafter. Hell is time arrested within and refusing to join in the movement of wind and stars. Heaven is the boulder rock unrolled to let new life out. It is man restored to all four of his seasons rounding for eternity.

So I went up to my brother, and putting both hands on

his shoulders said: "It's good to see you again, Ouboet—and still growing things."

He stammered: "Ouboet, I wish I'd known you were coming. I'd have liked to be there to meet you. But come on up to the house. You must be tired. Can you stay long?"

"No, Ou Boetie," * I said and explained quickly, "I've no right in a sense to be here at all. It's taken me a fortnight to get here, and I'll be lucky to be back to the front in time if I'm not to get into serious trouble. So I'm going back in a few hours to catch the night train north. I've been hitch-hiking my way by air down here. I've come here just to see you and spend these few hours with you."

"Really, Ouboet?" he said as if he could not believe his ears: "Is that really so?"

"Of course," I told him tightening my grip on his shoulders and feeling I had no time even to go through the conventional motions of such a meeting. So I went straight to the heart of the matter and told him I had come to tell him of a great wrong I had once done him and to ask his forgiveness.

"Oh, but surely, Ouboet," he began to protest, but more out of habit than real feeling I was sure. So I interrupted him, begging him to listen and went on, without pause or evasion to tell him the story of my betrayal as I saw it.

He listened without interruption and with growing intensity. A hush seemed to have fallen over the fast-approaching storm and not even a mutter of distant thunder broke through the stillness of the parched garden.

When I had finished he turned and stared at me and I saw that there were tears in his eyes.

"Ouboet," he said in a voice I had not heard since one of our moments of reconciliation when we slept as children under the stars. "You mean, you—you've come all this way,

* "Little old brother" in Afrikaans.

spent the only leave you've ever taken since the war began, just to come and tell me this?"

I nodded, too upset to speak. Also suddenly I was now afraid that what I'd said seemed too little for so much. I looked away to where beyond the withered orchards the dark clouds were uncurling ponderously in the diminishing blue wondering what I would do if he too should find my words wanting.

Then I felt my hands taken in rough ploughman's fingers. "Ouboet, you've done many fine things," he said gently, "but never a braver than you've done today." He paused. "I've been afraid of this all along, but I only knew it for certain that day when you shot Stompie."

He broke off, and I stared at him.

"You knew?"

He nodded. "But now we're free of it all, thanks to you."

I realized, with amazement, that further words were unnecessary between us. Then I heard my brother with characteristic solicitude saying quickly, "But you look dead beat. Let's get back to the house. You go on ahead. I just want to turn off the water. Can't afford to waste a drop."

At his words physical fatigue flooded me and yet somehow became part of a new warmth produced by the release of the old tenderness between us.

My brother's wife was waiting for me below the *stoep*, curiosity and anxiety joined in her tense expression. But before either she or I could speak I heard my brother begin to sing in the garden as I had not heard him sing since childhood. He sang the verse I knew which was of his own composition:

> *"Ride, ride through the day,*
> *Ride through the moonlight,*
> *Ride, ride through the night,*

> *For far in the distance burns the fire,*
> *"For someone who has waited long."*

Then he started a second stanza, which was new to me:

> *"I rode all through the day,*
> *I rode through the moonlight,*
> *I rode all through the night*
> *To the fire in the distance burning*
> *And beside the fire found*
> *He who had waited for so long."*

I was deeply moved by the song and the woman standing by my side also reacted almost violently. "Dear heaven," she exclaimed. "D'you know ever since we've been married he's never sung a note. I'd never have believed he could ever sing like that again."

At that moment the thunder rumbled deep and long from end to end of the hills in the great plain. It was as if heaven itself had spoken. When the sound died away in the silence that followed we could hear only the wind moaning in the distance. My brother's wife looked at me, her face suddenly grown soft as a young girl's. "I'm glad you came," she said quickly. "But come in and rest. I am so glad I happen to have got a rather nice meal today and I believe you've brought us luck. I believe it is going to rain at last."

We turned and looked at the sky above the garden. There could be no more doubt. The cavalry of the great army of cloud was rounding up the last stray bits of blue. Thunder rang out again and again loud and long and the lonely hills at the end of the plain went white with the advance mist of the storm. Then we saw the rain itself come up fast, rushing with a sound like that of the great wind of the first spirit of life once more taking up its quest on the parched and long-rejected earth upon which we stood.

6. The Sowing of the Seed

"The questions put in my mind by this disturbing document," Lawrence said to me when we were alone again in the afternoon, "come so fast that I hardly know where to begin. But the first one is: did he go back to the war? I gather from this account that he felt bound not to overstay his leave. But surely such a—a revelation must have made a difference to him?"

"It did and it didn't," I told him. "In a way he seemed to go on as before."

"That surprises me. It suggests a compromise—Can you explain it?" Lawrence looked close to disappointment so I hastened to tell him what I could.

It was not much really. I felt convinced that Celliers had meant to write more about his life but was prevented from doing so for reasons which would soon be clear. I could not say for certain in what state he was on his return from leave because by the time he got back to North Africa, the Japanese had struck in South East Asia and I was on my way to a job in Burma. In fact I had not seen him again until the Kempitai, the powerful Japanese secret police, had brought him, barely alive, into my prison in Java.

"Was that the camp under the notorious Yonoi?" Lawrence asked quickly.

Yes, I told him, it was. One afternoon I'd happened to be standing near the prison gates when the Japanese had

pushed Celliers, barely alive, into the prison without ceremony or warning. I had known from the behaviour of the
Korean sentries who, to our regret, had replaced the Japanese ones, that something unusual was going on. As Lawrence well knew this was an uncomfortable feeling to have
anywhere in prison but never so bad as under the unpredictable Yonoi. I had no idea of course of the reason for it. But
I'd been on the alert because I'd discovered that when one
had feelings of that sort sometimes doing something quickly
and at the right moment could help to ward off disaster.

"I know. Timing was all important," Lawrence agreed
with me quickly. "But how difficult it was to make some of
our chaps see it."

I went on to tell Lawrence that I'd been standing there at
the gates on watch when suddenly they had opened. I'd
half-expected a company of infantry to come rushing in on
one of their prison searches but it had been just a solitary,
tall, broad-shouldered figure, which had been pushed in
through the doors in a torn jungle-green uniform, with an
untidy head of long hair which, after our cropped heads,
looked lush to the point of obscenity. He carried an empty
shoulder pack dangling in one hand and a field flash on
his hip, while he tried to walk upright without the help of
two Kempitai privates at his side. Even the sentries were
surprised. They had seen comings and goings of secret police
cars and concluded that something far bigger than the release of a prisoner from secret confinement was contem-
plated. And in a sense they had been right for I discovered
afterwards that that day we were to have been summoned
to attend Celliers's execution but that largely due to Yonoi's
intervention he had been reprieved at the last moment.

"Yonoi intervened!" Lawrence exclaimed incredulously.
He half-whistled and then asked what seemed the most

inconsequent of questions: "Celliers was very fair in colour-
ing, wasn't he?"

I said "Yes" and then asked: "Why?"

He smiled one of his grave smiles. "I'll explain when the
right moment comes," he assured me. "But I think you've
given me the key to something that the enigmatic Yonoi
once asked me to do. Yes. I saw Yonoi myself on a later
occasion. But you'd left the island by then— Go on!"

I told him I had recognized Celliers at once, though
he was greatly changed. The change of course was partly
due to the fact that he had been tortured by his captors,
kept starved in darkness for months, and inadequately
doctored for acute dysentery and malaria. Indeed, knowing
nothing of his inner history as we now knew it, I put the
whole change down to that. However, I was wrong. But to
return to that afternoon: Celliers, weak as he was, recognized me and called out my name. Before I could respond
the corporal of the guard shook his hand imperiously at
me and shouted rudely: "*Kura! Lakas!* You there! Quick,
come here!"

Of course I went at once to be hit across the face with
the back of the guard's hand. Korean guards in front of the
secret police had to be more Japanese than the Japanese
themselves. But suddenly there was a loud bellow behind
me. Yonoi had appeared unobtrusively through a side gate
and, seeing what was happening, had shouted to stop it.

"I can see him doing it," Lawrence said. "He was always
a great stickler for discipline. He disapproved of punishment unless ordered by himself."

"On this occasion he went much farther," I told Lawrence.
"He told the corporal to stand to attention while he gave
him a terrible beating about the head and face with his
cane, that piece of Javanese rottang he always carried, remember?"

Just then, I am certain we both had Yonoi's face vividly before us. He was a striking person we both agreed, perhaps the most handsome Japanese we had ever seen. He had an ascetic almost a priestlike face, round head and an aquiline nose. His eyes were well-spaced and though slanted in the manner of his race, were brilliantly compelling. He was also taller than most, and straightly made. He was the tidiest Japanese officer I have ever known too, his uniform always well cut and spotless and his jackboots polished and shining. He carried himself with a conscious air of distinction which most of us put down to vanity but which I now said to Lawrence may have been concerned with some special notion of honour that was inaccessible to us?

Lawrence nodded his head in agreement, remarking that one understood nothing about Yonoi and his people unless one had some intimation of the deep moon-honour always beckoning them in the great darkness that surrounded their overcrowded little lives. That was one of the things which had made life so difficult for us as prisoners of war. We were separated from our captors by many things, not the least of them being different conceptions of honour. In Yonoi's code it was the abandonment of all honour for a soldier to be taken prisoner alive—— But he was digressing, Lawrence said, and begged me to continue.

It took Yonoi some while to recover his self-control after beating the guard. His face had gone white and he stood muttering sounds that came not from his tongue or throat but, rather like a ventriloquist's, straight from within his stomach. The Korean clearly expected the beating to begin again at any moment though the blood was flowing from his nose, ears and forehead. He just succeeded in standing upright and finally Yonoi turned his back on him and spoke to me. He was the only prison commander I knew who would try his tongue at English.

"You! Officer!" he asserted, speaking the words with difficulty and with great pauses for recollection and application between each. Then he pointed to where Celliers was swaying uncertainly on his feet. "That person also officer. . . . That officer very weak. . . . Take good care! Make well! *Lakas!* Quick!"

He watched me with narrowed eyes as I went to Celliers. Not until I had Celliers firmly by the arm did he turn to go back into the guard room where he began a loud reprimand to the entire guard. He was still at it as I helped Celliers towards the crowded cantonments we had converted into a hospital. As usual, when there was evidence of "a hate" about, my fellow-prisoners had all withdrawn out of sight into their barracks. I could hear their tense whispers behind the thin bamboo walls discussing what might come out of this row at the gate where Yonoi still growled like some angry animal.

"Well, Straffer," I said, trying to conceal my shock at the change in his appearance. "This is a surprise! You look all in—but we'll soon take care of that. We've got one or two first-class doctors in camp with us. Not too badly off for medicine either. And from time to time we can buy food for the sick from the Chinese merchants outside. We'll soon get you well!"

A slight smile played over his haggard, sun-creased face. "Lucky to be here at all. Thought I was going to have my head cut off today—in fact I was taken out this morning to be executed in public. But for some reason they didn't fulfil either my expectations or their intentions."

It was said with a free gaiety that at any time would have been remarkable. I remember that it occurred to me that the old "Straffer" Celliers I had known in the Western Desert wouldn't have reacted in quite the same way. Part of him might even have resented such an order of release.

However, at that time I had no idea how deep the change in him went so I remarked amazed: "But how did you get away with it? They've executed quite a few of us recently. How did you do it?"

"I didn't do anything," he answered, smiling again. "I think they let me off because they liked the look of me."

"He said that?" Lawrence exclaimed.

"And quite without bitterness," I replied.

"Well, in view of this"—Lawrence tapped the yellow manuscript on his knees with a long finger—"You must have thought that interesting?"

"But I hadn't read the manuscript then," I said. "All I thought at the time, if I thought anything, was that the new 'Straffer,' in the last analysis, was just as relieved to escape death as any of us."

I concluded by telling Celliers that one day he must tell me what really happened for he was not in a condition for it at that moment. Lawrence would know from his own experience what Celliers's physical state must have been like after prolonged confinement and torture—so I'd skip the details. But our doctors were amazed that he should be still alive and without permanent injury to his system. But physical well-being seemed to be Celliers's particular specialty.

With care and a liberal ration of our hospital fare which we were still allowed in those early days to buy from the Chinese for our invalids, he recovered. I saw him regularly since Yonoi asked after him daily when I went to his headquarters to report. That a prison commander should take such a close interest in a prisoner had never happened before and it made a great impression on me. I just couldn't understand it. I was increasingly confounded when the doctor reported to me that from time to time Yonoi would appear without warning in the open entrance of the hospital cantonment. He would stand there looking at the corner where Straffer lay, taking no notice of anyone else. He would just stand there staring at Straffer as if—as one Australian doctor put it to me—they were two of a kind. The doctor added: "Made me uncomfortable. Something not quite healthy about it."

The strange thing was that Yonoi's interest never brought him to speak to Straffer on any occasion. After standing there for some time he would summon the doctor in charge and say: "Officer there: make well!" Finishing in that expressive Malay word: "*Lakas!* quick!"

It seemed that Yonoi's spirit, too, was in a hurry of its own.

But to return to Celliers's story . . . I learnt from him in the days that followed that something of significance had happened to him which had sent him hurrying home on leave to South Africa. Celliers told me that for a time he had had a terrible struggle with himself to know what to do about the war. He had thought out many plans and had even thought of transferring to a Red Cross unit. But in the end he had rejected all these solutions. He had felt that a person with a history such as his could not suddenly contract out of a situation which he had helped to bring about, and seek some specially privileged solution of the spirit. He was convinced that we were all accessories to the fact of war, and that once war had become a fact we could not avoid our own role in it. I remembered a phrase he had often repeated in our discussions in hospital. None of us, he claimed, were pure enough to claim a special solution for ourselves out of "our own human and time context." We could none of us afford, without fatal excess of spirit, to by-pass any of the stages through which life itself was forced to go. The spirit's battle for life was so important that one had to accept the challenge on whichever level it was presented, no matter how exalted or how humble or horrible.

One had even to respect the need of the spirit for death in certain living issues and just take what decency and proportion one could lay claim to into the killing. Celliers made no pretence of thinking that this was the final answer but that was as far, he said, as he could carry it at the moment.

"Dear God!" Lawrence interrupted here, shaking his head sadly. "Haven't we all covered the same ground ourselves? But is that all there can ever be to it?"

I went on to tell him that by the time Celliers had returned to North Africa the Japanese had overrun Burma and Malaya; Singapore had fallen, and Java and Sumatra had surrendered almost without a fight. The future everywhere looked black. Then a gloomy Headquarters at Cairo had asked Celliers since he spoke Dutch whether he would be prepared to jump by parachute with a small select band into Java to keep up a "nuisance" guerrilla warfare against the Japanese. He had agreed and some months later he and four companions were parachuted into a remote valley in Bantam. He was reticent about what had followed. Of course we didn't have much chance to talk because he was not with us very long, and the experience also, I suspected, was very close and painful: it had been the reason for his long secret confinement and torture. The wound of the memory was still so fresh that any question tended to set it bleeding again. Still, he did unbend to me enough for me to gather that his mission had been a total failure.

All along it had been founded on the assumption that the peoples of the Sunda lands in Java would co-operate with him against the Japanese. In fact, not only did they keep him at a sullen distance but both his specialists were brutally murdered. The promise of the General Staff that support and supplies were to be sent by submarine was never kept. Even Celliers's radio signals were never acknowledged, though for two months he tried to call both Colombo and Delhi at the agreed hour on the prearranged wavelengths. He admitted all this without any special emotion: he appeared to have made his peace with it long since. He had had in all only one serious brush with the Japanese.

One day he had made contact with a platoon of Ambonese infantry wandering in deep jungle. Lawrence would remember those sturdy native soldiers from the island of Ambon for we had had many of them in prison with us. They were the finest of all the soldiers in the old Netherlands East Indies Army, devout Christians, and born mercenaries in the best sense of the word. They and the Menadonese, so akin to them, were almost the only Colonial troops there who had seen action. This particular platoon were on patrol in West Bantam when the frantic surrender came. Their Dutch officer had left them in charge of a sergeant-major and gone out for news of the surrender. He had never returned and the Ambonese made no secret of the fact that they believed he had deserted them to put on civilian clothes to escape internment. They had no clear idea of what would become of them but had instinctively remained together avoiding the Japanese. They had made straight for the wildest part of Bantam, getting rice from the peasants, and each night as the darkness fell they sang their sombre Dutch hymns. To meet Celliers, an officer who spoke Dutch even though he was in British uniform, seemed to them a direct answer from God to their prayers. They attached themselves instantly to him with a willingness that stirred him profoundly. Their supplies were almost vanished, their money and field medicines gone, and Celliers's small party were even worse off.

Realizing that they could not hold out for long in such a way, Celliers suggested that they ambush one of the Japanese convoys which ran supplies regularly from the roadstead at

Palaboehanratoe * to the highway's junction at Soekaboemi.†
They did so promptly but with mixed results. They got
the supplies, money and ammunition they needed, but the
Japanese escort made such a valiant stand that three of the
Ambonese and one of Celliers's officers were killed. Another
was so badly wounded that rather than abandon him to
the enemy, Celliers killed him himself with a lethal dose of
morphia.

Knowing that the Japanese would retaliate quickly and
in great strength, Celliers now withdrew with his party to
the west. Alone now with his staunch, hymn-singing yellow
soldiers, he went deeper into that dense silent jungle of
the southern Sunda land guarded by giant and reeking
volcanoes lazily blowing fumes like cigar smoke into the
faces of the great white thunder-clouds striding the high
sky above them. Each day the increase of air activity and
the way in which the peasants shrank from them while
even the children at their approach disappeared swiftly into
their elongated house of bamboo and straw mounted on
stilts above the flashing paddy water, warned Celliers that
agents of powerful enemy forces, determined on retribution,
were in the vicinity.

One evening they had made camp on a mountain top on
the edge of a lovely valley many roadless miles from any
known centre of Sundanese life. The mountain was called
Djaja Sempoer: "Peak of the Arrow"; the valley Lebaksem-
bada: "That which is well made." Celliers was confident
that they could indefinitely play hide-and-seek with the
Japanese in the immense jungle and primeval forests which
rolled in great waves through valleys and over volcanic tops
like green ocean water driven before a typhoon. The Ambonese soldiers were gathering round an old warrant officer

* "The anchor-dropping place."
† "The desired earth."

who was also their lay-preacher for the evening service. The sun was setting and Celliers remembered how tender was its light on the broken-off summit of the formidable volcano of Krakatoa just visible in the Sunda Straits far to the west. He was watching it, deep in thought, when the Ambonese began to sing in Dutch: "Blyft met my Oh! Heer!": "Abide with me, Oh Lord!"

Instantly Celliers had been taken far back in memory to the hills in Palestine and, in a moment of revelation, he had seen what he called his "betrayal" in other terms. As now I told Lawrence I could still remember the exact words that he had used: "Listening to those simple Christian souls singing among the pagan woods," he had said, "I knew then that I had not been obedient to my own awareness of life."

"My God!" Lawrence exclaimed, stirred for a moment out of his role as tense listener.

Yes, I emphasized, that was what he'd said, and later in hospital Celliers had explained to me that he had come to realize that life had no meaning unless one was obedient to one's awareness of it. He attributed the sense of meaninglessness which had afflicted his world before the war to just that fact: it had been disobedient to its own greater awareness. I asked him what "awareness" had meant to him as he sat there in the sunset hour on the Peak of the Arrow? He'd replied it was easier to say what it was not, rather than what it was! It was certainly not merely cerebral effort or achievement. It was not what we called knowledge, for, as he saw it, our knowledge tended to pin us down, to imprison us in what should be no more than a frontier position. What he meant by "awareness" was perhaps a sense of the as yet unimagined wholeness of life; a recognition that one could live freely only on the frontiers of one's being where the known was still contained in the infinite unknown, and where there could be a continual crossing and re-crossing of tentative borders, like lone hunters returning from perilous sojourns in great forests. It was, to put it pictorially, he said, a way of living not only by moonlight or sunlight, but also by starlight. He spoke with great feeling and said that as his men had been hymn-singing there on the mountain top he had realized that from henceforth he must learn above all to love the necessity of search for a greater wholeness in life. His tragedy, as of many of his generation, was that they had not been helped to think of love in its truly heroic sense. He, as they, were condemned by what he called the "betrayal of the natural brother in their lives," and could see little in the world around them beyond the hatred caused by their own rejections.

Here Lawrence pressed me hard to recall everything I could of the conversation, and I became rather embarrassed. At the time when Celliers was talking to me there was a lot that I hadn't understood as I felt I did now. But to try and explain it all to Lawrence made me feel extremely uncomfortable. My whole upbringing and tradition were against so naked a conversation. I think, towards the end, Celliers himself had sensed something of my unspoken reservations, for he had concluded rather abruptly by saying that, as he saw it, he felt the first necessity in life was to make the universal specific, the general particular, the collective individual, and what was unconscious in us conscious.

He had then returned to the progression of his story. He told me that it was just at that moment, on that evening on the mountain when he had felt himself to be striding across the frontiers of his own understanding, that he had heard the Ambonese singing suddenly break off.

The Ambonese had rushed for their carbines as a man from the valley below appeared cringing and terrified on the edge of their clearing covered with giant-ferns. He was one of a group of simple peasants who had never been out of their valley and who had sold some of their rice to Celliers some days before. He was now in a terrible state, for he had been badly beaten up. His chest was heaving so that he could hardly speak, and sweat mingled with the blood that ran down his coffee-coloured skin from wounds reopened by his exertions. He fell at Celliers's feet sobbing in broken Malay over and over again: "Tuan besar, Great Lord, please do not shoot me. Tuan Lord, I could not help it. Tuan, please do not kill me!" Only then did he dare deliver a letter that he carried in his hand.

The Ambonese surrounded them in a tight ring to listen intently while Celliers read the letter aloud. It was from the Japanese Colonel commanding the troops in the valleys below. It told Celliers curtly that the Japanese gave him until noon the next day to surrender. If he had not done so by then the entire village at the foot of the mountain would be shot for their treachery in supplying him and his men with rice. But if he surrendered the village would be pardoned and he would stand his trial before a military court. That was all. But Celliers knew enough about the enemy to realize they were not bluffing.

To his relief he found the decision at once: here was at least one universal he could make specific. He told the Ambonese as gently as he could that he would have to go down with the man of the valley to surrender. Some of them, in tears, begged him not to go. But he stood firm in his decision, asking them moreover to shed their uniforms, bury their arms and mingle with the indigenous population as they easily could, without discovery, until the end of the war. At that, Celliers told me, they looked terribly disillusioned. He said the hardest thing to endure that evening was the look of reproach in the eyes of his staunch little band of yellow soldiers. However, he collected his few belongings and turned to go down the mountain and into the valley below, already filled with enemy troops and brimming over with the shadows of the night.

After he had left the Ambonese, they started their hymn-singing again with even greater ardour than ever before, no doubt to overcome the feeling of loss and abandonment. He said there was a note of despair in the last strains of the hymn pursuing him down the slopes as if not only the night but the whole imposing structure of a proud epoch were crashing down on the peaks above. So deep was this impression that when the singing finally was overcome by distance and the silence taken over by the hysterical chatter of nervous apes in the lofty tree-tops around him, this new noise sounded like a welcome of devils to some new-comer in hell.

After that, there was little to tell about his capture. The peasants were not massacred and he was carried off to prison.

His Japanese captors were convinced that he was the forerunner of a greater invasion and knew its time and place, so for weeks before the trial he was tortured for information which, fortunately, he did not possess. Finally he was brought up for trial on the charge of "Wagamamma"—Lawrence would recognize the charge as the worst crime of which a soldier could be guilty in Japanese eyes—"the spirit of wilfulness." And there in court among Celliers's five judges sat Yonoi.

The moment Yonoi's eyes fell on him, Celliers noticed a look of interest, quickly transformed into something akin to alarm, appearing on his handsome face. The other judges too, stared at him hard and long though not so strangely as Yonoi. Celliers was certain they had formed a picture of him in their minds which he contradicted. They had already condemned him in their minds from the Kempitai record of his behaviour in jungle and prison as a foreign devil,

evil enough to show a spirit of wilfulness and disobedience
to the army of their Exalted Descendant of a Sun-goddess.
But from the start Yonoi in particular and the judges in general were disconcerted because his appearance instantly
predisposed them into liking him.

"That doesn't surprise me," Lawrence broke in here. "In
dealing with peoples whose language one cannot speak one's
physical appearance can be all important. And the Japanese
have a natural eye for beauty of all kinds. I can see clearly
how a fellow of 'Straffer's' looks would have set their imaginations in motion."

As the day went on Celliers saw the signs of the conflict
in the minds of his judges become more apparent. After that
first hard stare they tried not to look at him again. They
put their questions and listened to his answers with their
eyes focused on some point just over his shoulders. All day
long he watched this intangible struggle between seeing
and not seeing struggling for mastery in their imaginations.

This was something I understood fully directly Celliers
told me of it. I had learnt from bitter experience that immediately the Japanese showed a sudden reluctance to
meet our eyes in the course of our daily contacts we knew
that they were taking precautions to ensure that not a single
glimpse of one's obvious and defenceless humanity should
slip through their defences and contradict the caricature
some demoniac *a priori* image had made of us within them.
The nearer the storm came the more intense the working
of this mechanism became. I had seen its most striking
manifestation in the eyes of a Japanese officer who, with a
condemned Ambonese soldier before him, had had to lean
forward and brush the long black hair from the back of
the neck over the head and eyes of the condemned man
before he could draw his sword and cut off the man's head.
Before the blow fell he had been compelled to look straight

ahead over the doomed head seeing neither it nor us who stood, raggedly, in a long line in front of him. But the blow having fallen he was then free, if one could use such a word for so enslaved a state, to look us all once more in the face without danger of seeing us for what we were and certain only of finding in us confirmation of the terrible image which had provoked him from within.

All the same I was amazed that Celliers, whose first experience of the Japanese this was, could be so alive to such a subtle point. But when I told him this his answer immediately satisfied me. He had been a lawyer himself for many years in Africa, he informed me, and had often noticed, particularly when dealing with a black offender who was probably abysmally ignorant of the code, customs, laws and languages of the court, how often the judges would stare past such a man with exactly the same look as if to concentrate on the cold concept of justice entrusted to their keeping rather than on the frail flesh and blood arguing with such dumb eloquence against the sentence they were about to pronounce. Oh yes, Celliers assured me, he knew the look well! Ironically he had never really understood it until that day when it was he who was standing on trial for his life. He said that it was then too that for the first time he realized the significance of a greeting that many primitive black people in Africa give each other in passing. A stranger will call out: "I see you, child of a black mother, I see you." The other will reply: "Aye, I see you too, son of a black father, I see you." He realized then, that they greeted one another in that way because instinct told them there was reassurance for flesh and blood in truly seeing and being seen as such. The mere recollection of the greeting for him, on that fateful day, was so sweet that his eyes had smarted with it.

In that mood he had observed that most of Yonoi's colleagues succeeded in their efforts to avoid his eye, but fortunately for him, Yonoi did not. I asked why Celliers thought Yonoi had failed where the others succeeded. He had paused a long time before answering and then said slowly: "I guess Yonoi and I were birds of a feather caught in the same trap of our own bright plumage. He too was a fugitive from his own, inner law—just as I was." He forced a laugh. "Talk about loyalty to the old school tie. It's not a patch on the loyalty of the old Borstal knot."

As the day of the trial wore on, Celliers remarked how the handsome Yonoi was less and less able to resist looking at him with unguarded eyes. When finally the moment came for sentence (and Celliers had no doubt it would be one of death) Yonoi had found the courage to seize on some hair-splitting legality for a mitigation of sentence and to argue it with queer persistence and adroitness. Celliers explained to me here that the charge of "wilfulness" against him rested on the fact that he had gone on fighting after the superior officers on the Central Allied Command in Java had agreed to surrender unconditionally. However, Yonoi argued his special point now with such skill that finally the judge's president gave him permission to put some questions to the prisoner. For the first time Celliers heard his clipped, slow, implacable English:

"You!" Yonoi said: "You—you say you ordered come by parachute Java. Who ordered?"

"I received my orders from the Commander-in-Chief India," Celliers answered.

Pausing only to translate to his fellow judges Yonoi went on:

"You not ordered by General in Java?"

"How could I have been?" Celliers asked. "I came from Cairo to Colombo and flew from Colombo to Java two months after the surrender. I've never even seen the Commander-in-Chief of Java or had any communication with his officers."

As he spoke Celliers saw a flash of satisfaction in Yonoi's brilliant eyes. Yonoi turned to his judges to suggest with tact and passion that the charge of "wilfulness" could not be held because Celliers had obeyed, as any soldier must, the orders of his own Commander-in-Chief in India, who was still fighting. He had not received any orders whatsoever from the General who had surrendered in Java. This by no means pleased the judges though it did influence them. They over-ruled Yonoi in that they found Celliers guilty but agreed with him to the extent that they postponed sentence, presumably in order to consult a higher authority.

After the trial Celliers lay for weeks alone in his cell in semi-darkness, but he had a feeling that the doubt raised by Yonoi and the postponement of sentence had somehow let loose forces which were fighting staunchly on his side. I myself had noticed in prison that if ever something came between our gaolers and their spontaneous impulse to act they seemed incapable of concentrating on their resolve for long, and once they had hesitated the resolve tended to go by default. Time and again Celliers was told that he was to be executed, and taken out of his cell to see other unknown condemned men and women executed, yet he never believed it was going to happen to him until the evening of his release.

That day the Secret Police had removed him roughly from his cell, taken him to the guard room where the Kempitai officer who supervised executions and Yonoi sat side by side. Yonoi again gave him that strange, intense look but said nothing. The Kempitai officer opened his file and put some questions to him through an interpreter. That done the sergeant closed the file and looked at Yonoi. Yonoi, deeply preoccupied, nodded and continued to stare sombrely at Celliers. There was something new in that look,

Celliers said, yet when his guards threw him back in his cell with a laugh, saying in Malay: "Tomorrow you die!" he really believed it.

His reaction then, he told me, was really one of relief: relief that uncertainty was at an end and that his physical suffering would soon be over, but mostly relief that there could now be no further betrayal between him and his end. But, he told me with a smile, he had discovered that the human heart had its own dearest wishes even in regard to death. He found there was only one way in which he wanted to die. He had seen so many people executed, strangled, hanged, decapitated, beaten, starved to death, drowned and bayoneted. He wanted none of these ways of dying. He longed, with a passion he had never experienced before, to be shot with his eyes wide open to the natural and beautiful reality of day left to him. Once he reached that conclusion, he was concerned only with trying to persuade his executioners to gratify his final passion.

Instantly he thought of Yonoi. Yonoi, obviously, would have a great deal to do with Celliers's execution. As a last wish he would ask to see Yonoi and appeal to him. Somehow he was convinced that such an appeal would not fail: and after that he was at peace.

For a while he lay awake on the damp floor of his cell listening to the great nightly thunderstorm coming up. His cell at moments was so filled with lightning that it stood like a solid cube of gold against the purple Javanese night. He thought he had never seen light more beautiful nor heard sound more wonderful. When at last the rain fell and joined with the other storm sounds they brought him great comfort reminding him that, on the last tide, the abiding answer was not with man but with life; the true "power and the glory" were beyond all the comings and goings of man, no matter how imperious and impressive. Then he fell asleep and had to be shaken by his gaolers as the dawn broke.

However, the guards were gentler with him than they had ever been which only confirmed his conviction that he was about to die. Determined to love even this last necessity, he asked for permission to wash and shave before his execution, and one of the guards went and fetched him a bowl of luke-warm water and gave him a meagre piece of soap. He went up into the Kempitai guard room clean and refreshed. The officer-executioner of the evening before was already there with both guard and interpreter. He gave Celliers a quick professional appraisal, his eyes lingering on the prisoner's neck.

"Do you know," he asked Celliers through the sleepy interpreter, "what I think of when I see you?"

"I regret I have no idea," Celliers replied.

"I look at your neck, its length and its strength and the way it fits to your head and shoulders . . . and I think how best to cut through it with one blow of my sword!" He said it all merrily, laughing at the end as if it were a great joke.

To his own amazement Celliers found himself jerked out of the serene composure of the night by the gratuitous cruelty of the joke. The old "Straffer" flared again and he said quickly: "And d'you know what I think as I look at you? I think how pretty a hangman's noose is going to look round you neck when you've lost the war."

But the moment he said it he felt deeply sad that he had been jerked out of his previous serenity.

Meanwhile the counter-attack had been so unexpected that the laughter withered instantly on all Kempitai lips. The officer gasped and then furiously leaped forward and knocked Celliers down. As he fell Celliers thought: "That's torn it: there goes my last hope of being shot."

According to the Japanese pattern, all the others in the room should, at that moment, have joined in the beating-up of Celliers. But at that instant the Commander of the prison arrived. Everyone was forced to jump to attention and bow while Celliers himself tried to stand upright. He was left like that for hours, tottering on his feet, while all kinds of officers and officials came and went. One moment it seemed certain that he was about to be killed; the next that the end was still not in sight. At about eleven Yonoi appeared hurrying through the guard room and gave Celliers the same sombre glance before he disappeared into the Commandant's office. There followed another interminable wait and then the guard who had lent him his cake of soap whispered that Yonoi had asked formally that Celliers should be released to come and take over command of the prisoners in his camp. Yonoi claimed that none of the officers among his prisoners knew how to keep their own men properly in hand. He argued that only a person of Celliers's quality could impose the discipline needed.

When Celliers told me this, I had suggested at once that perhaps this could explain Yonoi's interest in him? But Lawrence now said instantly that he thought it to be only a rationalization of a more compelling identification with Celliers. Nonetheless Yonoi really had frequently made it clear to us how unworthy he found our ways in prison. I myself had been conscious that what we needed was a single inspired command, and Yonoi's rebukes had become harsher as well as harder to bear just before Celliers's appearance among us. Looking back I have no doubt that he intended to insist that Celliers should be given command over us all, using the argument he had put forward on that vital morning of the interrogation. However, the Kempitai, who had already hesitated too long to be truly concentrated on the issue, gave way instantly. Yonoi emerged from the Commandant's office to hurry past Celliers without the expected glance.

This, far from reassuring Celliers made him feel completely hopeless. But he was wrong. Some hours later he was released into our midst, and pushed unceremoniously through the prison gates in the way I have described.

For the first few days in our improvised hospital Celliers slept most of the time, seeming to take his medicine, food and injections without waking. But when he did wake he seemed set on the way to a quick recovery. He would have liked to get up at once to join the rest of us but the doctors insisted that he should stay in hospital for at least another fortnight. He accepted the ruling with good grace and thereafter spent most of his days writing on the sheets of toilet paper with which we supplied him.

All this time Yonoi's inquiries after Celliers became ever more impatient. It became no longer a tense question of: "Sick officer? Health, how?" but more irritably: "Sick officer not well? Why? Why not well? *Lakas!* Quick! *Lakas!*" One evening towards the end of Celliers's hospital term he was so angry when I reported Celliers as still unfit for prison duty that I thought he was going to hit me. He stood in front of me with a quick intake of breath, hissing between his teeth and rocking his head from side to side. A strange ventriloquist's growl began to rise in his stomach until he screamed: "Officer not well because your spirit bad! All prisoners' spirits bad! Spirit so bad nothing grows prison gardens! All, all, very, very bad."

He went on like this for a while but he did not hit me. Instead he confined the entire prison camp to its quarters without food or water for twenty-four hours in order that it could reflect on its evil spirit and purify its thinking.

We ended the twenty-four hours in an atmosphere which had sharply deteriorated. The general theory was that we were about to be moved to another camp, an event which always set the nerves of our hosts on edge, involving as it did inspections by higher authorities and a thousand and one other extra administrative chores. Since all moves were preceded by an intensive search of the camp, we took the customary precaution of burying our own essential records under the barrack pavement at night. Celliers's autobiography, which Lawrence now had on his knees, was buried with the hospital records by the doctors. But even before Celliers came out of his prison-hospital two days later it was evident to me that something more sinister than just a move from one camp to another was involved.

To my dismay, one morning when I went to Yonoi's headquarters to report, I found that even the friendly staff corporal was incapable of looking me in the eyes. Yonoi himself did not look at us once while he listened to the report, and disdained even to answer our humble requests. Soon the same incapacity for seeing us spread to the Korean sentries. That day and all the next the curious unseeing mechanism gathered momentum until it seemed to me as if Yonoi were moving like a medium fixed in a trance and the sentries goose-stepping between our prison-gate and their quarters like figures walking in their sleep with nightmare exaggerations.

We ourselves became affected with the state of mind of those who had us so absolutely in their power. The youngest among my troops, I noticed, would experience a need to take the nearest friend by the arm as if for reassurance that our prison reality was not an illusion of the insane. Indeed suddenly everything was so terrifyingly unreal and our daily round of circumscribed living so pointless that it needed a determined effort of will to keep our men clean, circumspect and active. Hungry as we all were, many suddenly found their appetites gone, and the very air standing so bright and deep above our opaque walls seemed to go sullen with a charge of new thunder.

That evening our doctors released Celliers from hospital because they felt his condition no longer justified them running any risks with Yonoi's growing impatience. I had no doubt that whatever was about to happen would happen soon and that nothing we could do would prevent it. That I was not alone in my feeling was evident from the unusual quiet among all ranks in prison. Everyone spoke in a subdued voice as if knowing that we were entering some avalanche country of the spirit where the slightest excess of sound could precipitate a deadly slide of snow and rock on all in the dark valley below.

After our evening rice I walked slowly with Celliers many times around our prison camp. I had already experienced many beautiful evenings in Java but none more beautiful than this. The sun was just going down and beyond our prison walls in the centre of the great plain below our prison camp the tide of purple light was creeping like deep sea-water drawn by the moon up the slopes of the great Mountain of Malabar. Its crown, so like the ramparts of the great Crusader Fortress of Krak des Chevaliers which Celliers had seen on the edge of the Holy Land, was blazing with light. The sky itself was a deep emerald ocean wherein an immense thunder-cloud was bearing down on the mountain, a very dreadnought of war, sails all set and swollen with the wind that drives so high over the becalmed earth of Java fragrant with the sandalwood and spice of the outer islands and smooth as silk with streamlined light. The dark base of the cloud itself shuddered with its burden of thunder like a hull with the shock of seas breaking over the prow, and the lightning flashed among the golden sails with the constancy of a signaller's lamp. Just beyond our prison walls the dark spathodias which lined the invisible roads outside were in full bloom and their scarlet flowers flickered like flames of fire from the tremble which the distant broadsides of lightning and thunder though inaudible to us imparted to the sensitive air.

The going down of the sun, the purposeful advance of the cloud and the stirring of those flowers among the dark leaves filled the evening with a great feeling of eventfulness and somehow stressed our own cast-iron exclusion from the normal rhythm of things. As it grew dark the bats one by one dropped headlong from their sunless attics in the dark trees and instantly began to beat about the dying day in their flight from one black hole to another. Soon they were joined by the Titans of their world, the flying foxes, and together they emitted sub-sonic shrieks of alarm that were like tears of taut silk in the throbbing silences. They made the evening feel ugly, bewitched and old, and I was relieved when Celliers drew my attention to the evening star which was hanging so large and bright in the faded track of the sun that it looked as if it might fall from sheer weight out of the shuddering sky.

"It's odd," Celliers was saying, "how that star seems to follow me around. You should have seen it as I saw it in a winter sky over the high-veld of Africa on one night over the hills before Bethlehem. I spotted it even in full daylight from the jungles of Bantam—but I've never seen it more lovely than now. There's light enough in it tonight to fill both one's hands to overflowing." He broke off to peer down towards the ground at our feet where the earth was still wet and glistening from a heavy downpour in the afternoon. "Look!" he exclaimed his voice young with astonishment. "It throws a shadow as well. Look just behind you in the wet. There's your star shadow following you faithfully around. How strange that even a star should have a shadow."

"Look, Straffer," I changed the subject abruptly because

Celliers's voice lately seemed to me to have too much of an undertone of fate in it. "You know, of course, you might be landed with the command of us all at any moment now?"

"I guessed so," he answered. "But I'll try to get out of it, unless you all wish it? What about the other senior officers if Yonoi insists on my taking over?"

"I don't know," I admitted. "We're not a united bunch at all as you may have noticed. You've joined us at a very critical moment. I'm pretty certain something frightful is about to happen and in the circumstances everyone may forget their differences and be ready to accept a new command."

"You say something frightful is about to happen?" Celliers stopped in his stride, turned quickly to face me and asked: "What? Why?"

"I don't know," I told him. "I've no idea. I'm not even certain that what I fear is about to happen to us. All I know is that we can do nothing to stop it coming—and that when it comes you may find yourself charged unfairly with the responsibility of dealing with it."

I spoke for once straight out of my feelings and to my amazement Celliers, for the first time since I had known him, gave me the impression that I had really succeeded in getting close to him. He took me affectionately by the arm and looked intently at me.

"Of course," Lawrence interrupted me. "I can guess why, can't you?"

I shook my head and he hurried on to say: "But surely it was because you were speaking out of your own experience, your own suffering, and so beginning to speak the 'idiom' he had learnt? If only we could all re-learn to speak out of our common suffering and need we too would be surprised to find how close we are to one another."

Lawrence's interjection threw much light on the turmoil

of feelings that had assailed me that evening when Celliers and I stood there arm-in-arm in prison with our star-shadows beside us in the night. I could still hear Celliers saying gently: "I wouldn't worry about the unfairness of what I might be asked to do, though I am most grateful for your concern. There are situations where personal 'fairness' and 'unfairness' are utterly irrelevant. And this may well be one of them. But please tell me—if you'll forgive so heretical a question—why you are so certain something unpleasant is about to happen?"

He used the word "heretical" with an intimate teasing note. I told him that the "unseeing" mechanism of the Japanese was once more at work in our midst. I was just finishing my explanation when a series of commands were shouted aloud to the sentries at the main gate.

"You hear that?" I asked Celliers. "Well, if you knew those sounds as well as I do you'll realize they're not normal. The guard is changing over as it does every night at this hour. But the voice of command is different. It's taut with tension, charged with the thing which is building up in them all, just like that thunderstorm beyond the mountain."

"I see," he said quietly. "And I'm afraid I agree with you. I recognize the atmosphere before an execution. We'll just have to wait until it comes and if it does and I have to take charge, I promise you I'll do so without hesitation. Thereafter we can think again . . ."

We stood there silent. In one of the hedgerows the fireflies began to come out like showers of sparks shaken by some fire deep in the earth. Again those strange solar-plexus noises of the guard at the gate broke on the night. The last light of day was gone and only the stars and the sweep of distant lightning was left to trouble the dark. The wet earth at our feet now was like an antique mirror and we stood with our feet among the stars.

Once more Celliers remarked quietly: "You know I can't get over a star, so steeped in the night as that one there, throwing a shadow."

Then arm-in-arm we went on slowly to complete our last round of the prison.

The trouble started the next day soon after our morning meal of thin tapioca gruel. I had just given Celliers a hat which had belonged to an officer executed a month before. What was more I had persuaded an Australian soldier who had brought it as a souvenir from the Western Desert, to part with the metal springbuck head that South African soldiers wore on their caps, and I had fitted this to the hat. The badge was slightly damaged, the tip of one horn being broken but so slightly that it was hardly noticeable. Yet Celliers spotted the damage at once. At the time I thought it was just another proof of his alert senses. Now I realized, of course, just as Lawrence did, that there was more to it than that. As he stared at the badge I have no doubt that he was thinking of Stompie. Indeed, after thanking me warmly, I seemed to remember him muttering something about "most strange . . ." However, at that moment the orderly of the day came up to me at the double to say Yonoi wanted all camp commanders immediately at his headquarters.

Soon we were standing in a row, the English, American, Australian, Dutch, Chinese, Ambonese and Menadonese section commanders, in front of Yonoi's desk. The clerk at the table in the corner, the sentry at the door and the warrant officer in charge, had none of them looked at us once since our arrival. Yonoi himself stood at the window, his back to us, silent for close on fifteen minutes, the ticking of the clock in the office so loud in the unnatural stillness that it sounded like a dentist's hammer tapping on the teeth in my head. When at last Yonoi broke the silence he did so with his back to us, speaking through an interpreter, always a bad sign because it suggested that a process of not-hearing was joining the one of not-seeing.

"So!" he said, "there are no armourers, gun-smiths or armament experts among the four thousand prisoners which the Imperial Japanese Army has been gracious enough to spare?"

He was referring to an order he had passed on to us from Army Command some weeks before telling us to render a full list of officers and men within these categories. The demand had struck dismay in the camp because it could only mean that the Japanese wanted to use men so qualified to help in their war effort. They had no right under international law to make such a request. Yet everyone knew from bitter experience that refusal to make a return would have appalling consequences for the men in our charge. Nonetheless some of us wanted to tell Yonoi politely but firmly that the order was illegal and that we could not comply. Others felt that we should tell a lie and say we had no armourers amongst us. For long hours the senior officers of all nationalities had debated the issue until it became clear that no agreement could be reached. Finally, by a majority vote, it had been decided to make a false return. And now the lying bird was coming back to its terrible roost in our midst.

I have said before that we lacked real leadership and I never felt it more as I looked at the silent row of anxious vacant faces of the officers beside me. To give him his due, Hicksley-Ellis (whom Lawrence had already described as a foreign cartoonist's idea of an Englishman with no chin, a rush of teeth to the front, a whispy untidy moustache, pink face and large popping eyes) seemed ready to act. Knowing his infallible knack of irritating Yonoi, I was about to forestall him when Yonoi, his voice barely under control, repeated his question and then, without waiting for an answer, ordered us to parade with all our men within five minutes on the open ground in the prison. We hurried from the building knowing that the worst was about to happen and our only chance of mitigating it was to carry out the order with dispatch and precision. I heard an Ambonese officer say to his Menadonese colleague: "Say your prayers quickly, brother, for God alone can help us today."

We were not yet back in our lines when the bell at the gate of Yonoi's headquarters started to peal frantically and the buildings outside our prison walls where guards as well as Japanese infantry were housed began to resound with those odd abdominal military commands. We were barely assembled on the parade ground, officers in front of each group of men, when all the gates were thrown open and the Japanese soldiery came running in from all sides. Except for their mortars they were armed in full preparedness for battle. They quickly set up heavy black machine-guns at all four corners of the parade ground, their crews going to earth in firing positions beside them while the rest of the sections began fixing their bayonets. For a moment the sound of the metal snapping into position and the machine-gun crews testing the mechanisms and magazines of their weapons rang out ominously all around us. But once that was done a deep silence fell over the camp.

We stood there thus for an hour, the blazing sun beating down directly upon us, looking at the silent Japanese infantry in firing positions, the black muzzles of their guns sighted on our dense lines and from time to time swinging along the crowded formations as the machine-gunners practised their aim. There was no sign of Yonoi or indeed of any officer in command. Each section must have been carefully briefed beforehand and stood or lay at the ready under command of its N.C.O.'s.

Again, stronger than ever, I had a feeling of unreality. The great glittering day opening out around us, the thunder-clouds coming up like explosions from the sea and rolling high over the reeking volcano tops towards us proclaimed the universe to be about its normal business. The birds around us were singing as clearly and urgently as ever. The shining air over the gleaming paddies outside was humming like a guitar string with the burning wings of myriads of dragonflies and water insects. And even in the great tree by the prison gate immediately behind one of the machine-gun sections the flying lizards had begun to glide gracefully down to earth from the branches where they housed to search for food. Only we seemed locked out from that overwhelming sea-swell of life around us and I felt black in my heart that all else should appear so unconcerned at our fate.

So a full hour went by in this fashion. We dared not speak since we knew from experience how easily any sound or movement of body could provoke our gaolers on these occasions.

But Celliers who was standing next to me did ask in a whisper: "What's the form now? Do they often do this sort of thing? What started it?"

I managed to tell him that it had never happened quite like this before with so great a show of force, and briefly explained the ostensible cause adding: "I'm sorry it's happened on your first day out. But it's no good pretending that anything might not happen at any moment. They might even be getting ready to massacre us all."

Out of the corner of my eye I saw to my amazement something close to a smile on his face. He said in a whisper so confident that I felt the dead heart in me grow warm again. "Nonsense. I won't let them massacre anybody. I think I know just how to stop them."

"You know?" I asked, my voice like that of a stranger in my own ears.

"I do. But be careful," he whispered back, long pauses between each phrase. "I don't like the way that bloke in charge of the machine-gun over there is watching us. His eye has not left my face these past few minutes."

We remained silent then until, at the end of the first hour, Celliers asked me: "I wonder if you can hear it too?"

"Hear what?" I asked alarmed by the urgent tone of his question.

"The music," he answered.

Puzzled, I listened more intently than ever. Apart from the normal electro-sonics of that tropical island and the throb of its volcanic heart beating at the temples of the thin-skinned earth of the island there was no sound to be heard.

I told him so but he insisted, saying: "There's the most enchanting music in my ears. It's all around us. It's lovely and it's everywhere."

Though still a whisper his voice was full of a strange exaltation. I stole a quick glance at his face and the look on it was hardly of this world. I imagined then (and did so until recently I went to Celliers's home and spoke to his brother's wife), that the horror piling up around us coming so soon after his suffering in the hands of the secret police was disturbing the balance of his senses. Now I am not so sure. His sister-in-law told me that after comparing times and dates—as Lawrence would know there was a wide difference between Javanese and South African time—she had woken up in the night at that precise moment and noticed her husband was not in bed beside her. Suddenly afraid she had tried to light a candle when he spoke to her out of the dark, saying: "Sorry, I didn't mean to wake you. I'm here by the window."

She could just make out his dark silhouette against a window glistening faintly like water with star-shine between him and the night. But his voice was uneasy and she asked: "Why are you standing there? What's the matter?"

"I don't know," he had answered. "I was woken up in my sleep by a sound of music. Can't you hear it too? It's still going on somewhere out there beyond the stars."

She shook her head but knowing her husband's gift of strange intuition felt more frightened than ever.

Then, before she could answer, he said again: "Dear God in heaven, can't you hear it? I wonder what it is?" He had paused and turned. "Oh! I'm so afraid for Ouboet suddenly. . . . For the first time I fear for him."

At that he had put down his head and begun crying quietly without a sound of any kind, the tears coming out of him, she said, so effortlessly that it was as if her husband was a vessel overflowing with water. She could not comfort him and they slept no more that night. But for close on a week he went about singing the little tune he had composed in his father's garden thirty years before, and once he had turned to her and said with quiet certainty: "I think Ouboet is in terrible trouble and needs me. I'm singing for him." After doing this for close on a week he suddenly stopped and sang that tune no more.

However, knowing nothing of this, I stood there in the full glare of sunlight beside Celliers on that terrible morning uncomforted by his belief that he was listening to a tidal harmony of sounds and voices. I said nothing because I felt he had already suffered enough and if he found comfort, like Joan of Arc, in hearing heavenly voices he deserved to be allowed to cling to it. Nor had I time to say anything for a series of commands had rung out at the gate and the guard was rushing to present arms. Yonoi, followed by his warrant officer, a veteran of the wars in Manchuria and China, together with an interpreter walked in. He barely acknowledged the salute of the sentries and came straight to the centre of the parade ground looking neither to left nor right of him. Once there he turned to face our ranks, placed his supple legs in shining jack-boots wide apart and firm on the ground, his hands clasped behind his back. He was almost directly opposite us and about fifty yards away. I was dismayed to note from the angle of his head that, although he was facing us, his eyes were glancing over our heads.

"I ordered you," he told us through the interpreter, his voice tight and thin like the lash of a whip and the s's hissing like a serpent on his tongue, "to parade all your men. You not only lie to me but are disobedient and wilful as well. You will parade all your men."

Before I could stop him, Hicksley-Ellis stepped out of the ranks and said: "But we are all here."

Without waiting for the interpreter, Yonoi, his handsome face almost aglitter with the resentment of a whole people and the outrage of a long history, hissed: "Come here!"

We watched the tall knock-kneed officer walk awkwardly to within a yard of Yonoi and then stop to stand facing him.

"I'm afraid that's done it," I whispered out of the corner of my mouth, my heart dark with dismay.

I had barely finished when Yonoi, quite beside himself, shrieked: "You! You lie again! I said all, all people! Where are hospital people?"

I thought he was going to draw his sword and stick Hicksley-Ellis there and then but he just slashed him about the head and neck a dozen times with his cane before commanding: "Now fetch all, all people!"

The order was instantly repeated by the interpreter. We were forced to get our doctors to move all the sick out of their improvised hospital and on to the parade ground into the most cruel of suns. They had tried to do so in

a way most considerate to the sick, the orderlies carrying
the worst cases out on stretchers. But Yonoi would have
none of that. Incensed with a sense of injury against both us
and life he walked down to the doctors and ordered all the
sick to their feet. The senior medical officer protested and
was immediately knocked senseless for his pains. Yonoi
shrieking: "You not sick, you lie! You, you all lie. Your spirit
bad, very bad. You not sick!"

Fortunately we had no operation cases in hospital that
day. Even so it was as bad as it could be. There were men
with temperatures close on hundred and five from the fever
which took such a heavy toll among a community as consistently under-nourished as we were. They stood swaying
like drunkards on their feet and before long several of them
fainted and lay moaning on the ground where they had
fallen. At first Yonoi tried to prod them to their feet but
when they failed to respond he just stamped his feet in disgust and left them lying there for he was eager to get to
the climax of his affair with us.

All this time Celliers went on standing beside me as if
hardly there, the look of light and height upon his face.
He was still, I imagined, listening in to his illusion of cosmic
voices and tidal music. But when Yonoi turned to face us
for the final account I found that Celliers after all was also
with us. He mumbled to me that Yonoi was only behaving
the way he was because, like us, he was doing just what was
expected of him. Celliers added that confronting Yonoi
with the unexpected alone could save Yonoi, his men, and
us. To be the mere opposite of what he was would do no
good. It would merely mean that we would all drown in
our spirits like swimmers locked in one another's arms.

"There's going to be more than just drowning in our
spirits," I retorted grimly finding this too euphemistic a
rendering of the situation. "Look! Here it comes!"

Yonoi had summoned Hicksley-Ellis to him in the centre of the parade ground.

"Ask him," Yonoi told the interpreter, "how many armourers and armaments officers he has in his group?"

Of course Hicksley-Ellis, as arranged, answered "None."

Then, Yonoi, being what he was, cracked inside. He had Hicksley-Ellis tied with hands behind his back and made to kneel bare-headed on the ground near him. Yonoi then stepped back, drew his sword, raised it flashing in the sun and with his lips to the naked steel said a prayer to it as I had seen other officers do before other executions. The machine-gun crews released their safety catches and all four guns clicked loudly as they rammed the first bullet into the firing breech. Nothing could prevent it coming now, I thought. One by one the heads would fall until someone broke—and even then it would not be the end. This appetite for disaster would have to be fed, and not until it was sated would the devourer in Yonoi and others desist. Whatever we did from now on would be wrong and only make it worse for those who survived the day—if any did.

In my despair I turned openly to Celliers.

Before I could speak he spoke to me in a low and reassuring voice as if he were still hearing the music in his ear. He said: "I'm going to stop it now. It'll be all right. But whatever happens do nothing about me. Remember, nothing. Good-bye."

I did not have time or mind to take in the significance of that "good-bye," nor recognize it then as a clear indication of his knowledge of what the end was going to be for him for as he spoke he stepped out of the ranks, his new hat at a rakish angle on his head and the sun flashing on its mutilated badge. He walked, as Lawrence had already remarked, most beautifully. Without hurry he advanced on

Yonoi as if he were going across a paddock at home to do no more than take a high-spirited stallion in hand.

The effect among our prison ranks was startling. No sound broke from us but the atmosphere became unlocked and flowing. I knew that without even looking round. Celliers's reputation had already spread throughout the camp and hope flared up in our ranks again. Even I, though I had no idea what he could or would do, found a too-sweet excitement going through me as I watched his easy almost nonchalant approach. It was truly wonderful; perfectly timed and executed. Anything faster would have alarmed them. Anything slower given them time to recover. Anything before that moment would have failed, for Yonoi and his men still would have been free to rush forward and stop him. But finding themselves abandoned by the conclusion they thought foregone they hesitated and just gaped at Celliers, waiting for Yonoi to give them the lead.

When Yonoi opened his eyes again after his short prayer to the spirit, the Maru of his sword, Celliers was barely fifteen yards away. Amazement like the shock of a head-long collision went through him. Going white in the process he stared in a blank unbelieving way at Celliers. For the first time in days he was compelled, because of the unfathomed identification between Celliers and himself, to see someone outside himself.

Amazement then gave way to consternation and he cried out a command in English that was also a plea: "You—officer —go—back, go back, go back!"

But Celliers went on to place himself between Hicksley-Ellis and Yonoi and said something quietly and unhurriedly to Yonoi.

Yonoi appeared not to have heard him. He shrieked again: "You—go back, back, back!" like someone trying to scare a ghost.

Celliers shook his head quietly and went on staring at him steadily as a disarmed hunter might stare a growling lion straight in the face. Perhaps more in terror than in anger, Yonoi raised his sword and knocked Celliers down with the flat of it. The crack on his head rang out like a pistol-shot to be followed by another exhortation to Celliers to go back. Dazed, Celliers struggled to his feet, swayed and half-turned as if to obey—then swung around suddenly. He took a couple of paces back towards Yonoi, put his hands on Yonoi's arms and embraced him on both cheeks rather like a French general embracing a soldier after a decoration for valour.

The shock of this strange action was unbelievable. I do not know who apart from Yonoi was shocked the most: the Japanese or ourselves.

"My God, what a bastard!" an Australian infantry officer behind me exclaimed bitterly.

Here, Lawrence, his face white, interrupted me. "Straffer went as far as that——"

I nodded and described how then Celliers had stepped back a pace from Yonoi and stood once more silently facing him. Of course, none of us will ever know what went on in Yonoi's mind but for the only time I had ever known he, who always had been so quick and in command of all situations, obviously did not know what to do. He looked as if lightning had struck him. His face had lost its colour and was like death with dismay. He trembled on his feet and might even have fallen to the ground if his warrent officer had not acted for him. It was this old veteran of several long wars who now suddenly uttered the anthropoidal yell which always preceded a Japanese bayonet charge, jumped forward and began beating up Celliers. His example was inevitably followed by the N.C.O., Commanders of the Machine-Gun Sections and the Corporal of the Guard. Our prison in the light of the high-noon sailing serene and indifferent overhead was filled with the noises I have only heard in a jungle trying to maul out of existence its fear of the falling night. Most strangely one and all tried to outdo one another in beating up the already half-senseless Celliers.

Yet not so strange, Lawrence commented here, for the whole incident would have become immediately an affair of honour. Did I not realize that Celliers had insulted Yonoi before his men? Did I not remember how kissing between men and women, even in the most natural forms, was regarded by the Japanese as the most obscene of gestures? Did I not remember how Hara censored the few novels we had had in camp by ordering that all the pages with a mention of kisses and kissing should be torn out of the defaulting books? Surely knowing that I could see now how deeply Yonoi must have lost face, so deeply that even the right to avenge the insult must have gone as well. Now only his men could do that for him and, in their code, that was what they would have had to do if they were not also to lose all honour with themselves. But what was far more important, Lawrence went on, could I understand that in doing this to Yonoi Celliers had made both us and the Japanese free of whatever it was that locked our spirits so fatally together? We had been there as two halves of the same thing, two opposites darkly dependent on each other, two ends of electricity equally inducing each other, until Celliers bridged the gap and released the fatal charge?

Indeed, I agreed with Lawrence, it was most noticeable how this whole situation immediately had become an issue between Celliers and the rest. The crisis that had brought us all out into the parade ground seemed to vanish behind us like waste thrown over the stern of a ship in a fast receding wake. Only one thing obsessed both Japanese and ourselves: the odd, unpredictable thing Celliers had done to Yonoi.

It applied as much to ourselves as the Japanese. I have already described the remark of the Australian officer when Celliers embraced Yonoi. Now while the terrible beating up with fists, boots and staves went on, in even the most imaginative of faces near me there was not only disgust at the punishment the man was receiving but also distaste for the way in which it had been incurred.

At this point, distressed at the recollection, I had to stop speaking.

Lawrence hastened to say: "Poor old Straffer. He was trying to contain a sea of dark possibilities in the nutshell of a single lucid deed. To use his own words: he was at last being obedient to his awareness and making a collective situation individual. And don't forget Yonoi! I would say it wasn't so much Celliers versus the rest as Celliers versus Yonoi. He'd forced Yonoi to face up to his identification with him. It was no longer a thing between races but a thing between two individual men. . . . But anyway, what happened then?"

It was soon over. Yonoi, though still like a person profoundly concussed, stopped the beating and ordered the guard to carry Celliers off to the guard house. Celliers by then was unconscious and only recognizable by his long yellow hair. Then, like someone utterly exhausted, Yonoi turned his back on us and, his eyes on the ground, walked slowly away and out of the prison gates. Shortly after the infantry sections too were withdrawn. We were left standing alone on the silent parade ground, afraid to speak. At nightfall Yonoi's warrant officer came and ordered us back to our barracks.

Officially we did not see Yonoi again. We heard no more of the issue that had brought on the affair but the next evening a new commander appeared in camp. By then a rumour was going round among our own interpreters that Yonoi had committed or was contemplating *hara-kiri*. In view of what Lawrence had said that would not have been surprising but (as he knew already) Yonoi did not do that.

On the morning of the third day after the scene with Yonoi we were ordered to dig a hole in the centre of the parade ground. At once I feared that it was Cellier's grave we were digging. That done our own carpenters were made to construct a stout wooden fence in a circle thirty yards in diameter round it and to put rolls of dannert wire against it as well. Immediately I knew I had been wrong and that the hole could not possibly be a grave. But for what else then?

We found out the truth in the afternoon when we were ordered to parade as before. There Celliers, more or less cleaned up but black in the face from his beating, doubled over and hardly able to walk, was brought out of his cell into the midst of a whole platoon of guards with fixed bayonets, who half-marched, half-dragged him right to the edge of the hole in the circle of steel and wood.

Just for a moment his hands were freed and, incredibly, he seized the opportunity to straighten his body and wave one trembling hand at us while he tried to smile. His hand however was instantly seized by a guard, jerked down, and then tightly tied with rope behind his back to the other hand. His feet were similarly bound and two guards then seized him and forced him upright into the hole. They held him thus, like two foresters transplanting a sapling, while some of their comrades piled their rifles and took up spades to shovel the earth, that rich, midnight earth of the central plateau of Java, back into the hole. They did this carefully and with a studied, ritualistic eagerness, pausing every now and then to stamp down the earth with their feet firmly all round Celliers until he was buried up to the neck with not the least chance of being able to make any movement. Only his bare head, chin, and neck showed above the ground but it was noticeable that the head was erect and that the face for all its bruising looked strangely composed as if it saw something beyond that moment which caused it, from time to time, to try and smile.

The living grave complete at last, two guards with fixed bayonets were posted at the entrance to the enclosure around it. Our new prison commander then read us a lecture exhorting us to look on Celliers and reflect on the consequences of our impurities of spirit and wrong-thinking. Then he dismissed us disdainfully from his sight. Not the least macabre of the many sinister touches to that terrible afternoon was the music which suddenly blared out from the loudspeaker of the wireless turned on in the guard room when the prison gates closed on the new commander. Broadcast from a worn-out record, Rene Clair's nostalgic accordion music "Sous les toits de Paris" rang out loud and clear from one end of the camp to the other. I nearly broke down at this gratuitous refinement of tragedy for the tortured Celliers.

However, I could safely leave to Lawrence's imagination the terrible toll in the feelings of men like ourselves who were so keenly aware of our utter powerlessness to help Celliers in the days that followed. No one in our midst could move on their normal duties about camp without seeing the bare yellow head and bruised face exposed all day long to the tropical sun. I said "yellow head" but it would be more accurate to say white because so fierce was the sun on Celliers's last days in the earth that his hair became as bleached as desert bone. Fortunately, or perhaps unfortunately, we could not get near enough again to see the expression on his face. The guards whose awareness of the terrible punishment inflicted on the man showed itself in a marked fear that we might be provoked into rushing them, kept us henceforth at a safe distance. Even so after the first day we could tell from the fallen angle of Celliers's head that he could not possibly last very long in those conditions. The second evening after his living interment the Padres of all nationalities held a special service for him, the whole camp joining in. The service ended with the singing together in many tongues of the hymn "Abide with me." The Ambonese and Menadonese sang with moving fervour and at the end of the service there was hardly a dry eye in camp.

Dangerous as the consequences could be for my fellow-prisoners I went straight from the service to the Camp Commander's headquarters to plead for mercy for Celliers. The reaction however was so outraged in every way (even an appeal for him to be given some water provoked a dangerous outburst) that I nearly revived the situation from which Celliers had rescued us. I remembered how he had beseeched me in that vital moment on the parade ground to do "nothing about him" and felt forced not to repeat my approach to our new Commander. We had to watch him slowly dying the most painful of deaths. Yet he himself seemed in no hurry to die, or rather that tenacious, resourceful body of his was in no hurry to depart. However, from the motionless drop of his head I felt that his spirit was not there at all and I hoped with all my heart that it was out of reach of the pain. No moan, complaint or cry ever came from him but the evening after the service, the guard having just gone to the gate for his relief, some Dutch soldiers felt compelled to go nearer Celliers, and they said they thought they heard him trying to sing. To their amazement, in a hoarse broken voice he was crooning to himself in some kind of Dutch, and they heard these words distinctly:

> *"I rode all through the night,*
> *And far in the distance found the fire,*
> *And beside the fire one who had waited long . . ."*

They would have liked to go nearer but the arrival of the relief guard at the gate forced them to hurry on their way.

Significant too in those final hours was the manner in which the guards themselves changed in their attitude to Celliers. At first they had looked at him without pity and turned to stand sentry with their backs to him. After the first day however, I was astonished to see that each guard coming for his turn of duty to the living grave would first face the buried man, come to attention and bow his head respectfully to Celliers. Finally, at the end of the third day the night-watch on duty in the barracks nearest Celliers reported the strangest thing of all.

The moon was full at the time and the parade ground brilliant with its light. At three in the morning our watch was startled to see Yonoi's elegant figure appear at the enclosure and send away the guard to the gate. For a moment he thought he was seeing ghosts because like many he believed Yonoi had committed *hara-kiri* some days before. Yet it was Yonoi, for his walk and build were unmistakable.

After standing in front of Celliers and looking at him for long in silence, Yonoi put his hand in his pocket and produced something which flashed like silver in the moonlight. Strange as it might seem our watch was convinced that it was a pair of scissors, for Yonoi appeared to bend down over Celliers, take his long hair in his hand and snip some of it off. . . .

Here I had to beg Lawrence, who was getting more and more agitated, not to interrupt while I stressed for confirmation that our watch distinctly heard the metal blades click in the moon silence. For a while longer Yonoi remained there in deep thought before bowing low to Celliers in the same way that the watch had seen him bow to the rising sun on the day of his Emperor's birthday. That done he walked slowly to the gate where he re-summoned the guard. And that was the last we saw of Yonoi.

By morning Celliers was dead. We were summoned to the camp headquarters after morning gruel to be told that we could have the body for burial. The new Commander could not have been more considerate at the interview. He looked us straight in the eye with an expression of someone who had suddenly been absolved from all sin and restored to an innocent vision of life. His gods had had their sacrifice and for the moment he was profoundly content. As pleased as a child before a feast he informed us: "I'll now show you typical Japanese morality for dead." A bugler and a military firing-party of infantry were ordered to do honours at the cemetery, The Tanah Abang, "the dead earth" as the Javanese called it, and so we buried Celliers that afternoon to the sound of the thunder he had loved so well rumbling over the purple citadel of Malabar.

After that I regret to say I tried to forget what had happened and looking back on it all now I realize I was not alone in my attitude. Deliberately we seemed to avoid talking in camp about this man who had suddenly flashed out of the dark into our prison lives like a shooting-star and had burned out so brilliantly and quickly before our eyes. I think the whole episode was so painful and tended to start up such imaginative thinking with disconcerting implications for our future lives that our overburdened prison spirit instinctively avoided it. When I met Lawrence months later I believe the incident was already so effectively repressed that I did not mention it to him, and on my release the excitement of my home-coming and taking up of a peaceful life again helped to encourage the repressive process. Yet I never forgot Celliers. At all sorts of odd moments he would be there in my memory as fresh and vivid as he had ever been in real life and raising for me the same eloquent issues he had raised with himself. When his manuscript reached me I felt compelled to go off immediately, seek out his brother, and tell him what I could of Celliers.

I was too late; the brother was dead. His widow was there alone on the farm with a son whom she said had been born to her late like Sarah's, just a year after Celliers's sudden visit. She was not really unhappy about her husband's death, in fact she said it had been right for him to die because his life had naturally come to an end when Celliers had died. They knew of his death, of course, though not of the details. She was deeply moved by my account. At the end of our interview her young son had come into the room from the veld with a gun in his hand and had startled me by his close resemblance to Celliers.

I had come back home deeply uneasy, feeling I could not honourably go on ignoring the implications of Celliers's story in my own life. I had not realized how deep it went until the night before when Lawrence had spoken to me of Hara. But now added to Celliers and his brother in my memory there were also Hara and Yonoi; the two were become four? What was I to them and they to me and what could I do about it?

Lawrence did not answer me directly. Instead he told me what obviously he had been wanting to tell me long since. After his release, when he went straight back on to active service, he was one day requested to come and act as interpreter for a war crimes investigator at a prison reserved for Japanese officers suspected of atrocities. There, among others, he had found Yonoi. He would not bother me with all the details but go straight for the main point. Yonoi, hearing Lawrence's fluent Japanese and attracted by his manner with the accused men, had spontaneously come up to him and pleaded to speak to him alone. Having heard about Yonoi's reputation, Lawrence was surprised to find him so subdued and oddly preoccupied. Still more had he been puzzled by Yonoi's business with him and had remained so until I had told him about Celliers.

The moment they were alone Yonoi had confided in Lawrence that, when the war ended, he had been in charge of a women's prison. That apparently had been the humiliating consequence of what had passed between Celliers and him. When he was arrested and searched in one of our prisons after the war something Yonoi valued more than anything in the world was found on him and taken away. Could Lawrence get it back for him? Lawrence had asked what it was.

Instead of answering Yonoi had looked him straight in the eyes and pleaded instead: "I am an officer and ready to die. Could you please be so good as to tell me the honourable truth. Am I to be hanged like the rest?"

"I don't know," Lawrence had answered. "I fear the chances are you may."

"In that case," Yonoi begged, "you understand us Japanese and will know how important it is to me. As my last wish would you recover this thing for me and send it to my home to be offered to the spirit of the ancestors in the shrine of my fathers?"

"I will if I can but you mustn't expect me to be definite until I know what it is," Lawrence replied.

Yonoi had paused, clearly aware that this might be his last chance to achieve a result of such overwhelming importance to him. But then he had explained in detail. This thing was just a strand of yellow hair. The British soldier who had found it on him, fed on stories of Yonoi's brutality to women prisoners, had thought Yonoi had cut it from the head of one of his victims, and had snatched it from him and hit him with his fist. Yonoi did not complain of that. All that mattered was the fact that the soldier was wrong. It was a man's not a woman's hair. It was a lock of hair from the head of the most remarkable man he had ever met, an enemy and now a dead enemy, but nonetheless a man so remarkable that he would never forget him.

He had cut that strand of hair from the dead head purely so that the spirit of the man should be honoured and given a proper home in the hereafter. It was his intention when the war was over to give a place in the inmost hall of his own ancestors to that strand of hair. But alas, from what Lawrence now had told him, he could not hope to do it that way. Instead, would Lawrence please do it for him, for only then could Yonoi die as he ought to die?

Lawrence had promised but in the end as Yonoi was given seven years in prison instead of the expected death sentence, he had recovered the hair from the other articles of evidence produced against Yonoi and kept it for him. When after four years Yonoi was pardoned and released, Lawrence had sent the hair to him in Japan. Yonoi had written back immediately with immense gratitude. The hair had been dedicated in the sacred fire of his people's shrine. It was, Yonoi wrote, a beautiful place at the end of a long cryptomeria avenue and among steep hills covered with maples burning like a forest fire on the autumn day of the ceremony. A long elegant waterfall poured out of the heights above the clouds and fed the stream and pools full of carp and wing-swift trout at the foot of the shrine. The air there was fragrant with the scent of leaf and pine and purified with so much water. He hoped Lawrence would agree that it was a suitable home for such a spirit. Finally he, Yonoi, had written a poem for the occasion. Presenting himself at the shrine, bowing low and clapping his hands sharply to ensure that the spirits knew he was there, he had deposited this verse for the ancestors to read:

> *"In the spring,*
> *Obeying the August spirits*
> *I went to fight the enemy.*
> *In the Fall,*
> *Returning I beg the spirits,*
> *To receive also the enemy."*

"You see," Lawrence said to me now, his voice low with feeling: "the seed sown by brother in brother in that far-off homeland was planted in many places. It was planted that day in your prison in Java. Yes, even in the manner they killed Celliers his enemies acted out their unwitting recognition of the seed of his deed, for they did not only bury him alive but planted him upright like a new young growth in the earth. Even the manner of their denial of the deed was confirmation of what was rejected. He was planted again by Yonoi on the hills and spirit of his native country and here again the seed is alive and growing in you and me."

I believe he might have gone on had my wife not entered the room just then and asked me to see to the windows and doors because a wireless warning had come through that a great gale was bearing down on us fast. When I came to check on the last window at the top of the house I stood there for a while looking out at the dying day. Yes, the great grey calm of Christmas was breaking fast. In the south-west against the pale yellow sky the clouds, ragged and torn, were coming racing towards us. The elements were loose and wild with movement and how good it was to know them once more on the move. I stood there with a heart full of welcome for the storm and it was as if Celliers had come again from all those many places in which he had been born, lived, died, been buried and enshrined, to stand behind me renewed and reintegrated, saying clearly in my ear: "Wind and spirit, earth and being, rain and doing, lightning and awareness imperative, thunder and the word, seed and sower, all are one: and it is necessary only for man to ask for his seed to be chosen and to pray for the sower within to sow it through the deed and act of himself, and then the harvest for all will be golden and great."

Christmas Night

The Sword and the Doll

The gale which bore down on us that Christmas night when John Lawrence and I carried the story of Jacques Celliers as far as we could, was one of the greatest in living memory. It was upon us almost before I could get down from the top of the house to re-join him in the drawing-room where the heavy curtains and shutters already were shutting out the last little light of day. He himself was sitting in semi-darkness by the large open fire and we remained there without speaking for long, listening to the rising voice of the storm. Words seemed utterly unnecessary just then, so much did the wind speak for Hara, Celliers, Yonoi, him, me and us all. Indeed no storm had ever sounded more eloquent and I pondered for quite a while on nature's need for violence in accomplishing the transition between the seasons. I wondered to what extent too it was part of the terrible necessity of our own world to experience storms of war sometimes twice in one generation. When I reached this point in my thinking I noticed something about this storm that before I had never fully realized: the strange harmony at the heart of it. At all sorts of moments, sometimes in the lowest trough of the wind when the voice of the storm was little more than a sigh, or again on some great Everest crest when the individual sounds were torn alive and screaming from the immense trees thrashing in our tender, elegiac English earth, all the many and various noises would suddenly blend and a moment or two of pure music would float over the heaving waters of darkness and chaos. Sometimes the music had a twang-like accompaniment as if plucked from a great harp; sometimes it was like a rounded blast of Roland's horn summoning the spirit of Man to turn about and stand; at others it was a scamper up and down the scales. But in its most gentle moments the sounds resembled the opening notes of a theme on the Shaku-hachi flute of Hara's own people, which sings not only the song willed upon it by the player but also out of its nature of the fountain of green which once surged up through its native shoots of bamboo.

We were still sitting there in silence listening to the harmony brought forth from such violence (as perhaps Celliers had heard the first intimation of music beyond the storm in our Japanese prison camp), when my wife came into the room, turned on the light and asked: "I wonder if you two would mind going up and seeing the children? I promised that you'd go and say good night to them."

Although we went upstairs at once we arrived too late. Christmas, of course, is notoriously exhausting for children and the twins, who had found sleep hard enough the night before and had been awake since early morning, were already fast asleep. In fact the little girl had been overcome by her fatigue in the act of trying to lift the Dutch doll her grandmother had given her from its miniature play-pen. Her fine black hair hung over the side of the little bed with the light in it a subtle night-sheen. Her outstretched arm held the doll firmly in hand and her face was buried deep in the white pillow. I settled her into a more comfortable sleeping position without waking her but could not loosen her grip on the doll. Whenever I tried to do so she protested instantly, moaning in her sleep. Afraid that I might wake her altogether I placed the doll, still clasped tightly in her hand, beside her underneath the eiderdown. The moment I did that a sigh of content broke from her, the flush of sleep in her cheeks deepened and her long dark lashes settled over the clear white skin.

The boy had been overcome in a more orderly moment. He still lay more or less in the position wherein his mother had settled him but he too had a hand out of the covers. It was clasping the toy-sword drawn from its sheath. His long yellow hair was disordered on the pillow and the lead soldiers were scattered over the bed where he had once more fought an enemy right up to the gateway of his sleep.

"What a wonderful sight," Lawrence remarked as we tip-toed to the door to switch off the light. "Odd that you should have had twins so opposite in appearance, one so dark and one so fair. But it makes them more complete in a way than if they had been born identical."

There was a deep undertone of envy in his voice. In this fluid, vulnerable state of our re-discovery of an intimacy tested on all sorts of occasions of life and death in the last war, his remark made me more aware than ever of the lonely role his way of life imposed on him.

But all I could think of saying was: "I wish you'd tell that to their mother. It might please her because I suspect she'd have preferred them both to have been fair."

However, he did not get a chance to do so just then. My wife, who had obviously awaited our return with curiosity, was the first to speak when we rejoined her.

"I wonder," she asked, "if the same thing struck you as it did me when you were with the children?"

"I thought they looked dead beat, poor little devils," I answered. "What a good thing Christmas comes only once a year!"

"Of course they're tired," she replied with some resignation. "But it wasn't that that I meant."

"They looked very happy," Lawrence answered when she looked inquiringly at him. "And very lovely too," he added: "and . . ."

"Not that either," she cut in smiling, clearly happy over his appreciation of the twins and perhaps not at all displeased that he too had failed to get her particular point, confirming her preconceived view that only a woman could really see in her children whatever it was she had observed. "But didn't it strike you that the girl's last thought, like her first, was for her doll; the boy's for his sword?" She paused. "How much better the world would be if managed by women. We'd soon have no wars. All this male aggression would disappear and"—she turned to me—"you know, I do feel you should stop giving your son a sword and soldiers to play with. I am certain that's where the trouble starts."

"Do you really believe that?" Lawrence asked before I could reply. "I know numbers of people would agree with you. But I myself feel they'd be wrong." He in his turn paused. "You say that if boys had no soldiers and swords to play with there would be no wars. Do you also carry that form of reasoning to its logical conclusion and say that if little girls were denied baby-dolls to play with women would cease to have babies?"

"I'm surprised at you," my wife exclaimed, her mind springing to its own spirited defence. "You're using logic in a typically male fashion for a purpose for which it was never intended and it's unlike you."

"I don't think I am," Lawrence countered laughing with her. "I spoke out of my own experience. Though I know many people would agree with you. I believe that the boy's sword and the girl's doll do not induce the states of mind that you suggest."

He stopped as a great blast of wind shook the house so that the thick walls seemed to sway around us. A sound as of horses' hooves and a battle-cry as if all the Valkyries of Germania were massing for war outside fell on our ears and the flames in the fireplace flickered low before Lawrence went on to say that both sword and doll seemed to him to be expressions of a pattern already deep in life. They were objects in the world without made to express a great invisible need of which both men and women were the subjects. It was only as apprentices of this master need, he thought, that the lives of men and women had any meaning. The two things, therefore, were not separate except as two halves of the same whole. That was why the two children had looked so complete to him, not only in being one dark and the other fair, but also in their choice of toys. Yes! sword and doll belonged to each other: without the sword the doll would have no life; without the doll the sword would have lost its meaning.

I noticed that my wife was becoming more and more interested but, suspicious of generalization and abstraction, she went straight for what was, to her, the heart of any matter: the human factor in Lawrence's explanation.

"You've just said you spoke out of your own experience!" she observed keenly, anxious to get on. "But what sort of experience? General experience of life, war and men? Or did you have a particular experience in mind?"

Lawrence did not answer at once. To one who knew him as well as I did it was obvious that my wife's question had found the inner mark of a hidden target. We waited in a silence wherein the sound of the storm spoke unimpeded to us, now howling like a pack of wolves, then suddenly throwing a bar of angel-song on the wild deep of air while the fire strained gallantly up the chimney against the down-blast of wind.

"I was speaking out of both, of course," he answered finally with great deliberation. "And I must confess that the feeling that prompted your question was almost uncannily right. I did have a particular experience in mind. Only I was not certain that I could speak about it. I was not sure I had come to terms sufficiently with the experience to discuss it with anyone, even those closest to me." He paused. "However, seeing the twins tonight has, I think, made the experience clearer to me. Not only that. It has placed it in the company of those other things we have been talking about in connection with Hara, Yonoi, Celliers and ourselves."

"Couldn't you please tell us about it?" my wife pleaded.

Lawrence hesitated. "I'd have to be intensely personal and more frank than I am both by training and instinct inclined to be."

"But it would be good of you." My wife made it unnecessary for him to explain more as she gave him an especially warm look.

I knew that look well and it never failed to move me anew. It was for me a sign of how greatly women long, in their deepest being, to help men to bring up into the light of day what is uncertain, fearful and secret within them. So deep is this instinct that they tend to be less afraid of the unpleasant facts of human nature than we are, and to mistrust profoundly only that which shuns the light of truth within us. No matter how unpleasant our secret or how awful the consequences of self-revelation may be for them, all that is best in woman feels triumphant because of the act of trust that makes emergence of the secret possible. So now, noticing the frank and warm look that she gave Lawrence (whom she had only met for the first time the day before) I knew for certain that henceforth all would be well between them.

As for Lawrence, he protested no more. Seeing my wife

settling herself deep into her chair, he started straight away on his story.

The particular experience he had in mind, he explained, took place during the war, in a gleaming green and purple island of Insulinde. But, of course, the experience also had been prepared within him long before the war. If there was one thing he found more and more difficult precisely to determine it was this matter of the beginning of things. He realized it was of the utmost importance to place the beginning as accurately as possible for the sake of shape and articulation, but nonetheless the determination of origins was as arbitrary an abstract from the continuity of life as any generalization to which my wife had taken such instinctive exception earlier in the conversation. This understood, he would place his point of departure in some such moment as the one wherein we had just left the twins. He could not remember a time in his own life wherein there was not the image of a sword shining with a most compelling radiance in his imagination. To this day he had never forgotten the shock that went through him at Mallory's description of Excalibur and King Arthur's finding of the great sword. From that moment the whole legend of Arthur had held an inexhaustible interest for him, right to the end where Excalibur was reluctantly returned to the waters and an arm covered in white samite raised a hand to pull it down into the deeps below. Even now he suspected there was still far more to the legend than he could ever decipher and learn. But in those early days he was not bothered by such considerations though he accepted the whole legend as a decisive event in the evolution of his own spirit. Even the naming of the sword had seemed right for to him it was never purely a thing of metal but an individual manifestation of living experience. He felt compelled, too, to give a name even to the first wooden version of his own sword. He called it, he said smiling at us, "Brightling" and looking back he would say it was this absolute acceptance of the living significance of the image of the sword which made him the first soldier in a family that had always been scholars, law-givers and churchmen.

When he began to do service abroad he was confirmed in his sense of the significance of the image of the sword for he noticed how different nations found it necessary to have their own distinctive shapes. He would not bore us with what might be over-refinements of interpretation but a few illustrations of what he had in mind might make what was to come clearer. Had we ever remarked, for instance, on the difference of the shapes of swords favoured by two great opposing systems of the human spirit: the Christian and the Moslem, the cross and the crescent? If we had, we must have observed how like a cross, how like its Crusaders' prototype was the European sword; and how like a new crescent moon slicing day from night was the shape of the scimitar. Only a few days before, flying to join us for Christmas, he had walked through the narrow streets of Damascus where the aeroplane had spent some hours, and had seen how the Arab aristocracy still moved in their purple shadows with a dagger, a miniature scimitar, dangling in a golden sheath like a new moon at their hips. There was no doubt in his own mind that the shape of the scimitar was inspired by the moon and this, like other Moslem practices showed what a great tide from the moon swung in the spirit of Islam. Again it was significant that another moon-conscious people, the Japanese, also carried a slightly curved sword. For him, of course, there was no sword like the European. It was for him the least incomplete. It was shaped like a cross which in itself was for him a cardinal image of the complete spirit; a graphic illustration of the truth that life must be lived not merely horizontally but vertically as well. His own feeling was that the European sword was inspired by the sun. He said this because even as a child he had observed sword-light in the rays of the sun. Once on leave from the Army in India he had been climbing in the Himalayas at fifteen thousand feet on an unusually still and clear evening. The sky was silver-blue and speckled with the shadows of peaks on the horizon like an antique mirror. Just before the sunlight vanished below the purple rim it threw the image of a cross on the still air flashing like a great crusader's sword over an immense black split in the far range. In Malaya too he was struck by the fact that the sword there was neither curved nor straight. Though pointed and two-edged it was shaped like a tongue of flame. The sound of its native name, Kriss, even re-echoed for him the hiss of the fire of the Malayan smith who fashioned it. He could go on at great length about these things for they had provoked his fancy for many years. However, to return to the sword. . . . Whether inspired by sun, moon or earthly fire the significant element common to all was the association with light. The sword was, he would suggest, one of the earliest images accessible to us of the light in man; his inborn weapon for conquering ignorance and darkness without. This, for him, was the meaning of the angel mounted with a flaming sword over the entrance to the Garden of an enchanted childhood to which there could be no return. He hoped he had said enough to give us some idea of what the image of the sword meant to him? But it was infinitely more than he could possibly say about the "doll." The doll needed a woman not a man to speak for it, not because the image of the sword was superior to the image of the doll. It was, he believed, as old and went as deep into life. But it was singularly in women's keeping, entrusted to their own especial care, and unfortunately between a woman's and man's awareness there seemed to have been always a tremendous gulf. Hitherto women's awareness of her especial values had not been encouraged by the world. Life had been lived predominantly on the male values. To revert to his basic image it had been dominated by the awareness of the sword. The other, the doll, had had to submit and to protect its own special values by blind instinct and intuition. Fortunately that was changing and in our own time the feminine values were emerging from age-old shadows. Men had begun to acknowledge their need of a woman conscious of her own special values. Yet the danger, as he saw it, was still lest men should set too great store by the symbol of the sword: that he should sacrifice life to the promotion of his own specialized awareness. We had only to reflect on the history of Europe to see how readily men had murdered one another for ideas to realize how far this male hubris could go. The danger to woman, he suspected, was in that she would sacrifice her own special awareness to her need of man and his sword. She tended to live her life through her men and children, bending them to her own dark unfulfilled mind, and preventing them, as she had been prevented herself, from living out their full specific lives. The balance between these two claims, Lawrence thought, had never been fairly struck and never could be so long as woman was just the annex to a specialized male need. Yet now he had a feeling that the need for the spirit of man for flesh and blood to live it out, and the need of the instant life of woman for swordlight to direct it were about to form a union. However, he was not there to philosophize or crystal-gaze on a stormy Christmas night. He hoped he had said enough to give us the general background of his state of mind on these things when the war came. It was now up to him to pass from the general to the particular.

He paused for quite a while and I got the feeling that,

useful as his talk doubtless had been in order to give the climate of his story, yet, it had served also another purpose. It had served also to postpone the moment when he would inevitably have to pass from the general to the particular. My wife also, when we discussed it afterwards, had the same impression.

It started on the last day of February 1942 in the heart of Insulinda, Lawrence began slowly. He wondered whether any of us could still clearly recall the kind of moment that that was for us in the war? He himself had to prod his memory with a great effort of will to realize what a dark hour it had been and, since the darkness of the hour was relevant to the experience, he hoped we would forgive him if he went to some trouble to remind us of it.

In Europe, in North Africa, in Malaya and the Pacific the war had been a lengthening series of disasters for us and our friends. Pearl Harbour, the destruction of *Prince of Wales* and *Repulse,* the invasion of Malaya and the Philippines and the tidal sweep of the Japanese southwards had come at a cruel and crucial hour for us. At that moment, like me, he had been pulled suddenly out of his regiment on the Libyan front. Because he spoke Japanese and had served in these parts he had been ordered to report to the South-East Asia Command which had been formed under Wavell to deal with the Japanese onslaught. So slight were our resources and so heavy the demands that he could find no aircraft to fly him to his destination. He was forced to make the journey in a cargo ship in a motley, slow-moving convoy. As a result, he had arrived at Wavell's headquarters only the night after the fall of Singapore. Coming as he did straight from a front where we had just experienced our first victory in driving Rommel back beyond El Agheila, he was instantly struck by the feeling of hopelessness in the military air. It was not that our own people had lost heart, not that they doubted our final victory, nor had the courage to make a stand. But they all knew clearly that Insulinda could not be defended successfully against the Japanese, nor even held for us to gain time to organize our defences elsewhere.

Of course, everything was done by the Chiefs of Staff to keep this sombre knowledge from the ordinary soldiers and civilians. The combined military Headquarters was perched on the slopes of a volcano called, Lawrence said, with prophetic aptness, Tangkubuhanprauw "the-Ship-turned-upside-down," for what else he asked could have been a more graphic image of the fate in store for those societies caught in that typhoon of war in the East? All round the Headquarters and to some extent within it, life was going on with an easy abandon almost obscene to one who had come from so austere a front as the Libyan desert. The hotels, restaurants, dance-halls and night clubs were always crowded with laughing, noisy, over-fed people. He had never seen a population so large and fat as were the Europeans in that island. What made their appearance all the more marked almost to the point of caricature were the millions of small, delicately made, soft-spoken, ascetic-looking native peoples who surrounded them.

There was no shortage of food or drink of any kind and at his hotel the first morning after a gloomy interview with a realistic though undismayed Commander-in-Chief, he was amazed at the numbers of men in uniform who started their day with a fiery Bols followed by iced lagers. He would watch them eat a breakfast of several kinds of smoked meats, eggs, several sorts of cheeses and breads and a pot of coffee, believing they would not eat again until nightfall. But at eleven o'clock in the morning, constantly wiping the sweat like water from their faces, they would reappear for more iced beer and large plates full of thick soup of pork and beans. At about two in the afternoon, preceded by more Bols, they would have a meal which was a banquet by peacetime European standards; at sunset they had more Bols, crackling Kroepoek and other oil-fried snacks, followed by another banquet, served again by spare, gentle and grave Javanese waiters. The strain put on their bodies by sheer excess of food and drink in a tropical climate was so obvious to Lawrence that he wondered how they would ever find strength and breath enough to march far against so spartan and agile an enemy as the Japanese.

And as he wondered he realized with dismay the meaning of such abnormal eating and drinking. These people were afraid. He was in the midst of a community caught up in a fear so terrible and deep that they could not even acknowledge its existence. These huge men and their women were trying to eat away their fear. All that eating was the grown-up equivalent of the child frightened in the dark of things without shape or name turning again and again to its mother's breast though it had long since fed enough. It was no use a resolute military command attempting to keep the population reassured by putting on a brave face, publishing optimistic communiqués and encouraging energetic preparations for defence. All the reticence of an Antarctic night cannot conceal the whispering of the ice of a fear that is encroaching and real. In the core of their being this community already knew the truth, and the knowledge was spreading fast through nerves and tissues: a great reckoning was near and a whole epoch and Empire were about to crumble and fall. Yet as they ate and drank hugely they sang over and over again their most popular ditty of the moment: "We zyn niet bang" (we are not afraid). They were protesting too much just as they ate and drank too much. They were, though they may not have known it, more afraid than they had ever been before. All else was façade and camouflage of the soul hiding from the consequences or an excess banished from recognition far too long. Lawrence's suspicion of what the moment of truth would do to them moved him deeply and left him without any desire to condemn or judge.

For instance once an air-raid alarm caught him on a main street. A large motor-car suddenly drew up beside him. It was driven by a huge civilian and held four, bright full-bosomed, plump young women, laughing much too loudly and brightly.

"Jump in and come and watch the bombing, we'll get a good view of it from that hill there!"

The driver's invitation was uttered in the bluff, faintly arrogant tone that prosperous Europeans in that part of the world tended to use to foreigners. More, he spoke as if he were conferring a favour on Lawrence and offering him a seat in the front row of the stalls on the first night of some new play. Lawrence declined politely, somewhat shocked by so unreal an approach to war.

As he walked on one of the girls exclaimed loudly behind him: "Oh, let the poor frightened Englishman alone! He's probably not yet got over his flight from Singapore and would prefer a nice safe little shelter."

She immediately followed up the remark by starting the inevitable refrain: "Maar wy, we zyn niet bang." The rest joined in and, singing, they vanished from his life.

Yet Lawrence could assure us that, insulting as the remark was intended to be, it failed to annoy him because he was by then convinced that the woman in the classic manner of the unaware was merely attributing to him the fear that she could not face in herself. Even so he himself did not realize fully how wide, deep and real this fear was until the morning after Wavell and his entire Headquarters had been evacuated swiftly and in great secrecy at dead of night.

The evening before the evacuation his Commander-in-Chief had sent for him. He was told that there was no doubt that the Japanese were about to land on the island. The Dutch and Allied warships and the Dutch aircraft in particular had fought gallantly to hold off invasion but had been so destroyed or damaged by vastly superior forces that they were now immobilized. He wished he could assure Lawrence that the land forces would do as well; but he feared resistance on the ground would be slight and easily overcome. *Yet it was of the utmost importance that resistance should go on for as long as possible.* Every day gained in delaying the Japanese was precious. Even when organized resistance ceased he was hoping that it would be possible to carry on a protracted guerrilla war against the Japanese. That was where Lawrence came in. He would not give Lawrence orders but merely tell him about the situation and then he could decide for himself—because as Lawrence soon would see it was a pretty grim proposition. He, the Commander-in-Chief, needed an officer who would take command of a group of volunteers from all units and nationalities on the island. Once the main battle was joined (as it still just might be) between the defenders and the Japanese invaders, he wanted this particular unit to slip around the flank of the enemy and harass its lines of communications from the dense jungle which bordered most roads in the island. If there should be no main battle and only a token resistance—and this had to be considered as a grave possibility—then it would be more important than ever that such a special force remained in being and continued activities from some jungle hide-out. Once the Commander-in-Chief was back in India he would do his utmost to get supplies by air and submarine to this guerrilla force; but he doubted if there would be much that he could do for a long time to come. Therefore the force would have to live off the country and rely on its own initiative and the wits of its commander to survive. It would be unfair to pretend that its chances of survival would be great against so ruthless an enemy. However, in such jungle-country it might just be possible. All he could say for certain was that if it succeeded in persuading the Japanese that there were sizeable forces still holding out in the depths of the jungle and so prevented them from diverting troops to reinforce their onslaught elsewhere, it would be invaluable to the wider plan of the Allies. Throughout the Commander-in-Chief took Lawrence into his confidence in the most complete and imaginative way to make certain that his officer could believe as he did that what he asked was truly necessary.

Even so, after replying that he would, of course, do what his Commander wanted, Lawrence had returned to his room in the nearby hotel which was still full of feasting and singing people, with a feeling that he had come to an end too. He was like someone who had walked into a fatal trap and had just heard the door shut on him. He lay awake most of that night listening to the convoy hurrying down the mountain road by his hotel as it carried the vast Headquarters Staff and their baggage to ships and seaplanes waiting for them in the one harbour on the south coast not yet blocked by the enemy's navies. As they moved out it was as if he heard a vengeful history move in stealthily on bare feet like a giant, knife in hand, to take their place. When the sound of the last truck had vanished down the road another sound took over. The night-watchmen in those wooden villages which, beyond the electric lights of the European towns, stand on stilts like sleeping herons over their own charcoal reflections in the star-filled paddy-waters, began to rap out urgent signals to one another on their bamboo alarm gongs. Lawrence was certain it was not his over-strained senses deceiving him: there was fear in that signalling too. At breakfast the next morning his apprehensions were confirmed. The laughter and defiance had gone from the red faces of the gin- and beer-swilling men like the text of the previous day's lesson which had been wiped off the school blackboard by some caretaker in the night to make room for the lesson to come. The expression that now greeted him was nothing but the dark face of the fear of which he had spoken. Also there was something else of even greater significance. All the Javanese servants in the hotel, the Sundanese hawkers in the streets, the Madurese cleaners and scavengers, the Sumatran clerks and intellectuals, had discarded the compliant head-dress of rich glowing turbans of blue, gold and brown batik, that they had favoured for centuries, and in its place they had donned the stiff, uncompromising, black hat of the emerging Nationalists of the islands.

It was bad enough that Lawrence had to go and collect his few personal belongings in the abandoned headquarters which, crowded and busy like a beehive only the day before was now empty except for himself and the cleaners. Everything around him emphasized how precipitate the evacuation had been. The floors were littered with discarded possessions, each room a still-life of the rejected and doomed. Second-best uniforms and soiled greatcoats hung limply over chairs and tables; socks, ties, shirts, worn shoes and boots covered the floors; half-open desks and drawers held torn files and empty official envelopes, and several volumes of Jane Austen and Trollope, books favoured by professional British staff officers who discovered amid the brutalities of the war a longing for the gentility and refinement of life, were scattered about. In an American naval office lay two books: *Forever Amber* (a title dumb with irony seeing that all the lights ahead had long since turned red), and a fat volume of *Gone With The Wind*. Finally there were the copies of *Who's Who* and de Brett in a British staff room. Both books looked to Lawrence to be scarlet with the discomfort of those mentioned within them because their kin had turned their backs on an Oriental enemy.

He himself had been through the chaos of retreat and evacuation before and could make his peace with all these reminders of how alone he was now. But it was not so easy to come to terms with the sight of the slight, silent, little men of the islands going from room to room and collecting what was of use to them, and all wearing those stiff, black caps on their heads. Beyond all need of words there, for Lawrence, was the slumbering meaning of three-and-a-half soporific centuries suddenly emerging in an undeniable image: a new hat to symbolize a new state of mind. Overnight the teeming millions of that lovely long necklace of the jewelled islands of Insulinda had been transformed in one moment of darkness and fear into a whole people of judges— and like judges at a trial for murder they were putting on their black caps in readiness for the pronouncement of sentence of death on the culture and the men and women who had imposed it on them, from without, for so long. Today, Lawrence turned to us, we could judge how accurate was that fear, by what had happened in those islands since. Whenever people tried to blame the Japanese, British, Americans or Communists for the course this piece of post-war history had taken, he had only to remember the black hats of the humble cleaners in the great abandoned buildings on the slopes of the mountain of the "Ship-turned-upside-down," to realize how false was such blame. He would then see again vivid in memory those lithe little sweepers wielding their brushes like new brooms of history to sweep the litter of centuries clean from the door of a future of their own. Not by persuasion of any invader but out of a people's

own inner nature and texture of being was the future born
that day, and for good or ill a tide in all our histories turned.
Lawrence stressed all this, he now said, because, looking
back, it was of the utmost importance to what followed in
his story. It had been difficult enough to command his own
heart in a battle against a growing sense of his individual
doom. We could imagine then how doubly hard it was to
hold it intact when a sense of the doom of an age and a
cancellation of such a long confident assertion of the purpose of a great Empire, were joined to it. For the first time
in the war, he, Lawrence, had been in danger of seeing no
meaning whatsoever in what he was about. And thereby
hung his tale. . . .

He left the forlorn Headquarters, therefore, as soon as
he possibly could and went about the business of collecting
his unit with a bleak heart. Just before noon he set out with
the advance party of the little force so clearly predestined
for disaster, to take up a preliminary position on the fringes
of the great raised plateau, the formidable natural fortress
which the self-indulgent masters of the island had claimed
with unabashed melodrama they would "defend to the last
drop of their blood." His road out of town took him past the
island's most fashionable hotel. The wide veranda was
crowded with Dutch staff-officers and their women. Their
noonday gins apparently had done something to revive their
spirits because seeing his trucks go by some of the men
started up a large chorus of "We zyn niet bang: we are not
afraid." But he had heard more convincing performances
of the ditty before, and in particular he noticed that the
women no longer joined in and that somehow added another dimension to his own private dismay.

The road towards the expected "invasion area" twisted
among steep forest-covered hills and along golden valleys
between great grey volcanoes asleep in the hot sun. Yet

they were active enough to give the impression that if he went nearer he would hear their fires snoring within. The sky above was a great unblemished mother-of-pearl shell, and the beauty of the day sparkled and glowed over an island earth so rich and generous that it rewarded the people who tilled it with five harvests of rice every two years. All seemed to mock the darkness within him, Lawrence said. At moments he felt as if he were in a nightmare dreaming of war and of his trapped, pre-ordained role within it. As the afternoon went on over the gleaming paddy fields immense thunder-clouds formed to do and undo their long volcanic hair like gods regarding their own reflections in the quick-silver water. There was no wind (just as there were no seasons in that part of the world) only an endless repetition of this same still fecund, mother-of-pearl moment in the ardent volcanic nature of the land through which he was moving. The only traces of movement were a tremble of heat in the air as of transparent poplar leaves shivering in a breath of summer, and a constant throbbing imparted by the urgent beat of the deep volcanic heart of the earth to the silence singing in Lawrence's ears. By every paddy field tremble of heat, shiver of light and throb of earth were encouraged by the agitation of the dense swarms of blue and silver dragonflies, zooming over the burning waters on transparent wings. In each paddy water slender women stripped to the waist, their faces purple under the shadows of their wide hats of yellow straw, moved rhythmically, hip to hip, as women had done for a thousand years of planting new rice alongside the old. Always somewhere behind them a great water-buffalo moved with ponderous steps like a statue of the Beast in some ancient legend come to life. Always too a naked little boy with a burnished skin sat like an image of the young Buddha on the broad back of the buffalo whose immense power seemed to have found direction and meaning in the service of such delicate companionship. Beautiful as the scene was, Lawrence stressed, it made him feel increasingly unrelated to what he was doing. He had not realized until then how much one depended in moments of trouble on the support of the earth and the familiar sights and sounds among which one had been born. He longed desperately for a miracle to give him a glimpse of even the most commonplace of his native English scenes: a lane between water meadows, spotted cows chewing the cud in the grass and buttercups while the pale sun drew haloes round their backs and behind them a lath and plaster cottage grew blue smoke like a plant in a red chimney pot. That would have been enough, he had thought, to bring him back to centre and destroy this devastating feeling of unbelonging which was biting so deeply into him. But all that remained was that great shining day utterly indifferent to him and his mission. Even some sign of recognition from the people in the fields would have helped, but though they could not have failed to hear the noise of his trucks they did not pause in their work to glance upwards from beneath their big hats as he hurried by. Once he waved and called out a greeting in Malay to a little boy washing his buffalo which was lying, eyes shut ecstatically, in a stream within a few yards of the bridge where Lawrence crossed. But the boy gave him no answering sign and went on splashing water over the buffalo with his quick, brown hands as if he had not heard. The boy, the woman, the silent sleeping mountains, the shining earth, the smoking jungle and its lofty unruffled plumes of palm all stood as if deliberately with heads averted, oblivious both to him and his mission. Open and frank as day and scene both appeared, yet such aversion made them secretive and subversive. There was not, he observed, any darkness so great as darkness in the sun. Thereafter in the odd villages he passed it did not need the sight of clerks or street vendors in black caps to make it quite clear to him that this was more than just peasant indifference to change. It continued thus until evening, when at last he came to the village on the lip of the plateau where he planned to wait for the Japanese invasion: only there could he judge how best to commit his little force.

The village was built on the side of an immense Janus-headed volcano looking both ways: to the purple highlands from which he had just come, and also towards the sea. At that hour with the red sun going down between Krakatau and Java Head in the Sunda strait and its light setting on fire one huge summit of cloud after the other, the earth below by contrast looked black and already abandoned to the night. The plain and the redeemed marshes below the village and between the volcano and the sea were no longer visible, but he could tell the whereabouts of the islet-locked ocean by its effect on the northern sky where the sunset fires were abruptly extinguished and the moisture-charged air rose swiftly to hang like a thick mauve curtain between the day and the night. It was its exalted situation above the malarial plain and its nearness to the sea which had made the village a favourite health and pleasure resort of the more privileged persons working in the great port on the coral coast. The village contained several big luxurious hotels and the roomy holiday houses and week-end villas of many prosperous merchants and higher officialdom. But there was no holiday atmosphere about it on this evening of fire in the western sky and darkness on the earth. An air-raid alarm had sounded just before Lawrence arrived and no light shone in the fast deepening twilight to welcome him. The streets were silent and empty. At the entrance to the village square the challenge of the policeman who stopped the convoy rang out with a loudness which sounded almost profane. Luckily the policeman knew about the con-

voy. He was there, in fact, to conduct the men and officers
to their billets.

It had not been easy to find decent rooms for them, the
policeman explained. The hotels and houses were full to
overflowing with fugitives, mostly women, children and old
men who had been pouring in from the outer islands. It had
been terrible to see them coming in because most of them
had left their homes, husbands and belongings at a moment's
notice in order to escape the Japanese who had an uncanny
knack (he said it with a trace of acid cynicism) of always
showing up a hundred miles ahead of where only a few
hours before the lastest official communiqués had placed
them. The refugees had arrived packed like cattle in trains
with few belongings other than what they stood up in and
not knowing what had become of the fathers, sons and husbands who had been left behind. Though he was dutifully
polite and scrupulous in his attention to the needs of Lawrence and his men the policeman explained all this with an
undertone of accusation as if he, too, blamed the British
and their failure to hold Malaya for everything. When all the
men and officers were under cover and at last provided for,
he escorted Lawrence to the most modern hotel in the village. Lawrence would have preferred to remain with his
men but he had no option since he had been ordered to be
night and day at the end of a reliable telephone until the
battle with the enemy was truly joined and this hotel had
been chosen, the policeman said, precisely because it had
the best telephone system in the place.

By then the darkness was almost complete. Only the lightning flashing from some yellow head of curled cloud, filled
the black night with profound unrest and made the silence
stutter with the distant mutter of thunder. Out of smoking
hedges swarm after swarm of fireflies began to break like
sparks blown from the great blacksmith working his forge

in that volcano towering purple against the sheets of lightning which flared from time to time behind it. Whenever
his eyes recovered from the flashes of light, Lawrence was
amazed how dense and how near the jungle crept even
to so long-established a settlement. In a state of heightened
perception brought about in him by that immense world-
drama so swiftly sweeping to its climax, the jungle appeared
like a tiger crouched patient, watchful and at ease in the
night, ready to spring on the village the moment the back of
man was turned. From it, as from the fields, streams and
paddy waters, rose a noise of ecstatic crickets, singing lizards
and booming bullfrogs that was deafening. It sounded as
if all the small, secret forces of creation, whose enemies
prowled by day, were joined there in the chorus of gratitude
to the night which alone gave them their chance of fulfilment. Immediately above Lawrence was a great patch of
clear sky. When the lightning flared it was like a deep lagoon
ringed with coral strands of cloud but in the darknesses between it was charged with the same unrest of creation which
vibrated in the earth around him. The Milky Way emerged
too with a profuse deep-sea phosphorescence as if the mother
of light were spawning in those coralled waters there.

Then near the hotel this urgent rhythm of sound and
light and this song of the unrest of secret creation was
joined by a new sound. The shock of it made him stand
still for a moment, and listen to a thin, protracted wailing.
He looked around and could just make out the dark outline
of a long veranda running right round the L-shaped wings
of bedrooms which branched out from the main body of the
hotel and stretched right up to the entrance from the road.
There a shimmer of light (which provoked a wordless grum-
ble in the policeman's throat), shone behind a curtained
window. The wail suddenly ceased, to be followed by a
fresh-born sneeze and a murmur of relief and a volume

of subdued but satisfied and affectionate whisperings. Obviously a child had just been born to some refugee mother. But so bleak and locked-out did Lawrence feel himself to be from all creative processes that the realization merely added to the pressure of his apprehensions of the horrors to come. Indeed he stood there instinctively repeating in his mind, as he was destined to many times in the days ahead, the last verse of his favourite psalm: "The Lord is my Shepherd." But that did not really help much just then, and he walked on to the main building noticing as he went up the steps the shadowy outlines of slight Indonesian ayahs moving to and fro along the verandas with babies in their arms all of whom they were trying to rock to sleep in the fresh air outside their tepid blacked-out rooms. The shuffle of their feet was only just audible in the glittering sound going up from the earth to the spawn-star sky with its urgent pulse of thunder and wings of lightning beating the bounds of night.

Inside the hotel reception hall he found the proprietor making a perfunctory show of working by candlelight at his desk. He was obviously in a tense nervous state because as Lawrence walked in, he jumped up nervously. To Lawrence's dismay he was another huge fat man smelling strongly of drink. Yet he was not drunk. That was one of the odd things about the island. Lawrence had not seen a single drunk among the island Europeans though many among the British and American troops who could drink only a fraction of the liquor that people like the proprietor could consume.

However, reassured by Lawrence's uniform and the presence of a policeman whom he knew, the proprietor now greeted him with meticulous politeness. That done he apologized for the darkness inside the hotel saying that as soon as the air-raid alarm was cancelled he would switch on the electric light. He explained that on such sultry evenings he and his guests would rather have little light and open windows than bright lights with doors and windows shut against the blackout. He suggested, therefore, that as the air-raid alarms had never lasted long he would show Lawrence to the hotel drawing-room, give him a drink and leave him there in comfort until he could occupy his bedroom by proper light. It was not much of a room, he added, because God knew, the hotel was hopelessly overcrowded with distraught women, feeble old men in their dotage and tired overwrought children, but at least it had its own telephone and . . .

He broke off suddenly to ask out of longing for reassurance against the shadow of the intolerable fear which was darkening the intuitions of the island community: "Is it true that the American Navy has destroyed the Japanese invasion fleet off Bali and that fifteen divisions of Marines are now landing at Sourabaya to help us?"

Knowing what he did Lawrence could have denied the rumour outright but he did not have the heart to do so. He merely answered that he had heard nothing either about so stupendous a naval victory or so great a landing. Whereupon the man, his bloodshot eyes tragic in the candlelight, sighed deeply and exclaimed: "*Ag!* Even if the news is not entirely accurate, there must be something in it. No smoke without fire, you know! In any case I believe we'll have good news soon. It cannot go on like this, always being bad, then worse and yet still worse. I'm certain the Americans won't leave us in the lurch, as . . ."

Lawrence believed he was about to add "as the British have done" but he stopped and cut short a note of rising emotion just in time in order to ask artlessly in the eager voice of a fundamentally kindly and simple person: "Do you know whether it is true that Princess Juliana gave birth to a son last night?"

Lawrence replied again that he was sorry he could not confirm the rumour. At that he was led into a large, dimly lit veranda-room and shown to a chair by a small vacant table. It was the last empty place. The room was crowded with people indistinct in candlelight made dimmer with cigarette smoke. Judging by what he could see as well as by the quality of subdued voices surging around him, the people in the room were mostly women. No one appeared to have noticed his entrance and he sat there for half an hour undisturbed, listening to the conversation and from time to time seeing the unheeded lightning like an archangel messenger alighting on the sill of an open window.

Everybody as far as he could gather was talking about the war and from time to time being bitter about the British. Indeed, he felt uncomfortably like an eavesdropper. However, more striking and significant to him was the undercurrent of fear tugging at the sleeve of the uncomprehending spirit of these islanders, and over all the air of tension produced by a stubborn determination to go on as if the present were but a brief interlude and nothing in their lives really had changed for ever. At all sorts of odd moments this fear would break through their conscious defences. Some apparently meaningless trifle from their recent experience, the insignificant shell enclosing the subtle poison of decline and fall, would appear in the surf of their conversation like a small unpalatable crustacean dragged to the shore in a fisherman's net. Thus he heard a woman near him suddenly put an end to a conversation about the Dutch royal family by saying: "You know an odd thing happened the morning we left our home outside Palembang. Just before the news came through from the Governor's palace that all the children, women and old men were to hurry to their evacuation centres, the eldest of our Manduers * came

* Malay foreman.

to the estate office and asked to see my husband. He had been with us for thirty years and was the head of all our coolies. I can't tell you how good, decent and respectful he has always been. But suddenly there he was at the door of the estate office, asking, if you please, for three dozen tins of condensed milk!"

"What on earth are you saying, Mevrouw?" the voice of an old man exclaimed in the dark nearby. He sounded outraged as if there had been some enormity in the head coolie's request. "What are you saying? a Manduer made "zo 'n Brutale verzoek" (such an impertinent request?).

"Indeed, he did." The woman confirmed emphatically. Evidently reassured because someone else found the episode as untoward as she did she went on more confidently. "What's more, my husband asked him why he wanted the milk. Was he not satisfied with the lavish rations he had drawn all these years? But the man just looked past my husband, and said he had no particular reason for asking: he just wanted three dozen tins of condensed milk!"

"I hope your husband told him where to take himself and his impudence," that blurred old voice or another one intervened.

"Not at all," the woman replied her voice riding high with emotion. "That was the strangest part of it all! A week before my husband would have dealt most firmly with the Manduer because we've been far too good to him to justify such demands. But my husband, completely taken aback, just stared at the man for a moment or two, then took out his keys, unlocked the store and tamely gave him the milk!"

"That was a mistake, a grave mistake," the tired old voice again commented, and went on without respect for the purity of its metaphors. "That milk was just the thin edge of the wedge trying out your husband's grip on this confused situation. I bet that chap was back within the hour asking for more! Give these fellows a teat and they take the whole cow! Hé, hé, hé!"

He cackled, please with his joke. But no one else joined him.

"I'm afraid I don't know whether he came back or not," the woman said. "The alarm came through almost immediately after. Within the hour I was gone with the children. But ever since I've been quite unable to get the thing out of my mind. I feel it means something but I don't know what."

She stopped speaking, her words darting through that dim-lit room like a bat carrying in the twilight hour the full message of the night about to fall. So quiet had it become, Lawrence said, that you could almost hear the silence squeak. He had just time to think—this is meaning in pantomime: it was the milk of human kindness that these indigenous people were thirsting for all these years—when the voice of another woman broke in: "And I'll tell you something else that I can't understand: the owner of this hotel allowing these waiters to go about in those awful black hats and doing nothing, absolutely nothing about it at all?"

"Hush, hush, my dear," another woman exclaimed as a waiter moved deftly without a sound on neat, small bare feet into the room. Silently, he tripped his way between the tables to serve drinks to some people near Lawrence. Ice fell with a sudden, precise, cool and utterly impersonal tinkle in several glasses, and the waiter vanished through the open door but not before Lawrence had seen clearly outlined against the glow within it the black hat on his head. Then the voice of appeasement spoke up again: "Hush! my dear, you must really be more careful! I know we never speak Dutch to these people but they must have picked up a phrase or two by now and could easily understand what you're saying. . . ."

"And what do I care if he does? I would like all the world to hear!" The woman who had started it answered shrilly, with an overtone of hysteria in her voice: "If that proprietor were only half a man, he would never have allowed such insolence to begin, let alone tolerate it for so long. *Ag!* Dear God! What is to become of us with only such men left to protect us?"

She started to cry without restraint so that the whole room was affected by it. Lawrence feared they would all lose their self-control and join in but just at that moment, the siren of a nearby sugar-mill proclaimed the end of the air-raid alarm. At once all the lights went on, and the shock of light was as good as a slap in the face and removed the danger of any spread of that particular form of hysteria. The women sat up straighter in their chairs, automatically patting and smoothing their dresses.

Lawrence then saw that the room was filled with women of all ages, except for the one old man who sat crumpled over a drink in his chair, his red-rimmed eyes blinking at the light. At a table opposite Lawrence a middle-aged woman had her arms round a younger one and was trying to comfort her. As Lawrence watched her sobs grew less and presently she allowed the older woman to help her to her feet and begin leading her from the room.

As she did so, someone at a table behind Lawrence made a remark he could not catch. It was uttered low but in a tone of such unusual quality that Lawrence turned his head to look. He heard another woman loudly rebuke the owner of the voice: "It is easy enough for you, my dear, to disapprove. If you had three little children to think about as she has, poor dear, you would understand her outburst better. Believe me, you are very, very lucky not to be married and to have no husband and children to worry about at a time like this: very lucky indeed!"

Lawrence heard the reply distinctly: "I wasn't disapproving. And it was precisely because of the children that such hysteria worried me." The voice paused as if in two minds to go on or not, then decided to do so. "And my dear, what strange ideas human beings have about luck." It was said quietly without bitterness or reproach but with a strange sort of nostalgia.

So interested were the women in each other that Lawrence was free for a moment to watch them unobserved. What the one woman looked like he had no special recollection except that she resembled many others present: a large, full-bosomed matron, the worthy wife no doubt of another experienced planter in the outer islands, and with an air of basic well-being which even the anxieties of the moment could not altogether obscure. Of the other, the owner of the voice, the detail was extraordinarily fresh in his memory.

She was young, perhaps twenty-two or -three, and tall for a woman. He could tell that even as she sat at the side of the table, one long, well-shaped bare leg over the other and hands with unusually broad palms and long fingers together in her lap. She had on leather sandals and unlike any of the other women in the room, wore a loose skirt of native material, a deep, rich, brown batik with blue and yellow butterflies and flowers printed on it. Tucked into it like a blouse, she had on a boy's plain white open-necked shirt, a red silk handkerchief nonchalantly inserted in the pocket over the heart, and the sleeves neatly rolled up to just above the elbows. On her left wrist she wore a bracelet of burnt Djokja silver and round her throat a delicate gold chain with a locket of what looked like a virgin Sundanese nugget, the size of a pigeon's egg. Her shoulders were neat, her neck long and elegant; her head well poised and shapely. Her forehead seemed high and broad for a woman, her face longish and inclined to an oval. She was not thin and yet had nothing fat about her. The cheeks below their high almost Mongolian bone, indeed, were slightly curved inwards. Her wrists and ankles were slim and the bone beneath the skin of hands and face gave him the impression of being so fine that she looked in that assembly, a well-bred hunter in a paddock full of cart-horses. Then her mouth was full and the eyes well apart, big, slightly slanted and of a blue so intense that they looked almost purple. Her hair was extremely fair, thick and yet of so fine a texture that as it fell straight from the parting in the middle to her neat shoulders it shone like lamplight about her head. She used no make up of any kind and the clear, even European skin had not yet been stained by the climate to a weak coffee colour, as those of the other women present were. In fact it was still of a whiteness so fresh and intense that he could only describe it as brilliant. There was indeed, Lawrence now told us, an early Marie Laurencin painting of which she might have been the model. Though Laurencin was by no means his favourite painter, she was the only painter who had conveyed something of the impression this young woman made on him. Laurencin's vision, whatever else one might care to say against it, was fundamentally of woman as woman saw herself and when her own vision was still fresh she had painted a young French girl who looked just like that refugee girl, sitting with her long hands in her lap in the hotel drawing-room in Insulinda, the face a little heraldic, but with spirit behind it, vivid as a dream; woman in fact he would suggest, before her encounter with man. Yes, that was how she had appeared to him, in that blinding moment immediately after the lights were turned full on, not only a woman but the woman in all women. Tired, preoccupied, filled as he was with a sense of fast-approaching disaster and totally unready for such a reaction, an emotion as of having made a great discovery possessed him.

Long as it takes in telling, all these impressions were contained in the briefest of moments, because very soon the woman became aware of him too and looked up straight into his eyes. He had felt forced to turn quickly away then, but not before he had seen her interest at seeing a stranger in strange uniform watching her so closely startle the clear look in her eyes like water on a still bright day troubled by a cats-paw of wind. He hoped to look at her again but just then the proprietor came to take him to his room. As Lawrence walked out, the rest of the women too saw him clearly for the first time. They stopped talking at once and watched him amazed; even the crumpled old man came erect in his seat. Lawrence was not out of the door before the sound of excited speculation about him and his purpose there broke out like a beehive resuming work at dawn.

It was to be in any case a night of great interest. Twice before midnight his telephone rang and woke him just when he might have slept. Each time it was his liaison officer at the Dutch military headquarters, still on the slopes of the sleeping volcano of Tangkubuhanprauw, giving him the latest dispatches. All showed that the iron noose about the island was closed and rapidly tightening. The last light of day had disclosed two vast Japanese fleets of warships and transports making for the island: one coming up fast from the north and aiming at the middle of the long coastline; the other from the west heading for the harbour and railhead on the Sunda strait, not far from Lawrence's position. Not a single dispatch hinted at even a remote chance of help or hope of relief. Indeed when Lawrence asked what was the feeling at Headquarters the officer on the far end of the line hesitated before he blurted out: "Well, sir, if you really want to know what I think: they've had it, and if we don't find a snug spot of cover in the jungle, we shall soon be gone for a Burton."

All this was made more disconcerting for Lawrence by the manner in which it had to be conveyed to him. Lawrence had arranged with the officer beforehand that since they had no time or staff for codes or cyphers they would speak to each other in schoolboy gibberish, hoping that would be enough to confound any foreigner listening in. So he had to smile hearing the cool Sandhurst voice on the line rendering "We shall be gone for a Burton soon" as "E-way all-shay e-bay one-gay or-fay anna-way urton-bay oon-say."

Then again there were the night-watchmen in the villages and hamlets in the jungle nearby. Their great bamboo gongs, full of portent and fear-fever, went tok-tok-tokking all through the long hours in between the telephone calls. Once when his own unrest took him to the window of his room he suddenly heard the urgent noises outside overwhelmed by a deep, continuous vibration rather like that of the waters of a great river in the distance falling infinitely into some unimagined chasm in the earth. He touched the glass of the window with the tips of his fingers and felt it shivering as with cold. For an hour or more this deep abysmal agitation troubled the night and then as suddenly as it had begun, it ceased. He had no doubt from past experience that the disturbance came from big guns firing far away to the west and that it was direct intimation that his own particular hour, whatever it was to be, was near. With that realization the image of the woman, complete with the startled look when she had first noticed him, came vividly to his mind and he heard again that voice exclaiming: "My dear, human beings have strange ideas about luck."

He was up very early and hurried down to his breakfast so that he could get to his men as soon as possible. He had thought he would be the first in the dining-room but already she was there. She was sitting at a table alone, waiting for her food, her hands folded characteristically in her long lap and breathing in deeply the fresh air from the window at her side, while the morning wove the young light through her hair. He sat down several tables away, also by an open window, facing her. A waiter, wearing the inevitable black hat, appeared silently at his side. He ordered his breakfast, asked the waiter to be as quick as possible, and glanced up to see the girl watching him intently. She made no attempt to avoid his look and he found himself standing to attention, in the way men did in those islands, and bowing to her. Slowly her left hand came up and was held briefly in a kind of boyish greeting above her neat shoulder.

At that very moment the proprietor, shuffling along at a portly double came into the room, calling out loudly: "Colonel Lawrence, Colonel Lawrence, quick! quick! You're wanted by Headquarters on the phone. They say it's most urgent."

"Curse the man!" Lawrence exclaimed to himself as he dropped his napkin on the table and turned sharply away to follow the proprietor: "Why not just say I'm wanted on the telephone and leave Headquarters out of it."

However, he had no chance of speaking his mind to the proprietor just then for the bleary-eyed man, still smelling of gin and beer, seized him by the arm and impelled him towards a public call-box in the hall.

"I bring your call to this box," he explained in his breathless throaty voice. "You'll be alone there and save time running upstairs to your room."

With that he opened the glass door, pushed Lawrence inside, shut the door on him and then walked backwards to take up position about four yards away where, with arms folded and feet apart, he could keep his eyes on the face of the leading actor. Almost at once he was joined by his waiters, all in black hats. When Lawrence put the receiver to his ear and leant back against the glass wall of the box, a finger closing the other ear in order to shut out all external sound, he saw this strange little gathering standing there, hypnotically united in a trance induced by their sense of impending disaster as they had never been in normal life.

"Hallo, Lawrence here!" He tried to say it as if he were expecting no more than an invitation to dinner.

"Is that you, sir?" The voice of his liaison officer was unmistakable for all the long-distance crackling on the line. It too gave an imitation of unconcern. "I think this is it, sir. The Nips are landing now in a big way on the north coast between Semarang and Surabaya. Then the last of our fleet, three crippled warships, ran into the main western invasion force in the Sunda Strait last night, did heavy damage but were all sunk in the end. The Nips have got the railhead at Merak and are landing in force on the beaches for miles around. So far there is no report of any land skirmish or action of any kind and . . ." The voice hesitated and then resumed, "And look here, sir, I think I had better come clean on this . . . I don't know for certain but I believe these fellows have no intention of opposing the Nips at their beach-heads. I think they're going to pull back all their units on to this plateau as fast as they can, and if they fight at all, fight in the hills and passes along its edges. I think you must be prepared to see the Nips on your doorstep pretty soon now."

"Good! Good! Well done! That's all very clear," Lawrence answered with exaggerated emphasis in plain language for the benefit of those faces peering through the glass of the telephone-booth like conspirators into a soothsayer's crystal, as well as for those ears without doubt listening in at all exchanges along the line. "Just go on talking. Say anything you like but keep the line busy while I just sort out in my mind what you've told me."

Then he stood there for a full minute, telephone to his

ear, pretending to be listening intently but not hearing a word of the gibberish pouring into the receiver. He did not really need the minute for himself. This is what he had expected all along and tried to discount in advance. He knew exactly what he was going to say but he wanted to give the impression of being casual and unhurried so as to counteract the atmosphere of crisis produced by the proprietor's behaviour. In the end he told the officer with great deliberation: "You had better hand over to your Dutch opposite number at once. Tell him to keep us posted here. Then collect the rest of the unit and come here as soon as you can. Any questions?"

"No, sir, none. I entirely agree. I'll be glad to be back with you." Nothing could disguise the relief in the officer's voice.

Lawrence rang off and stood for a moment watching the proprietor and his staff like an actor on the far side of the footlights. As he did so he noticed a shadowy flutter of a reflection on the glass beside him. He looked around and there, alone, her face almost against the glass, was the girl with her blue eyes and all their wide, candid expression contracted into a single question of some overwhelming intent. The look stirred him deeply because it was of quite a different order to that on the faces of the proprietor and his staff. But if he remained within the booth any longer it would be counteracting the impression he wanted to create. So he opened the door slowly and stepped out. Immediately the proprietor was at his side and wanted to know if Lawrence had heard any news he could tell them. He knew, he said, that he had no right to ask for any military secrets but could not Lawrence just indicate whether it had been good or bad?

Lawrence told him quietly that it was news concerning his military mission. It was like the calls in the night, a routine one from his superiors, and there would be many more of them. As the proprietor knew, he was an English officer and a stranger to the country. It wouldn't be at all right for him to pass on what could only be his own inadequate impressions of the general situation. The Dutch authorities were the only ones who could do so without distortion and he was certain that when there was anything of importance to be announced it would be announced soon enough over their own wireless. Meanwhile if the proprietor would excuse him, his breakfast was waiting and he had a great deal of work to do.

The man spread his large hands out in front of him in a melodramatic gesture of submission to what he regarded as unnecessary military reticence. Grumbling that if the news had been good Lawrence would have let it out soon enough, he worked off his disappointment by clapping his plump red hands and ordering his waiters peremptorily back into position beside empty tables. They tripped back lightly, almost girlishly, into the dining-room to stand there so still and preoccupied with their own impressions of what had just occurred that had it not been for their black hats they might have been images carved out of their native djati by the hereditary sculptors of Bali.

Lawrence was left alone with the woman still standing and still watching him, her eyes gravely beseeching. She was the first to speak in the tone he had first heard only more muted than ever. Holding out her hand as if importuning for alms she asked: "Please, what did you hear on the phone?"

"You've heard what I have just told the proprietor. I'm afraid . . ." he began automatically.

"Oh, please don't say things like that to me!" she interrupted and for the first time the shadow of a personal defeat showed in her wide eyes. "You can't say 'no' to me." She stopped as if the truth of this passionate assertion were self-evident and looked him straightly, even a little defiantly, in the eye. Yet at the same time she put her left hand to her heart as if ready for the support it might need.

"Why not?" Lawrence asked the question abruptly.

Trained in a school of life which regarded all natural emotion with suspicion he feared he had no great "finesse" in dealing either with his own or that of others. Now, however, the unaccustomed emotion evoked in him was made more formidable by a feeling that he stood in a special relationship of responsibility towards this woman. That was the most confusing part of the encounter because at that time nothing could have appeared more absurd and irrational. Looking back, however, he realized how accurate the feeling had been. He had recognized a quality in her of which no one else among her companions, judging by the reprimand from that comfortable matron he had overheard the evening before, was in the least aware. The recognition laid special responsibilities on him for were we not all ultimately charged to live not according to general rules but by our own specific recognition of one another's quality? However, having the courage of one's recognitions was a lesson only slowly and painfully to be learnt and on that early morning in the hall of the hotel he was aware only of conflict between his upbringing, a long established sense of duty, and this strange new feeling about the woman. All that made him sound curt, almost rude to her, whereas he was really only being rough with himself.

To his amazement she seemed to see straight into the core of his predicament and even to be encouraged by it.

"Why not?" She repeated his question and went on straight away to answer it. "Because I have to know. I can't go on any more with rumours. I shall be utterly lost if I can't somewhere find not the whole truth—I'm not asking that—but just one real fact to build on. You've no idea how we've been deceived and lied to these past months. . . . They say it's for our good, as if we are children in need of pretty bedtime stories to lull us to sleep. . . . That may be true of men like the proprietor and these poor unhappy women and their worn-out children—but it's not true of me. All my life I've feared only the dark . . . only what is secret and hidden. These others may have to cling to their illusions. They may need lies to guide them to their moment of truth. They might panic if they knew what I believe you know. I would not. Only one thing can make me panic—not knowing."

Her voice had not faltered but it struck a deeper note that nearly blurred its clarity as she begged him to tell her the truth and so help her to be stronger. She emphasized that he was the only one who could help and so, as she saw it, he had to help. There was no alternative to the soul of honour which she took him to be. Then she added persuasively: "Besides, you can't tell me anything that I don't in a sense already know. You can only give the horror a name, a time and a place. However frightful your knowledge may seem to you it couldn't be as great as this nameless terror I've carried about inside myself these past few months. Oh! I wish you could know for how long I've felt disaster creeping down on us. For weeks I've even smelt death in the air and today I know it is very near. But I promise you I shall not tell a living soul. No matter how bad it is I can hold it all." She made an eloquent gesture with her hands like a potter demonstrating he had black clay enough to shape a vessel that would hold securely whatever life chose to pour into it.

Moreover, she had spoken all this, Lawrence said, not only with a passion that carried its own conviction but also with a certain instinctive poetry that would have sounded out of place in a drawing-room and doubtless was normally foreign to her, too. Yet in that sombre moment in the evolution of the vengeance of outraged fate, in that Far Eastern version of a world Eumenides into whose ancient chorus fate had conscripted them both, no other language would have been so appropriate. And—Lawrence added it with a tone of pleading for our understanding—he was utterly convinced by her. He was suddenly convinced that of all the decisions he had had to take in his life this slight choice of whether to speak or not to speak was the most fateful. He did not hesitate. He did not even feel it necessary to pledge her again to secrecy. Against all the rules, against all his training and upbringing he told her. Looking straight into her eyes and quietly so that his voice did not carry beyond her, he said: "They've landed."

"I thought so," she replied without change of expression. "When and where? Near here?"

Lawrence told her what he knew and was amazed how for a while emotion vanished from their exchanges. Conversation became spare and matter-of-fact.

In the end she asked, "But were not the landings opposed by our Dutch troops?"

"I'm afraid not," he answered.

"Is there any chance of the Japanese being driven back into the sea?"

"I don't think so."

"What are the chances of help from outside?"

"None, I fear."

"Have we any hope at all of holding out somewhere until help can come?"

"I fear not."

"I see." She paused then to stare past him at the day unfolding over the blue, smoking, reeling earth. Then, her voice lower than ever, she asked: "You said one landing was near here, at Merak. How soon before they get here?"

"I don't know. That depends on the resistance put up by the army."

"You sound unconvinced, as if you think our soldiers won't fight. Is that so?"

"Not on the coast . . . but perhaps here."

"Only perhaps?"

"Yes. Only perhaps. I don't know for certain. So far the signs have not been good. But the natural place to fight would be along the rim of your great inland plateau. Perhaps that is what your commanders have been waiting to do. If that is so and all goes well this village should soon be in the front line of the battle."

"If all goes well?" she exclaimed sharply repeating his phrase as if not believing she'd heard it correctly.

"Forgive me!" Lawrence hastened to explain, smiling for the first time: "I was using the word 'well' purely in a special military sense. Militarily speaking it is terribly important that the enemy should be made to fight for this island. The harder and the longer he is made to fight here the more time we shall have to organize the far greater campaign in the world outside which will enable us, in the end, to win."

"So we'll lose here but win elsewhere?"

"Whatever happens here, we shall win in the end."

"You really believe that?"

She asked this, Lawrence said, neither out of doubt nor the need for reassurance, but because for so long she had been tricked into accepting counterfeit that now she rang each new coin of thought on the counter of her mind before taking it up. There was indeed, he said, something most noble about her determination not to let one single aspect of the truth evade her. Compared with such dignity of spirit he suspected that there was much in his response that must have appeared inadequate and unimaginative. But one thing still consoled him. He had not fallen for any temptation to hold out false hopes to her. As he looked at that lovely young head poignant in its youth and innocence he was moved as he had never been moved before.

Yet he answered truthfully, although in a voice he hardly recognized: "Yes, I believe it. More. I also know it . . . as you have known all these months past of the horror which is upon us now."

It was her turn now to be convinced and there was no hubris of doubt left in her. Her spirit for all its suffering and disillusionment had the humility to be capable of conviction. The expression on her face lost its tension.

To his amazement she took his hand in hers between fingers that trembled, and said almost inaudibly: "Thank you for what you've done." She raised his hand, held it for a second against her cheek, then let it fall and turned quickly about as if to make for the stairs at the far end of the hall.

She did this all so swiftly that Lawrence feared her to be overcome by what she had heard. Instinctively he caught her by the arm and held her back. "I've upset you."

Again she turned to face him. He thought his fear to be justified because tears were bright in her eyes.

But she replied, "On the contrary, you've helped me no end."

"Why the tears then?" he asked.

"Don't you know? There are all kinds of tears," she replied, trying to smile. "These are tears of a strange, uncomfortable sort of relief."

"But the proprietor and the waiters who have seen us talking won't know that."

"My God!" she exclaimed, startled. "That'd be awful after you've trusted me so."

"It would help I think, if you came with me now and had your breakfast as if nothing unusual has happened," Lawrence stated.

She made such a face at the prospect that he laughed and said: "I know how you feel. I've never had to go into action without feeling I could never eat again. But I always force myself and it's extraordinary how it helps. Have a try."

"I shall, I promise you, but you know I suddenly feel like having another bath," she replied, "and putting on different clothes. It won't take me long. Then you'll see me eating the biggest breakfast I've eaten in days!"

With that she turned and went up the stairs. Lawrence hoped it was not his imagination but her step seemed lighter.

But whatever she did, it took so long that Lawrence was forced to leave the hotel and hasten to the billets of his officers and men. Before she had reappeared there he called his group together and told them, too, what he knew. His experience of small independent commands had long since taught him the necessity of sharing as much as possible his own information and plans with those under him irrespective of rank. He told them that the rest of their unit would join them before nightfall. He wanted them to overhaul their vehicles, check their supplies and, except for a duty group, climb up and down the great volcano snoring there in the sun beyond the village. When their routine fatigues were done they were to do this every day because their lives would soon depend, in great measure, on their physical powers of endurance. Meanwhile he himself and one other was going forward in the direction of the enemy to study the situation at first hand. He was certain the telephones henceforth would be buzzing with fantastic rumours and that personal reconnaissance would be their only means of getting accurate information. Nonetheless he appointed an officer to take his place at the end of the telephone in the hotel. Whenever possible he would communicate with him, but they were not to be surprised if they did not hear from him for a day or two.

Lawrence explained that he told my wife and me all this not because he had any intention of inflicting on us the story of his military adventures, but just to make certain that we understood, in view of what followed, why he was unable to do anything more about the young woman to whom he had in such a confused way admitted a certain responsibility of heart and imagination. Yet despite his lack of time and his desperate professional purpose before leaving, he did write a note to the proprietor of the hotel begging him to get in touch with the appropriate Dutch authorities and implore them to evacuate without delay the women and children to the main town in the centre of the plateau. Their only safety, he was convinced, would be in their numbers and in being far enough away from the fighting so that by the time the Japanese did reach them the battle-fever of their soldiery would have declined. He knew that if this were done he would probably never see that young woman again: and the thought pained him. Since he had only seen her for the first time a few hours before, his reaction appeared absurd and out of proportion. Yet he had to admit to himself that if it had not been for her he might not have written that letter to the proprietor since the matter was not in his military business. Finally, having made certain that his unit would be in readiness to move off at instant's notice, he set out on the main road towards Merak on the Sunda Strait where the enemy had landed in the night.

He was gone several days and nights. There was no need really to into the detail of his journey. All that mattered for the purposes of what followed was that as the great indifferent mother-of-pearl days passed to be succeeded by nights glittering with the unrest of creation and resounding with the alarm signals of frightened little men, the devastating feeling of unbelonging and pointlessness which had threatened him ever since he landed in the island, deepened greatly. This was not helped by the retreat of the well-equipped, well-fed Dutch coastal division with which he became briefly entangled. His worst fears were confirmed for this division was pulling back as fast as possible in the direction of the blue and purple uplands behind him without having fired a shot at the enemy. Yet on the return journey he had taken heart because he spent an hour at the field headquarters of an incomplete brigade of his own kin. There in the long level light of a sinking sun under a sky solemn with thunder-clouds and with a view of the jungle stretching as far as he could see to where it was ultimately lost in a smoke of rain on the horizon, he watched a small force of Australians digging in for battle. The men had no fat on them and were unusually tall. They were an extraordinarily young and fine-looking force. The men worked at their defences stripped to the waist, their shoulders burnt a deep tan from two years of war under a foreign sun. They seemed cool and unafraid and though, like Lawrence, they were new arrivals in the island, they moved about calmly and purposefully rather as he imagined the Spartans must have done in the pass of Thermopylae.

Lawrence then told their commander, a V.C. of an Expeditionary Force of the First World War, what he had seen on his travels. The Brigadier smiled the smile of someone who had long since made his peace with his fate and said he knew it all. He and his men were there in order to keep the road from falling into Japanese hands until the Dutch forces had safely withdrawn into their inner defensive ring. That done his orders too were to break off battle—if he could—and follow suit. The "if he could" was uttered with a homely Australian twang and accompanied by a wry smile.

Lawrence asked when he expected the enemy to attack? The commander replied that fast as the enemy was sweeping towards them he did not think it would be before dawn the next day. He thought the best plan would be for Lawrence to keep his unit where it was. The moment the Australian had contact with the Japanese he would communicate with Lawrence and suggest a position which offered the best chance of getting round and behind the enemy when, and if, the battle was broken off.

Before sunset Lawrence was back with his unit. Near as the Australian positions had appeared to the village on his map it was a shock to find that it took him barely twenty minutes by car to reach it. That decided him immediately to send a dispatch rider of his own to the Australian headquarters in case the enemy infiltrated in the night and cut the telephone lines between them. He posted extra sentries on the roads leading into the village and detailed a Signals warrant officer to take over the telephone exchange in the hotel. He also gave orders that the entire unit was to breakfast at first light and stand to, thereafter ready instantly to move off. To give them a clearer understanding of his orders he told them, in the least negative way possible, what he had learned on his reconnaissance. He dwelt at some length on the presence of the small Australian force and stressed how impressed he had been by their spirit and bearing. With luck and good management, he ended, the next forty-eight hours should set them free of entanglement with retreating forces and safely in their own native guerrilla element of the jungle. Then taking his second-in-command aside he told him he was going to the hotel to try and get a good night's sleep which he had not had for some days. He was not, he emphasized, to be disturbed unless it was absolutely imperative.

By that time the sun had vanished below the horizon but the whole western sky was still aflame with its light. One thunder-cloud in particular glowed from base to summit with a vivid pomegranate fire. In the ditches and along the hedges the fireflies were massing for their nightly fiesta and bats and flying foxes in prodigious numbers beat the brown air around him, emitting as they did so that strange silky squeak of theirs. Unlike the night when he had first arrived, not a glimmer of light showed anywhere in the hotel.

"The proprietor's done then what I asked and they've evacuated the women and children," he told himself. The conclusion was confirmed by the officer who had stood in for him at the hotel during his absence. Lawrence met him taking the air at the main entrance to the building. Lawrence took his report and before dismissing him asked: "Why is it so quiet round here tonight?"

"Oh! don't you know, sir? They've been evacuating the women and children these past two days," the officer answered. "I believe the last of them went off just before sunset. The hotel is practically empty and if the proprietor's to be believed most of the native staff have deserted as well."

Lawrence left him to climb slowly up the stone steps leading to the hall where the telephone booth stood. "So that's that. They've all gone, rats and all!" The bitterness in his thought surprised him until he saw its meaning. He was merely telling himself in the plural that "she" was gone. Though he had done what he could to make certain that the girl would be moved to safety when he returned, he must have secretly nourished a wholly inconsistent and wildly improbable hope that she would have remained.

"All the better," he tried to tell himself. "I need all I've got to concentrate on my job ahead." But he was not at all convinced by himself.

Then from the direction of the entrance of the office at the far side of the hall he detected his first glimmer of light. At his desk, his head sideways on his arms, the proprietor was fast asleep, snoring loudly. Lawrence first called to him and when he did not respond, walked round the desk and shook him. He smelt of gin. After a while the man opened his eyes, smiled feebly at Lawrence and muttered something meaningless. Then the smile deserted him and, despite his obvious drunkenness, his one chink of consciousness showed in his face the full tide of horror welling up fast within him. So terrified was the look that Lawrence believed the proprietor already may have been in the grip of some mysterious intimation of his end. Thirty-six hours later, on the pretext that he had not bowed low enough to a Japanese officer, he was to be bayoneted on the steps of his hotel and his body propped up for days in the village square. But the look of terrible awareness quickly passed, the red eyes shut and the head fell back on his arms. He was asleep again.

"Poor, poor devil!" Lawrence thought not trying to awaken him again. "Sleep all you can while the going's good."

He turned and retraced his steps towards the veranda-room to see if he could find a waiter who would take an order for dinner. The glass in the windows still burned with the last red of day and the big dark room looked abandoned and empty until out of the shadows at the far end came a very old waiter, his face, with its amber cheeks and skin wrinkled like an over-ripe grenadella, looking most incongruous under his brand-new black hat. He came towards Lawrence, bowed impersonally but elegantly as did all the indigenous peoples of the island and said gently: "Good evening, Tuan. Good evening, Lord."

"Could you get me some dinner in half an hour?" Lawrence asked.

"Yes, Tuan. What would the Tuan like?"

Lawrence ordered a light meal and at the end asked: "What's happened to the other waiters? Are you alone on duty?"

"The *jongens*," the old man said, using the term for boys which the Dutch applied to their native servants, "the *jongens* have all gone to their homes. There's only the Tuan proprietor, the Tuan telephone, the operator, old Abdul and his wife in the kitchen, and I, left, Tuan."

"And why haven't you gone home too?" Lawrence could not resist asking.

"We are very old, Tuan," he answered, "and this is all the home we know." He paused, then hastened to add as if further diversion into his private world with a superior would be too great a breach of native good manners. "Is there anything else the Tuan would like?"

"Perhaps you would bring me a drink," Lawrence answered, suddenly aware of how tired he was and feeling that a drink before his bath and meal would do him good.

He seated himself by an open window and listened to the urgent night sounds of the abundant earth starting up without. Some Gibbon apes, afraid of the dark, settled themselves in for an uneasy sleep on the highest trees in the jungle at the back of the hotel and he heard their barks fade to a series of whimpers. The ape-sound was extraordinarily human as if it came straight out of the world's beginning like a cry of anguish from the first man when he found himself hemmed in by powerful enemies. How old was the pattern wherein he was caught, Lawrence thought, and how deeply discredited. Yet when and how would life break free of it?

At that point he heard someone coming towards him. He

thought it was the old waiter bringing his drink and did not trouble to look round. He preferred, face to face with so overwhelming a night, to keep his eyes on what fire was left on the horizon in the west.

Then a voice he recognized instantly said from immediately behind him: "Good evening!"

That he had had no premonition of her coming, always seemed to him proof of how deeply he had accepted the fact that he would never see her again.

Startled, he came to his feet and blurted out: "What on earth are you doing here? I thought you'd all gone."

"No," she answered calmly, not at all put out by his rough manner. "There are a few of the younger ones still left. There was not room for us all in the convoy this afternoon. We are due to leave in the morning—if it is not too late." She paused, trying to make out the expression on his face in the dim light, failed, and then asked, rather in the tone of the first request she had ever put to him: "Is it too late?"

He drew out a chair and offered her a seat beside him. It was, he told her, very late, dangerously late but perhaps not too late. Only she must make certain that she did not delay beyond the next day. If there were no cars or trucks or trains available he begged her to get on to the main road and start walking inland. The road was soon bound to be full of friendly military traffic who would not refuse her a lift. Everywhere the land forces were retreating inland and whatever happened elsewhere this one road was going to be kept safe for a while by men whom he knew would fight. He did not know how vast the Japanese forces deployed against these men would be but, judging by the enemy's past form, he thought it would take him twenty-four hours, if not two days, after the first contact to gather force enough to break through into the main road.

What soldiers were those of whom he was so certain they would fight? When last time they spoke he had not been confident at all that the Japanese advance would be resisted? She asked this, her voice younger than ever with inquiry.

He tried to study the look on her face but it was indistinct in the gathering dark beside him. He was aware only that its brilliant whiteness had been sombred until it glowed like a strange flower which unfolds only in the dark. Below that lotus white of her face there shivered a sheen of gold from the nugget at her throat and a shimmer of silver from the bracelet on her wrist as she raised her hand from time to time to finger her necklace.

He told her about the Australians a bare twenty minutes away by car and described how impressed he had been seeing them at work so calmly in the long light of evening.

"How wonderful—and yet how terrible," she exclaimed. He felt rather than saw her stiffen in her chair as she gripped the rush-work arms tightly. "The thought of what is about to happen is almost more than I can bear. How then can they be so brave?" She paused. The day had now gone utterly and lightning was beginning to flash at the windows. The sound of the night was brilliant, the fever of creation mounting high in the temples of the dark. She asked: "When do they expect the enemy?"

"Knowing your appetite for the worst," Lawrence tried to answer lightly: "I must confess at once that the battle may even now be on. But I doubt it. For at this short distance we ought to hear the firing if it were at all prolonged and heavy. The Australians themselves believe their battle will come early tomorrow morning or at the latest tomorrow evening."

Her response to this intelligence was indirect. She told Lawrence that the women she had been with ever since they were abruptly evacuated from Sumatra were always bewail-

ing the fact that they had left their sons and husbands behind, bewailing the fact that they had children who might
have to endure a Japanese occupation. She could only say
truthfully that she envied them, thought them lucky to be
so rounded and equipped for the disaster ahead. She wished
she had a child and a husband to take his place with those
tall Australians of whom he had told her. Even if her man
were to be killed, even if she and her child were to suffer the
misfortunes of the damned, it would give a point to all these
ghastly circumstances that were coming down on them like
a pack of wolves. Even as a child, she confided, she had
never doubted that life, whatever her own fate, would prove
itself worthwhile. Even in the despair and disintegration
which followed the Nazi occupation of Holland from which
she had escaped barely a year before she had never doubted
that all in the end would be worth it for those who were
given the privilege of being able to endure. Her belief in
the unending continuity and flow of life from before and
beyond any rhyme, reason, idea or temporary arrest of it,
was so deep, Lawrence stressed to us, that it appeared to
be not a form of belief so much as an irrefutable kind of
knowledge built into the heart of that woman. Accordingly,
she despised those women who because of the terrible
world situation proclaimed that they would bear no more
children to suffer as they had suffered. Life was a woman's
answer to the enemies of life, she said. Men like his Australians might have to fight death with death just as, she understood, in Australia they fought bush fires with fire. That was
a man's answer to the death about now and she respected
it. But a woman could only answer death with more life.
Yet could a man respect the answer from woman irrespective
of the form wherein it was given, just as she respected and
accepted the brutal necessity of the man's? All this was
uttered with the passion of a proud and pent-up spirit. Yet

she did not wait for an answer to her question but put another directly to him, personally: "And you? What are you going to do when the battle down the road starts?"

"Join them," he answered. "I'm just waiting here at the end of a telephone for news that it has begun and for direction as to where I can most effectively join in with the Australians. I am afraid my summons may come at any moment."

"I can't bear the thought of you going out there to be killed," she exclaimed with an anguish that was illogical in the case of a stranger like Lawrence seeing she had only so shortly beforehand expressed the ardent wish that she had had a man of her own to take part in the coming battle. "I just can't bear it!"

She put her hands to her face as if about to cry, then quickly dropped them and suddenly stood up. "Please," she said, taking Lawrence's hand and pulling at it gently. "Please come with me, please."

Her hand was trembling violently like that of a person in a fever. So stirred was he by her concern for him that he too stood up without a word. Taking her left hand in his he went with her out of the room. The journey from there through the hall, past the office wherein the proprietor still was slumped asleep with his flushed face on his arms, up the stairs and down the long corridor at the top of the landing, was not far. But so eventful, so full again had his feeling for life suddenly become, that it seemed to take a crowded hour. His whole being appeared to have become magnified and even the smallest perception of time and space, the most microscopic details of his surroundings, became more than life-size on the screen of his senses. Their footsteps on that empty staircase and along the night-lighted corridor rang out in challenge like the taps of a drum, and the night-sounds from without fell on his ears like the cre-

scendo of an insect chorus. Her eyes, as she pushed open
the swing doors of lattice-work with which all rooms were
equipped, seemed great, dark and bright with vivid feeling
under the corridor light. But inside her room the night
was more profound than ever. He could just make out
against the sheen at the open window the faint, creamy
shape of a mosquito net suspended over a bed. Then a flash
of lightning flew in and he saw one forlorn little suitcase
on the luggage rack against the wall which presumably
held all she possessed, and a nightdress hung over a chair.
The lightning passed swiftly. It was blacker than before,
the room a vast palace of darkness in which he was lost. He
turned about, almost colliding with her as he did so.

"I can't bear it," she said again and put her arms round
him, her head against his chest beseeching him in that muted
voice of hers to hold her.

At once his arms went round her and she was about to
say something but it was as if she discerned his intention
as soon as it was conceived and begged him: "Please, do
not speak. Please don't say anything. Just hold me like this.
It is wiser than any words you or I could find."

As she spoke the distant rumble of thunder from the
lightning which had greeted their entry into her room broke
over their heads like a wave finding the shore. Never, Lawrence said, had he heard so commanding and holy a sound,
as if it were the authentic voice of life itself exhorting them
to obey. More wonderful still as he stood there holding this
strange woman to him she ceased to be a stranger and
separate from him.

He was utterly taken aback therefore when suddenly a
small low voice breaking the rule it had just made said:
"I expect you will despise me for this!"

He thanked heaven he was not taken aback for too long,
and quickly interpreted the question to be her way of

banishing a final fear and so making that sense of oneness between them complete. Up to that moment he had not had time really to think about what was happening, and in the end he was grateful for the question because of the light it shed on the turmoil on his own feelings. It made him realize that from the start the impression she had made on him was that of a singularly true person. The little she had said to him had been enough to reveal an essentially feminine sensibility and intelligence. She had courage too, in the way only that women have courage, and now in this deep concern for life which had made her turn to him she had not shirked a most unorthodox challenge to the special integrity of her sex. Somehow he had taken it for granted that all these feelings that were so strong within him would have been common knowledge between them, and that was his only reason for being taken aback.

Touched by her concern for her honour, in his imagination he would have liked to tell her that he could kneel down before her as a sign of how he respected her and beg her forgiveness for what men had taken so blindly and wilfully from women all the thousand and one years vanishing so swiftly behind them but all he could hasten to say was: "I would have to be a poet and not a soldier to tell you all that I think and feel about you. . . . I can only say that you are all I imagined a good woman to be. . . . You make me feel inadequate and very humble. . . . Please know that I understand you have turned to me not for yourself, not for me, but on behalf of life. When all reason and the world together seem to proclaim the end of life as we have known it, I know you are asking me to renew with you our pact of faith with life in the only way possible to us."

That, almost word for word, Lawrence told us, was what he had said to her, and we could judge for ourselves how inadequate it was. But it was the best he could do. The hell of it was that he longed for the ability to express the many complex emotions he had about her in a simple and intelligible way, but all he seemed able to do was to put into rough words only the simplest and most arbitrary of his feelings.

Then the suspicion that as he spoke she had started to cry alarmed him. He put his hand to her face and felt the tears on her cheeks.

"Forgive me," he exclaimed, "for hurting you. But if only you could see inside me you—you would be blinded by the vision I have of you."

"I've told you before there are all kinds of tears." Her voice was overflowing with a new tenderness. "You've not hurt me. I'm only crying because I am overwhelmed by my good luck, first in finding you here and then in finding such understanding in you."

She raised herself, clasped her arms round him and kissed him with great tenderness.

Life, Lawrence said, can have no more than a passing regard for the conventions which men create as preliminaries for these occasions. But in the deep of itself life is profoundly traditional and when all else breaks down it has its own inner pattern of ceremonial of heart and mind to take over so as to confirm, solemnize, bless, dedicate and make whole what happened then between them. From that moment the night became peculiarly their own. He had, he hoped, told us enough about the nature of that island to show how eventful it was. He had never before experienced a nature in the physical world so packed as was that island with events of fire and earthquake, of upsurge of plants and volcanoes, of cloud, thunder, lightning and rain in the sky, and of the unending music of the small first things of life, celebrating with scraping legs, beating wings, and brilliant little voices the various urges of creation minutely entrusted to each of them. Yet that night was even more eventful than any crowded moment he had yet lived through, and each event within it seemed designed to bless and make the two of them more meaningful in each other's arms. There were times when they were both so stirred by their nearness to each other and to all other living, singing, flashing and shining creatures that they made love close to tears, until finally, utterly resolved they fell into sleep as if they had all life before them.

On the verge of sleep the girl suddenly asked: "What's your name? I know your surname is Lawrence. But your own, your Christian name?"

"John," he replied gently stroking her cheek with the side of a finger: "John."

So near was she to sleep that all her responses were as if anaesthetized. After a pause she said so indistinctly that he could hardly hear her: "John, my favourite disciple . . . how strange! John of the Cross and John of the Revelation, too." She sighed, and said not "Good night" but "*A Dieu*—to God, John."

She said it not as we do nowadays as a single perfunctory word of farewell but as two, so that the expression seemed to recover its original meaning, but the last word was barely audible and carried her right over the threshold into her sleep.

It was only then that he realized fully how tired she must have been and that recently she must have had even less sleep than he. Indeed she was so quickly asleep that he had no chance to ask for her name and up to that moment it had never occurred to him to do so. It was as if he had assumed that he knew it, so particular did she feel to him and their intimacy of such long standing. Indeed he felt as if he had known her before birth and could go on knowing her beyond death. Thinking, "I'll ask her later," he drew her closer into his arms and he, too, fell asleep.

He slept deeply and long until he woke many hours later, his first thoughts being of intense unease. Yes! The telephone in his room next door was ringing loudly in one long, unbroken chain of urgent sound. She was still happily fast asleep. He managed to leave the room without waking her.

The Australian Brigade-Major was on the line. "That you, Colonel Lawrence? Good." The officer spoke with a suspicious nonchalance which Lawrence knew well came to his kind only in moments of extreme crisis: "Thought you'd like to know our night patrols have just come in. The Japs are coming up fast on a broad front. Thousands and thousands of the little bastards everywhere, on foot, on bicycles and in trucks. We shall be at it any moment now and the Brigadier asks me to tell you he expects to give you the directions you asked for yesterday within half an hour."

Lawrence thanked him and told him that he and his men would be ready to move whenever the Brigadier chose. He then spoke to his own operator, told him to leave the line plugged through to his room and to go at once to his unit, alert his second-in-command and bring a car round to the hotel for him. That done, he hastened back to her room. Thank heaven she was still asleep. . . .

Quickly he collected the rest of his things, went back to his own room, dressed and took out his dispatch book to write her a letter. Hardly had he got his indelible pencil to the paper when he heard faintly but clearly in the distance the sound of gun-fire, spasmodic at first but soon continuous and swiftly gathering in volume. But this as clearly as he could remember was what he wrote.

"Dear, beloved child of life, the attack has started and I have to go. Here below is the address of my mother in England. Please communicate with me there when the war is over if we do not meet before. In case you should lose this write to me as soon as you can care of the War Office, Whitehall, London. Should I be killed please go to my home and see my mother. My only regret is that I have had no time to tell you all I feel and think about you and how deep my sense of our belonging to life. I take the thought of you wrapped around me like a warm blanket on a cold winter's night. *Please* make haste to get away from this place today—I too shall see what I can do to that end before I go. Somewhere in life there will be a dimension wherein we shall be together again. Until then, as you said last night, to God—A Dieu, my dear—John."

Short as the letter was it was almost too long because the last sentence was scribbled to the sound of the telephone ringing again. He hurried to pick up the receiver.

It was the Brigadier himself this time: "That you, Lawrence? Good. Note this map reference. I'll have an officer waiting for you there. He'll give you your orders. Get there just as soon as you can."

Lawrence put the receiver down. The sound of distant fire was much heavier and more sustained.

He went back to her room. She was still asleep. He placed his note carefully on the worn little suitcase, placing one of her sandals on top to prevent some draught from blowing it away. Should he wake her? No. His instinct was emphatic. She would be woken soon enough. Let those subtle partners, chance and circumstance, which had brought them so mysteriously and accurately together now also separate them unaided. Separation coming then would be kinder than if he made his own words of farewell accessories to the fact. But it was not easy. In fact it was about the most difficult thing he had ever had to do. His last look showed her deeply asleep, a flush as of dawn in her cheeks, and the light of the expanding morning new in her hair. He had not seen such a look of fulfilment on a human face before—and he did not see it again until he saw it on the face of our own daughter asleep upstairs with her doll in the bed beside her twin brother.

Down below Lawrence found the proprietor just stirring. "Look," Lawrence ordered the man who was more frantic than ever now with drink and premonition. "Before you do anything else get on to that telephone to your authorities. I don't care what you say or how you do it but you've got to get the last of the women away from here at once. Tell them if you like that it is an immediate order from the Australian General. Should this fail you, get the women on the main road walking inland as soon as possible. They'll pick up a lift before the day is out. But get them away. And as soon as you've telephoned get the women up and break-fasted. The Japanese are attacking down the road and I promise you you'll be lucky if they are not here by nightfall."

As he was watching the alarmed proprietor obey these orders his car drew up outside. He gave one last look at the big red-faced man and was reassured to see him talking with determination into the phone. Then he stepped into the car and drove off. At the gates he glanced back at the window of her room. All he saw in it was the sunrise burning in the glass.

What happened to him afterwards then was of no importance to his story except for one thing. He had not driven far, in fact had not even reached his unit before he realized that despite his own desperate personal feeling of separation from the woman, it was a sense of separation designed to make him aware of a feeling of greater belonging. Gone was his terrible feeling of meaninglessness and despair. He no longer felt trapped. The earth, sparkling like a rounded deep-sea jewel below the opening shell of the day, no longer appeared indifferent. In the night he had been reborn native to it all. He had come home again to life, and in the days that followed, grim as they were, these feelings grew. He would only have to think of the woman and their brief encounter to find the most bitter of circumstances relieved with a living and poignant distillation of sweetness. Yes, even when he was kept in solitary confinement for months in a Japanese cell, tortured, and then condemned to death, the sweetness of the memory would be so acute that it outsmarted the agony and misery of mind and body. The sense of continuity derived erased the effect of what seemed then to be his own inevitable end. Without what that woman had given him out of her own prophetic intuition of life he could not have come through; would not have been sitting by the fireside on a Christmas night speaking to us as frankly as he had done. He had felt that she, too, had found their meeting healing; he only wished it could be more than a feeling.

Lawrence stopped, not so much as one who had reached his conclusion as one not knowing how to continue.

We waited in silence for a while in the hope that he would resume. Then afraid lest he might not do so unless encouraged, my wife asked a question. I had been back so much with Lawrence in Insulinda that I had become impervious even to the voice of the great storm outside now reaching its peak. But as my wife spoke I heard it again and I leant forward to make certain I did not miss anything of what she was saying.

"Does that mean that you didn't see her again?" she asked.

"I have never seen her since," Lawrence replied.

My wife remained silent for a moment. Then she said slowly: "So she might have had a child by you?"

"Yes! of course," Lawrence replied, looking straight into

the fire. There was a long pause before he added, "But I am afraid she did not."

"Why do you say that?" my wife asked quickly. "Did you have news from or of her?"

"No, I never had news from or of her," he answered. "But I feel certain that if she had had a child I would have seen or heard from her again."

"I don't wish to be brutal," my wife said gently. "But she might have had a child and died under the Japanese before she could let you know. After all, thousands of women and children died in prison camps in those islands."

"I don't think she died," Lawrence answered confidently.

"Then what do you think happened to her?" my wife insisted. "And what did you do to find her—for I can't imagine that you didn't try to do so at the end of the war."

Lawrence answered the last part of her question first. Yes, he had tried to find her but his effort had everything against its success. We must remember he did not even know her name. He did not even know what happened to her after he left her that early morning asleep in the hotel. It was nearly three and a half years later when he himself came out of a Japanese prison. He went straight back to the hotel to find that the proprietor had been killed by the Japanese, the Eurasian operator vanished, and the old servants who might have remembered them both were either dead or gone. Even so he had visited all the women's camps possible but many of them were already half-empty because after the surrender of the Japanese in 1945, although the situation was still perilous, numbers of women had left the camps without waiting for official permission or assistance. He knew enough of her not to doubt that her urgent spirit would have made her one of the first to go. He had interrogated one emaciated woman camp-commander after the other, and they were all desperately anxious to help but without her name, without even a photograph or snapshot to help his description she had sounded like that of many others. His only hope was that she would write to him. He had warned both his home and the War Office to that effect but as the months passed and he did not hear, he despaired. For long he thought the only explanation was that she was dead, but gradually the certainty grew in him that she was alive and had come through as he himself had done.

"But if that's so," my wife exclaimed, "what on earth's the explanation of her silence?"

It was to be looked for, Lawrence told her, in that young woman's conception of what she had called luck. Looking back at the little time he had had with her and poring continuously over the few words they had spoken to each other, he was amazed how often she had referred to it. All put together it was clear to him that she had thought deeply and reverently about the nature of luck. As a result he was pretty certain that she would have left the decision as to their re-meeting largely to the chance which had brought them together. For instance he was convinced that had she had a child, she would have regarded that as a sign from life that her relationship with Lawrence was meant to continue. If not, then their experience, so unique in its context of time and circumstances, was complete in itself. It was as if she knew intuitively what he himself now believed consciously, that by freely forfeiting a renewal of their relationship that relationship could become more complete. Did we know, he asked, that poem of Manley Hopkins:

. . . *The thing we freely forfeit, is kept with fonder a care;*
Fonder a care kept than we could have kept it, kept
Far with fonder a care (*and we, we should have lost it*),
 finer, fonder
A care kept . . .

He was sure that something of that profound faith in chance, fate, coincidence of life or whatever we call these mysterious and incalculable manifestations of the will of God, had made her decide not to see him again. Men had a terrible tendency to institutionalize life. Fear of life, born from their own wilful estrangement from it, made men build fortresses to hold what they had chosen to select from life. Instead of striving to make permanent the passing forms and shapes of meaning it would be more creative if they entrusted themselves to the natural processes of change and so refused to become ensnared in surface patterns. One of the many things for which he had to thank this woman was that her silence since had taught him not to bend life to his own narrow will. It was amazing how once he had believed he understood her silence how alive and near to him she had become again. He could hardly feel closer to her than he was now. All the time he had spoken to us it was as if she had been standing beside him whispering the words he was to use. There was not a day that passed wherein he did not hear her voice again in the wind, not a year wherein he did not see her face in the spring and witness her fulfilled in summer. It was in one sense inadequate even to think of her as having been childless. Looking back to their brief time together he had come to realize that what he was today, what he could become tomorrow was, in a sense, the child of their union. He was reborn through it into a timeless dimension.

And that was his end but not ours. My wife, as he finished speaking, had got up and quietly gone to him. Taking his head between her hands she kissed him tenderly on the forehead. It is difficult to express how happy that made me. I had not mentioned before my anxiety as to how she would accept Lawrence in our relationship, since she had only just met him, but it was real and deep. I knew now I need never fear again in that regard. The image of the young woman of Insulinda, and her insight into the nature of chance and circumstance, I felt had joined us too for good. Even the voice of the storm outside in that silence seemed to confirm it. I mentioned at the beginning the strange harmony at the heart of the storm. Let me end with it because at that moment all the confused and frantic tides of noise outside were gathered together and resolved as if into the music of a vast orchestra combining to render a single theme which rose high above the tempest and the night.